FROM SCRATCH

BLUE PLATE SERIES

RACHEL GOODMAN

PRAISE FOR RACHEL GOODMAN

"Goodman's debut Southern contemporary is smart, sexy, and funny. [She] piles on the Southern charm to make this story a winner." --Publishers Weekly on *From Scratch*

"Debut author Goodman enters the world of foodie fiction with a "bam" that would make Emeril proud." --Library Journal on *From Scratch*

"The chemistry between Ryan and Margaret is genuine, and the quaint vineyard backdrop and small-town atmosphere Goodman creates will enchant readers." --Library Journal on *Sour Grapes*

ALSO BY RACHEL GOODMAN

Blue Plate Series

From Scratch

Sour Grapes

Copyright © 2015 by Rachel Goodman

Sour Grapes excerpt copyright © 2016 by Rachel Goodman

First paperback edition 2019, ISBN: 978-1-7342198-5-2
Second ebook edition 2019, ISBN: 978-1-7342198-2-1

First Pocket Star Books/Simon & Schuster ebook edition 2015, ISBN: 978-1-4767-7469-5 (out of print)

Cover design by Najla Qamber, Qamber Designs

For David, my everything and the cherry on top

LIP SMACKIN' DELICIOUS FLICKERS IN RED NEON above the diner's door.

Salivating addicts are crammed in the entryway and spilling onto the sidewalk, all vying for their Blue Plate Special fix. The chalkboard menu posted behind the register says today's offering is the James Beard—a dish dripping with enough cholesterol to clog even the healthiest arteries. Served all day and only seven dollars.

I elbow my way through the horde, careful not to maim someone's toe with my stiletto. The air inside feels as heavy as sausage gravy and smells of it, too. The sounds of my childhood surround me: forks clanking against plates, snippets of conversations, and a Bob Seger tune blasting from the Wurlitzer jukebox.

Scanning the crowd, I search for the familiar mop of black hair that belongs to my father. All I can see are shiny bald heads, gray hair, and baseball caps as they line the stainless steel counter, obstructing my view of the kitchen. But I know my father is there. I can hear his boisterous laugh booming over the noise.

Turner's Greasy Spoons is my father's pride and joy, his existence. He's been running the joint for the past twenty-five years. The regulars have dubbed him Old Man Jack. Right now, he's on my to-die-painfully-by-butter-knife list.

Weaving around tables, past servers carrying pitchers and balancing dishes, I spot my father standing over the flat-top grill, flushed and grimy from oil splatters. He wipes his forehead with his sleeve. I march toward him, and when he notices me, a grin spreads across his face.

"Folks, Lillie Claire Turner, the best damn cook in Dallas and my only child, has arrived," he says, gesturing at me with a metal spatula.

Swiveling around on stools, patrons nod and tip their hats.

"Your only child wants to know why you're not in emergency surgery," I shout as my father disappears from view. A beat later he steps out from the kitchen and meets me behind the counter, wrapping me in a hug. I inhale the scent of hash browns and coffee. I pull away. In my five-year absence, he's aged tenfold—deep creases around his mouth, salt-and-pepper hair, tired hazel eyes, lanky build.

"I went to the hospital and the house, and this is where I find you?" I try to quell the frustration and anger sweeping through me.

He furrows his brow. "Course it is. The surgery isn't happening for another three weeks."

I shake my head. "You're unbelievable." Fishing my cell phone out of my suit pocket, I put his voice message on speaker.

"Hey, baby girl, I don't want to worry you, but I'm here at the doctor's office. I've been feeling run down lately and my bum knee's been giving me trouble again. Anyway, he's saying I need surgery . . . Ah, Doc's back with the paperwork for the hospital. I gotta go."

"See," he says. "I never said it was scheduled for today."

I huff in exasperation. "I called you seven times, Dad. *Seven times* without an answer."

"I got busy with the breakfast rush," he says, then *shrugs* at me, as if this whole thing is a simple misunderstanding. I have a brief, out-of-body moment where I see flabbergasted, crazy-eyed woman about to kill her father.

"You scared me," I say, recalling my dash through O'Hare, the restless flight to Dallas, my panicked drive around town to locate him. "You made it sound like this was an emergency."

A bell rings and plates appear in the kitchen window. My father trays the order. "Well, listen, I'm sorry about that, but I told you not to worry."

I throw my hands up as a fresh wave of anger swells inside me. "You mentioned hospital paperwork, and then you didn't pick up your phone. How could I not envision the worst?"

"Easy there, baby girl. Calm down. It's just a simple operation to fix me up," he says, tapping his kneecap with his knuckles.

"So it's not even serious?" I ask.

"Doc says after some intensive therapy, I'll be shining brighter than a freshly minted penny. Now let me look at you." My father clutches my arms. "You're skinny as a green bean. Don't people eat where you live? And why are you dressed like one of those stuffy lawyers on *Law & Order?*"

"Because I was at work prepping for an important meeting," I say, my voice rising. At this very moment, I should be on the thirty-eighth floor of the United Building, overlooking the Chicago River, presenting to the executive board of Kingsbury Enterprises about their product launch. I'm the senior consultant on the account, the success of which determines if I make partner. "I dropped everything to be here, and you're acting as if I'm the irrational one."

"You don't belong in that job anyway. It's about time you came home. Five years in that frozen tundra is long enough. Now, how about some real food? No more of that bird crap you've been eating." He winks, and his lips curve up into a bright smile.

The fire burning inside me dies, replaced with exhaustion, and I slump against the counter. "I'm not hungry."

"Sure you are." My father pops his head into the kitchen window and speaks to Ernie, his right-hand man and short-order cook. "Can you plate up a James Beard for Lillie?"

"Coming right up, boss."

"Make sure you add extra syrup and bacon."

I cross my arms. "Dad, no. I—"

"You love this stuff." He pats my wrist.

"I'm not a little girl anymore."

"I know that. But you're never too old for tradition," he says, pointing at the wall on the far side of the diner.

Intermixed among rusted diner signs—with phrases like *If you're smoking in here, you better be on fire; Unattended children will be towed at owner's expense;* and *Jack Turner's diet plate: half the food, half the calories, full price*—are candid photographs from years past and framed high school newspaper columns written by yours truly.

Most normal parents tape their children's accomplishments to the refrigerator. Not my father. No, he creates menu items about them. Like today's Blue Plate Special, for instance. Inspired by my first column for *The Bagpipe* about legendary food pioneer James Beard's famous quote, "I've long said that if I were about to be executed and were given a choice of my last meal, it would be bacon and eggs," the special consists of three strips of bacon piled atop eggs scrambled with cheddar cheese and fresh vegetables, all drizzled with Vermont maple syrup.

The column was part of a monthly feature called "The Yummy," which focused on simple, delicious foods. Of course, I wrote those columns back when I cared about things like developing the perfect hush puppy recipe or discovering the key ingredient that made a pasta dish unforgettable. Back before I outgrew the diner and cooking altogether.

Ernie rings the bell and places a steaming dish in the window. The scent of hickory smoked bacon tickles my nose, and my stomach rumbles. *Traitor.*

Before I can protest, the plate is on the counter in front of me and a fork is in my hand. "Dig in," my father says.

I stare at him, refusing to cave.

My stomach rumbles louder. Bacon has always been my kryptonite. I've never been able to resist the mesmerizing sound of it sizzling in the skillet, the way its intoxicating down-home aroma wafts through the air, how the succulent flavors of juicy fat and crispy meat explode on the tongue.

"Go on," my father says. "I know it's your favorite."

My mouth waters until I can't handle it anymore. I take a bite. My eyes flutter shut and a moan slips from my lips. *Double traitor.* Somewhere around my fourth strip of pork heaven, I faintly recall my promise to eat no more than one.

"Slow down. Nobody's going to snatch it from you," my father says. "Heck, when you're in charge, you can sneak as much bacon as you want."

Freezing midbite, I look at him. "What?"

"You're taking over the Spoons."

His words hit me like a sucker-punch pie in the face. Usually I can sense when my father's about to hurl one my way—trickery and unwelcome surprises have been his standard operating procedure for getting his way since I learned to crack an egg on the edge of a mixing bowl—but I guess I'm out of practice because I never saw this one coming.

Once upon a time, the diner was as familiar to me as my own heartbeat. I said my first word, "cookie," crawling across the stainless steel counters. Lost my first tooth when I tripped and collided face-first with the walk-in pantry door. Solved my first fraction while measuring ingredients for a boysenberry crumble.

As a little girl, I gravitated toward the diner's kitchen, basking in the sweet and savory smells swirling around me. For hours I'd sit on the prep counter watching my father chop, dice, and slice, mesmerized by the careful cadence of the knife. As I got older, my life *became* food—experimenting with it, creating it, indulging in it—and a deep-seated passion for forming something with the palms of my own hands took root.

But that's my past, a past I duct-taped in a memento box hidden underneath my childhood bed five years and a lifetime ago.

The fork slips from my hand and clatters on the counter. I push the plate aside. "Are you delusional? I'm not managing the diner."

"Yes, you are." My father says it so matter-of-fact I almost believe him.

"No, I'm not," I say, anger building inside me again.

He steals my last strip of bacon and eats it. "Doc says with my surgery I'll be out of commission for a long while, so you can't expect me to run things while I recover."

"You can't expect me to do that either," I say through

gritted teeth, thinking I really will stab him with a butter knife.

My father pretends he doesn't hear me, rambling on as if this was always the plan. "You can spruce up the joint a bit if you want. Do some small renovations. But keep the red booths and the checkerboard tile. The jukebox is a classic, so don't even think about getting rid of it. Though I suppose you could paint the walls a different color and replace the counters. Maybe order some new neon signs. The kitchen could use a new icebox—"

Pressing my eyes shut, I breathe in deep and count backward from ten. "I'm not moving back to Dallas. My career, my life, is in Chicago," I say, thinking about how far I've come.

When I first arrived in the city, heartbroken, scared, and alone, I took a thankless position as a receptionist in a dentist's office to pay the rent and studied for the business school entrance exam at night. After two years of grueling coursework and a massive amount of debt, I graduated with an MBA at the top of my class from Northwestern, landed a job at White, Ogden, and Morris—the best consulting firm in the area—and worked my way up from a lowly analyst. Now I'm the youngest senior consultant being considered for partner, assuming I haven't ruined my chances.

But I won't let that happen. I love my job: the satisfaction of winning a new client, the excitement of finding the missing puzzle piece to a complex problem, the thrill of closing a deal—it gives me a rush.

"My daughter shouldn't be living in a place with a baseball team that hasn't won a World Series in over a century. Those Cubs look more like a bunch of high schoolers, if you ask me."

"I'm happy there, Dad."

My father twists his mouth so that the whiskers of his mustache touch his nose like he does when he disapproves of something. He grabs the coffeepot and walks down the line, refilling people's cups.

Trailing behind him, I continue, "I love that it has four true seasons and deep-dish pizza and Oprah. I love the fog that rolls off Lake Michigan, its crystal-blue waters, and the fact that I'm minutes away from Oak Street Beach. I love how the river turns green on St. Patrick's Day and that the city's residents are unpretentious people who never sugarcoat their words with fake southern politeness and 'bless your hearts.' "

True, with my career taking off the way it has, I don't experience these things as much as I'd like, but I still love them on principle.

"Nonsense. Nothing's better than Texas. We even got the best state fair and Tex-Mex in America to prove it. Ain't that right, folks?" my father says to the patrons at the counter. They nod and murmur their agreement between bites of greasy burgers and slow-cooked pot roast.

I step in front of him. "Drew is in Chicago."

Frowning, my father returns the coffeepot to the burner and tosses a dishtowel over his shoulder. "You're still with that boy? I told you he ain't right for you." He always says this. My father thinks I belong with someone who's not a blue-tie-wearing, *Wall Street Journal*–reading, Cubs-cheering accountant. Someone more like Nick—my first love, the man who shattered my heart, and one of the driving forces behind why I left Dallas. But my father only remembers Nick as the vibrant, passionate boy I fell in love with as a little girl, and not the bitter, angry man he's become.

Besides, my father hasn't even met Drew. He doesn't see the way he complements me. He doesn't understand that we prefer to spend fifteen minutes shuffling through stacks of delivery menus, contemplating our dinner options, promising to one day stock our fridge with something other than bottled water and yogurt, rather than prepare a home-cooked meal. Or how our idea of a fun Saturday afternoon is sitting on the couch working on our laptops with work documents scattered around us and the History Channel on in the background.

"Yes. You know we're still together," I say. What my father isn't aware of is "that boy" recently proposed and I accepted. It's not as bad as it sounds, I swear. I just haven't been in the mood to listen to my father's grumblings. I will tell him, but not right now when I want to strangle him.

My father crosses his arms. "Well, I get what you're saying about . . . all that, but since you're already here, you should reacquaint yourself with how we do things at the Spoons. Three weeks will be here sooner than you realize."

"Dad," I say, softening my tone. I move closer to him so that maybe he'll see me—*really see me*—and finally grasp that I can't do what he wants. "Please don't ask me to do this. This place isn't me anymore. You have Ernie, and I'm sure there are plenty of people around town who would love to help out while you recover. All you—"

He quiets me with a look—the one I received countless times as a child—that indicates if I don't shut my mouth, I'll be on permanent potato-peeling duty. It's embarrassing how, at almost thirty years old, that look still strikes fear in me.

"The Spoons has been in our family since before you were born. I'm not trusting it to anyone else but flesh and blood. You're still a Turner, even if you live in a different zip code."

The firmness in his voice, his insistence, sets off an alarm in my head, and an uneasy feeling settles in my stomach. "There's more happening here than what you're telling me," I say, now certain that whatever is really going on is the real reason he called me this morning and why he wants me to manage the diner. "What is it?"

"I'm not sure what you're referrin' to, baby girl. I'm having surgery in three weeks and need you here to run things. Simple as that," he says, but I don't believe him. Over the years, I've come to realize that my father is a vault of secrets. Whatever his true motivations, he won't share them until he's good and ready.

"I'll work from Dallas until your surgery"—*or at least until I find out what you're hiding*—"but that's it."

"We'll see," he says, then picks up another James Beard special from the window. I notice the slight limp in his stride as he delivers the dish to a little girl in pigtails spinning around and around on a stool taller than her. Maybe it is just his knee, and this whole thing is some convoluted way of bringing me home permanently.

Around me, the life of the diner goes on as usual. People crowd the doorway. Servers hurry by, carrying pitchers of sweet tea and delivering orders. Several patrons lounge in booths, rubbing their stomachs as clean plates sit discarded in front of them.

My gaze drifts to the dent in the counter where I banged a rolling pin after messing up a piecrust. I spot the doodles I scribbled on the wall in the prep area. The tile grout under my feet is stained from when I spilled beet juice.

When I refocus my attention, my father's prattling on about how folks have been begging for my recipes. "Just the other day Gertrude Firestone commented how she misses your four-napkin Sloppy Joes," he says, straightening a pair of salt and pepper shakers. "And none of the regulars like my version of your mother's peach cobbler as much as yours."

My heart drops to my stomach as anger rises up. It happens anytime my mother is mentioned. Someday I'll learn to brace myself for it.

I have few memories of my mother, each one fragmented and fuzzy, as if I'm seeing them through a glass Coke bottle. I recall skin that smelled like honeysuckle, the soft swish of her apron, and long, graceful legs gliding about the kitchen.

I used to miss her in a bone-deep aching kind of way. When I was younger, I'd imagine what her voice sounded like. Soft and gentle as a whisper? Or maybe bright and lyrical with hints of mischief. Either way, I'd pretend I could hear it in my head, keeping me company, guiding me. "That one looks delicious," her voice would say, as I flipped through the pages of a cookbook. "Or maybe try the recipe with the clementines instead." No matter the task, her voice followed.

At night, in the silence, I'd curl up in my twin bed and wish she were there next to me, combing her fingers through my hair and humming pretty sounds until I drifted off into dreams. It was easier than wondering what I'd done wrong to make her disappear all those years ago and never return.

But as I got older I realized I couldn't miss someone I didn't remember.

"Time to prep for the dinner rush," my father says, ripping me from my thoughts. "Go get washed up. There's an apron for you in the back room. The carrots need chopping."

My chest tightens. Only my father can make me feel like everything I've worked so hard for is slipping away. I squeeze my eyes shut and force deep, steadying breaths into my lungs.

"You coming, baby girl?" my father calls over his shoulder on his way to the kitchen.

He expects me to follow. I don't. I can't. I may have been raised in this place, but that doesn't mean I belong here now. Instead I make a beeline for the exit, careful not to knock into anyone or anything on my way outside. I don't want to add another mark. I've already left too many.

2

I COLLAPSE ONTO THE ROCKING BENCH THAT'S ADORNED
the diner's entrance for as long as I've been alive. Terra
cotta pots overflowing with flowers dot the sidewalk.
Burying my face in my hands, I rub my eyes. Any moment
now I expect my father to start hollering or storm out here
to drag me back inside.

"Well, hell's bells, if it isn't Lillie Claire Turner in the
flesh," says a voice that immediately gets my attention.

My gaze locks on a familiar face twisting into a broad
smile. "Wes!"

He pulls me into a bear hug and swings me around
until everything is a blur. A wave of nostalgia washes
over me.

Wesley Blake may be my oldest friend, but most of the
time he acts like a tormenting older brother. We share the
same birthday—Wes two years older—and he never lets
me forget it.

He moved from Tennessee into the house down the
street from my father's when I was four. After a misunderstanding over the ice cream truck's last Creamsicle, we

quickly became inseparable. Together we embarked on adventures in his backyard tree house, built forts using the diner's tables and chairs, and dreamed of conquering the world. Wes has been a welcome thorn in my side ever since.

He also happens to be best friends with Nick.

Wes places my feet on the ground. I lean back and take a good look at him. He's bigger, stronger, more solid than before, but his kiwi-green eyes, curly brown hair, and dimples are still the same.

"Damn, it's good to see you, Jelly Bean," he says in his slow, lazy drawl. Wes gave me the nickname when I dressed up as a tutti-frutti jelly bean for Halloween in fifth grade and it stuck. "What're you doin' here? I thought giraffes would learn to fly before I ever saw you back at the Spoons."

"My father faked an emergency."

Wes furrows his brow. "What kind of emergency?"

"He led me to believe he was being rushed into surgery when it's actually scheduled for three weeks from now."

"That's typical Old Man Jack for you," he says with a laugh.

I nod. My father's like a whisk, always whipping up trouble. "But does he have to be so underhanded about it?"

Wes cocks his head to the side and gives me a sly grin. "You're the dumbass who fell for it again."

I scoff, narrowing my eyes at him.

"Come on, Jelly Bean. Jack's been pulling these stunts for years. Remember when he made us volunteer at that high school bake sale while he went fishing? You were so pissed I think you actually grew horns."

"Can you blame me?" I say. "He signed us up for that stupid thing after I specifically told him I'd rather eat liver.

Then he conveniently forgot to mention it until the morning of the event."

"At least we got a Chubby Bunny contest out of it."

I laugh. "And then you threw up marshmallows all over the gym floor. Mr. Sherwood almost murdered you."

"That's better than the time we got kicked outta 7-Eleven for destroying the candy aisle. I thought for sure the owner was going to send the cops after us."

"He did send the cops after us. We hid in your Jeep behind that Fancy Fingers nail salon."

Wes shakes his head. "I forgot about that."

"So what's with the outfit?" I ask. He's dressed head-to-toe in blue and red Southern Methodist University Mustangs gear.

He flashes his dimples. "You're actually looking at the new linebackers coach for the football team. Of course, you'd know this already if we talked more often." He tugs on my earlobe until I slap his hand away. Then, in typical Wesley Blake style, he says with an exaggerated sniff and quivering lip, "We don't call each other. We don't write. My heart's crushed, Jelly Bean."

When I first moved to Chicago we kept in near-constant contact, but as time progressed and our lives drifted apart, our communications drifted as well. Now Wes and I only exchange texts and phone calls every so often; our last conversation was almost six months ago.

"I know. I'm sorry," I say. "It's been too long."

"It's okay. I get it," he says. "You can make up for it by eating a slice of pie with me."

I laugh. Wes has never been one to hold a grudge, not even when I threw his favorite old-fashioned Leather Head football into White Rock Lake because he wouldn't share his Starbursts with me. Instead, he waded into the smelly, murky water to retrieve the waterlogged mass, then apologized as he climbed out and offered me the candy anyway.

"Deal," I say, smiling.

Bumping my shoulder, he says, "Stay here. I shall return with the goods," then walks inside the diner.

Reclaiming my seat, I lean my head against the weathered wood and rock the bench back and forth, the old joints creaking. The wind picks up, carrying the scent of grass shavings mixed with freshly brewed coffee. Somewhere down the street a motorcycle engine rumbles to life.

Wisps of hair have escaped my bun and cling to the nape of my neck. October in Dallas is anything but cool. Some years autumn gets passed over altogether, jumping straight from a sweltering summer into a mild winter. The leaves never even have a chance to change color before the tree branches are bare and the surrounding lawns and sidewalks are crowded with their decaying remains.

The hinges on the diner door squeal as Wes's head pokes out. I smile as he walks toward me with a piece of pecan pie in each hand.

"Scoot your butt," he says, tapping my leg with his shoe.

I slide over, the boards scratching my skin. He plops down next to me, and for the next few minutes, the only sounds are forks scraping across porcelain and the steady creaking as we rock slowly back and forth.

The first time we ate pie on this bench was the day Wes's parents finalized their divorce, a couple of weeks shy of his junior peewee football tryouts. He showed up at the diner, cheeks wet and shoulders slumped, and asked if I wanted to share something sweet with him. We built a triple-decker blueberry pie sandwich and layered each slice with homemade marshmallow crème and crushed-up Heath bars. We stayed outside for what seemed like hours, planning our next great adventure and wishing on shooting stars.

At least this part of our friendship has stayed the same.

"So Jack said you're moving home," Wes says around a mouthful of pie. "Is this because of his operation?"

I nod. "He expects me to run the diner while he recovers, which means forever. But there's no way I'm doing that."

Squinting up at the sky, I think of Drew and our Sunday strolls around Chicago. How we like to find cozy spots at Millennium Park and toss day-old bread for the birds roosting on Cloud Gate. The way we hold hands as we walk along the lakefront and watch the fireworks explode over Navy Pier. When we venture to Chinatown for a picnic in the Chinese gardens.

"At least think about it," he says. "The diner could use some of your cooking."

"I can't move back here, Wes," I say, keeping my focus on Drew, our life together, and the things I adore about him. His boyish good looks. How he opens car doors for me and always lets me pick dessert—even pistachio ice cream, which he hates. The way his body molds against mine when we curl up in bed at night. Falling for him had been easy, comfortable, like lounging in a hammock on a summer day with a cold glass of lemonade. "I can't."

"Then don't."

I look at him, surprised he'd concede so easily.

"I think you belong here, Jelly Bean. But if you want to go back to Chicago, go back to Chicago."

I sigh, mashing bits of crust between the fork tines. "What about my father? And the diner?"

"Listen," he says, licking some crumbs off his finger. "Old Man Jack's survived without your help these past five years. I imagine he can survive a few more."

He's right. Except we both know it's not that easy, not when my father's involved. My father's the master puppeteer pulling my strings, and I have no choice but to obey.

We sit silently for a few moments, me pushing pecans around my plate until they resemble a four-leaf clover and him stuffing them into his mouth, polishing off the last of his pie.

"I don't know about you, but I'm craving a cookie." Wes pats his stomach. "Wanna split a chocolate chocolate chip?"

"No, thanks."

Wes studies me as though I'm a math equation he doesn't understand. "When have you ever refused a cookie?"

I shrug. Chocolate chocolate chip used to be my favorite, but now they taste too sweet, too decadent. Or maybe, like the diner, I've simply outgrown them.

"*Okaaay,*" Wes says when I don't respond. "More for me, I guess."

I laugh and pinch his side. "Maybe you should cut back before Annabelle complains about a muffin top."

Wes flinches, and his Adam's apple bobs. He picks at a small hole in the hem of his sleeve, his eyes glued to a smudge on the sidewalk. When he finally meets my gaze, I'm stunned by the grief written on his face. He takes a deep breath, as though bracing himself for something horrible.

"Annabelle isn't . . . we're not . . . didn't she . . ." he says, fumbling over his words. "We ended things this past spring."

The air leaves my lungs in a long whoosh, rendering me speechless. Wes and Annabelle are a modern-day fairy tale—childhood sweethearts hopelessly devoted to one another. Their edges fit.

Or so I thought.

Wes may be my oldest friend, but Annabelle has been my best friend since she sat next to me in Mrs. Hubbard's fourth-grade social studies class with her Lisa Frank unicorn folders, all rosy cheeks and glasses and lace-trim ankle socks. We talk on the phone every week, but not once during our conversations did she ever say, "Hey, Lillie, remember Wes? That guy I've been slaphappy in love with since he held my hand on the Texas Star Ferris wheel in seventh grade? Well, we broke up six months ago. Kisses!"

Why didn't she say anything?

"I'm sorry, Wes," I say, biting my lip. "She never told me."

He kicks a stray napkin with the tip of his shoe. "It's all right. She obviously doesn't want to talk about it, and I really don't want to, either." He opens his mouth like he's going to say something else, but then he closes it.

"I've got a good one for you," I say, remembering the joke I heard from a little boy at the airport.

"Yeah?" I see his shoulders relax, the tension flowing out like salt from a shaker.

"A friend got some vinegar in his ear. Now—"

Wes clamps a hand over my mouth. "Now he suffers from pickled hearing."

My jaw drops open. That weasel stole my punch line. "How did you . . . ?"

"Please, Jelly Bean. That was third-grade level," he says with a smug smile.

"Fine." I cross my arms. "Bet you can't guess this one. Why did the sesame seed refuse to leave the casino?"

He taps his chin. "I give up."

"Because he was on a roll."

Wes laughs, his eyes crinkling at the corners. "Damn. I missed you. Those jokes never get old. Wait till Nick hears them." His grin falters, as though realizing whose name he said. Nick, the one person we don't talk about and the only one I wish I could forget.

A fist squeezes around my heart. I've been so careful, tiptoeing around Nick's memories so as not to trigger them like land mines. But now they're surging up, pulling me under—him, bleary-eyed and exhausted, dragging into our living room after another brutal shift at the hospital. Me, desperate and pleading for him to listen, tears tumbling down my cheeks. The two of us staring numbly at each other across a chasm so wide it could never be bridged. Nick's angry words and my whispered good-bye as I walked out the front door, leaving him behind.

The images seem like snippets from someone else's life.

Proof this isn't home anymore.

Not for me, anyway.

3

Wes agrees to distract my father so I can sneak away. I have a career to save and precious time has already been wasted. As much as my father would disagree, my life doesn't stop for his whims or demands.

I set up a makeshift office in the Prickly Pear, a café-slash-used-bookstore-slash-live-music-joint and an old favorite haunt. After ordering a large, extra foam, skim, vanilla chai latte, I claim the corner table and boot up my laptop.

My inbox is flooded with emails, most of which are from Ben, another consultant on the product launch. He'd never miss an opportunity to gloat, especially after he was put in charge today. In my absence, he pitched the distribution concepts to the Kingsbury Enterprises executive board.

I can see him in his three-piece suit and horn-rimmed glasses presenting my ideas, taking credit for my hard work, gobbling up the attention like Garfield with his lasagna. I shouldn't be shocked—he's been after partner since starting at White, Ogden, and Morris a year ago.

With my sudden departure, he'll do anything to secure the promotion I've rightfully earned.

I'm the one who arrives early and stays late, the one who works most Saturdays, who accepts the tedious, mundane assignments no one wants while seeking out new opportunities to develop my skill set. That position will be mine.

As suspected, several emails are from Ben gushing over himself, bragging to the team about what a stellar job he did at the meeting. How the executive board *ooh*ed and *ahh*ed over his extensive research and creative solutions —*my* extensive research, *my* creative solutions. But it's his last email, written in his normal condescending tone, that makes me want to tie him down and force him to lick mold off cheese.

I'm the senior consultant on the account, and yet he's taken it upon himself to dictate duties to the team. Next to my name he's indicated I'm responsible for an updated report on market demographics, the newest financial projections for the first-quarter sales, and a detailed roll-out schedule. He's also added this gem:

LILLIE, WHILE YOU HAVE CHOSEN TO GO ON AN IMPROMPTU VACATION, THESE ITEMS MUST TAKE PRIORITY, AND I BELIEVE A WEEK IS AN APPROPRIATE TIME FRAME FOR YOU TO ACCOMPLISH THEM.

The nerve of this guy. I *chose* an impromptu vacation? If only that was the case. Maybe he'll finally die from a paper cut or choke on a pen cap. Ordinarily I'd tell Ben where to shove his undermining attitude, but he's copied Thomas Brandon, our boss and the head of the committee that decides who makes partner. I don't want to further jeopardize my chances of a promotion, so I need to be a team player.

I take a sip of chai, allowing the earthy clove and cinnamon flavors to calm me, and settle in for a long evening.

Hours later, my back aches from hunching over the computer and my stomach is grumbling from skipping dinner, but I've finished Ben's tasks. As I send off the documents, I can't help but feel vindicated and a tad smug. Ben underestimated how much I like a challenge.

As I am packing up my things, a buzzing noise comes from my purse. Digging out my phone, I glance at the caller ID—Thomas Brandon. I sit up straighter, pull my shoulders back, and answer.

"I assume your emergency's been handled?" his stern voice barks into my ear, skipping all pleasantries.

Cringing, I say, "Not quite. I need to stay in Dallas a little while longer. No more than a few weeks."

"A few *weeks?*" The way he says "weeks" sounds like he thinks I'm a sleazy car salesman selling him a lemon.

"But not to worry," I say quickly. "I'll be working from Dallas until I return. In fact, I've already submitted several documents for your review. They should be in your inbox as we speak."

"Good. I expect nothing less from you." Thomas Brandon hates excuses and doesn't tolerate apologies. Do it right the first time, every time, no exceptions. "I'll permit you to remain in Dallas as long as you're back in the office by early November, ready to hit the ground running. We can't afford a slow ramp-up period."

"Why? What's happening?" I ask, hoping it's not a demotion.

"Despite the unprofessional way you left Benjamin to cover today's presentation, Kingsbury Enterprises is quite impressed with the effort you've put forth into their product launch thus far. They've asked for you personally to lead the next phase."

"That's excellent, sir. Thank you."

"This is the firm's biggest account, so I shouldn't have to remind you what's at stake if our client's expectations aren't met."

"Absolutely. You won't be sorry," I say, an idea forming in my mind. The diner already runs itself. All that's needed is someone to ensure back-of-house operations continue— shift scheduling, payroll, communicating with suppliers, placing and tracking purchase orders—and that can be facilitated from anywhere. I could be back in Chicago by early November, working on the next phase of the product launch for Kingsbury Enterprises, all while overseeing diner business.

It's a win-win solution for everyone. I'll be partner by New Year's Eve.

"I know I won't, Lillie," Thomas Brandon says in his no-nonsense, nasally voice. "In the meantime, I'll rush some documents over to your address in Dallas so you can get started. Don't screw this up." He hangs up without a good-bye.

By the time I park my rental car on the street in front of my father's house, the night has turned cool, promising rain. Nestled in the middle of southern Rockefeller mansions decorated for Halloween, my father's humble two-story home stands like a stale gingerbread house. Peeking out from under a thick layer of grime, white trim adorns the brick facade. Black shutters frame windows in desperate need of a cleaning. Even some of the shingles are peeling away from the roof. I wonder how my father let it get to this state of disarray. Growing up, he took pride in having the only original house left on the block, polishing our quaint little abode until it sparkled brighter than the stainless steel counters at the diner.

I take a seat on the worn front steps and dial Drew.

"There you are," he says, concern edging his voice. "I've been worried."

Stability floods my body. I catch the jumbled chatter of the television in the background, and I picture Drew lounging on our leather couch, his suit jacket and tie banished to the floor and his dress shirt untucked as he watches sports highlights.

"Sorry it's so late," I say. "Today has been such a mess."

There's a shuffle on the other end, and the background noise disappears. "What's going on? Are you okay?"

"Better now." Picking at a weed growing through a crack in the steps, I launch into the day's events. Drew listens intently, murmuring his support, as I rehash how my father expects me to drop everything to manage the diner without any consideration for my life, my dreams, while he recovers from knee surgery.

After I've finished, Drew tells me he loves me and says, "What are you going to do?"

I sigh. "I'm not sure . . . I'm still figuring it all out. I mean, obviously I'm not moving back here, but I can't leave him right now. I need to stay until I figure out what's going on with him."

"That's understandable. Want me to come down there? I could see where you grew up. Help out for a bit."

Even though he can't see me, I shake my head. Drew knows the basics of my childhood. It's not something I've ever tried to hide, but I don't speak often or openly about it either. It's a part of me best kept separate from him and our relationship.

"I want you here, Drew," I say, biting my lip, "but it's

only for a little while. There's no reason both of us should get behind on work. Besides, someone has to keep our plants alive."

He laughs, then lets out the cute groaning sound he makes when he's stretching. "Did you pack enough clothes when you left this morning? Do you need me to send you anything?" That's Drew, always so caring, so thoughtful.

"That'd be great," I say, and ramble off a list of items that don't include business suits or stilettos.

"Did you tell your dad our news yet?"

There's no accusation in his voice, only that hopeful sincerity I adore so much, but I still feel a pang of guilt as I say, "Not yet. With everything being so hectic around here, I thought I'd wait until after his surgery. Once life has settled down."

"Okay. But I have to meet your father eventually, preferably before he's walking you down the aisle."

"Ha-ha. I promise I'll tell him, but not right now."

"It's going to be weird sleeping alone tonight. I miss you."

"I miss you, too." And I do. I miss the way he leaves little notes scattered around our apartment just because. Or how his pillow still smells of him long after he's left for work. Or when he surprises me at the office with takeout from our favorite Thai place if I'm stuck in the middle of a project. But above all that, I miss the easiness of him, of our life together.

We talk for a few more minutes where he rehashes his day and I complain about Ben before wishing each other good night. I put the phone back in my purse and push open the front door to a roaring crowd singing "Take Me Out to the Ball Game" during the seventh-inning stretch. My father is asleep in front of the Rangers game, an arm flung over the back of the couch, a foot resting on the coffee table. From my vantage point, I can see a big toe peeking out from a hole in his sock. The television flickers, and shadows dance across the ceiling, casting the living room in a faint glow.

My father stirs and mutters under his breath nonsensical snippets about balding watermelons and fuzzy raspberries. Laughing, I cover my mouth and creep toward the couch. By the time I bend down next to him, he's rolled onto his side and started snoring, the sound as jagged and harsh as a steak knife. Tucking a blanket around him, I notice how he seems more like a scrawny boy I would punch on the playground as a little girl than the man who taught me to chop an onion and used potato-peeling duty as punishment. The diner has not been kind to him these past five years, and I imagine his knee giving him trouble has only added to wearing him down.

Slinging my bag over my shoulder, I tiptoe upstairs to my childhood room. The space feels strange and smothering now, as if the pale yellow walls are closing in around me with no chance of escape.

Boy band posters are plastered over the mirrored closet, staring me down. Medals from baking contests I won drape over the corner of a bulletin board cluttered with pictures and ripped concert stubs. The dresser and nightstand now look like dollhouse furniture next to the queen bed crowding the room where my twin used to be. I expect to find a fine layer of dust covering the desk and bookshelf, but they've been polished so they gleam, the scent of lemon cleaner heavy in the air. My father's obviously been preparing for my arrival.

I hear the television turn off and heavy footsteps pounding up the stairs. A floorboard creaks outside my room, followed by a knock on the door.

"Baby girl?"

"Yeah?" I say, preparing myself for another one of my father's infamous surprises.

"Oh good, you're here." He pokes his head around the doorway. His graying hair is sticking up at all angles, and the skin around his eyes is dark and wrinkled as a raisin. "You know better than to run off like that. The Spoons doesn't wait for anyone."

"Neither does my career."

"Then it's time you reprioritize. And don't think I didn't recognize Wes tryin' to distract me. I may be aging, baby girl, but I'm not stupid. Now before you get buried under quicksand with all this diner business, mind doing your old man a favor and meeting me at the lawyer's office tomorrow afternoon? There's some paperwork I need you to look at."

I sigh. "Sure. Leave me a note with the address." What's the point of arguing? He doesn't listen to me anyway.

"I scheduled myself for the early shift tomorrow, and there's some banana pudding in the fridge if you feel so inclined. Sleep tight." He winks before shutting the door with a soft click.

"Don't let the sour candies bite," I finish, reciting our old nightly bedtime ritual as I listen to him pad down the hallway.

Outside, the moon hangs low in the sky. The overgrown oak tree scratches against the bedroom window, the wind rustling its leaves. My eyes land on the stone mansion beyond the fence where Nick used to live.

Do you want to count the licks to the center of a Tootsie Pop with me?

Those are the first words I ever spoke to him, hours after his family moved in next door, the moment he slipped into my heart. We were an unlikely pair from the start. I was the spunky five-year-old girl who spent her time fooling around in the diner's kitchen, while he was the golden boy—two years older and son of the beloved Dr. Greg and Charlotte Preston—who attended private school with Wes and dressed like he belonged in a yuppie children's clothing catalog.

Kneeling on the bed, I touch the thumbtack wedged into the windowsill, once a part of our secret messaging system consisting of a pair of recycled soup cans and a long piece of yarn that ran between our windows. My mind flickers to a memory of a gap-toothed boy and a pigtailed little girl, soup-can phones pressed against their ears in the dead of night, trying not to laugh too loudly so they wouldn't get caught.

Pieces of Nick are scattered everywhere. My eyes lock on one of the photos pinned to the bulletin board. With shaking hands, I pull it free. An ache spreads through my chest.

The picture was taken at the base of Turner Falls, the lush Arbuckle Mountains flowing with clear, spring-fed streams behind us. Annabelle was piggybacking on Wes, hands resting on his shoulders, a cheek pressed against his. They were bright smiles and freckled noses and neon sunglasses. Beside them, Nick and I were wrapped up in each other's arms, not a gap between us. His eyes were closed as he kissed my forehead, while mine were squinting against the sun, a silly, stupid grin on my face, my blond hair dancing in the breeze.

I remember that Labor Day camping trip so clearly. Wes had driven the four of us north in his Jeep until SMU and the Dallas city lights faded into Oklahoma country sky. The guys constructed two tents while Annabelle and I unloaded the car. For three days, we splashed around in swimming holes and explored caves and hiked the trails that ran through the park. At night beneath the stars, with the sounds of waterfalls and the wilderness surrounding us, we told ghost stories and sang along as Nick strummed on my father's old Taylor acoustic guitar and roasted marshmallows around the campfire. And when bedtime came, Annabelle and Wes crawled into one tent while Nick and I retired to the other, spending the hours we should have been sleeping memorizing every inch of one another's skin.

The version of me in this photo would tell you without hesitation that Nick and I would last forever, we'd been so swept up in each other.

There was a time when one look into his deep blue eyes would make me feel like I was drowning, when a smile from him would send my heart skittering in my chest, when a feather-light touch from his calloused hand would ignite a fire inside me.

When I believed he would never let me go.

But that was the love of youth and idealism. All-consuming feelings like that could never keep a relationship together—they certainly weren't enough to save us. There's something to be said for stability, companionship, comfort.

Everything I have with Drew, I tell myself as I pin the picture to the board and take a deep breath, the ache in my chest dulling. *Everything I want.*

4

———————

THE NEXT MORNING, ARMED WITH AN ARSENAL OF BINDERS
and papers I stole from the diner's office, I return to the
Prickly Pear. It's busier than yesterday, but I'm still able to
snag the corner table near the windows. With its purple-
painted brick, cascading chandeliers constructed entirely
from recycled eyeglasses, and vintage movie posters
decoupaged onto the floor, there's a coziness to this place
that helps me concentrate.

If I plan on overseeing diner business from Chicago, I
need to devote some time familiarizing myself with the
diner's records. Otherwise my father will be badgering me
with phone calls every two seconds while he recuperates
from surgery when my focus should be on executing the
product launch for Kingsbury Enterprises.

I order my usual chai and get to work. Only everything
is disorganized. Payroll records are outdated and incomplete. Daily sales figures are missing for weeks at a time.
Purchase order requests are only partially filled out, and
even then, with incorrect shipping instructions. Distribu-
tors' catalogs are ripped with chunks of pages missing and

several suppliers have sent outstanding payment notices for deliveries made months ago.

So much for the diner running on autopilot, I think as I flip through page after page of chaos. How does it even function with record keeping like this? Is it even turning a profit?

The sound of hollering yanks my attention away. I glance around and see four guys that look like they stepped straight off a bus from Nashville—guitars slung across their backs, cowboy hats pushed down low over their eyes, tattoos covering their arms—jabbing each other's shoulders and laughing as they walk into the back room, where the stage is set up.

I recognize them as members of the Randy Hollis Band from the various posters hanging around the Prickly Pear. They must be performing tonight. I remember in high school and college watching musicians shuffle through this place, paying their dues, living off tips stuffed in empty coffee mugs, cutting their teeth trying to make their dreams a reality.

The same way Nick did, I think as sudden images of him playing the songs he wrote to a crowded room crash into me. I shake them away. I don't want to remember him. Or what happened between us.

I turn back around and continue sorting through the diner's files, keeping my focus where it belongs. Three hours later, I'm still trying to make sense out of something, anything, in this mess. My father's chicken scratch, haphazardly scribbled in the margins of almost every page, mocks me. Claiming defeat, I toss my pen onto the table and stretch my arms above my head. A bowl of teeth-rotting cereal calls my name.

In the room adjacent to the café is Couch Potato Corner, the perfect place to catch a quick mental break and where I spent many late nights with Annabelle after all-day studyfests. Distressed leather sofas surround old-school televisions, complete with built-in legs and rabbit ears. A breakfast bar flanks the back wall filled with glazed doughnuts, cereals reminiscent of childhood, and Eggo waffles begging for a toaster oven and a bath in Mrs. Butterworth's. Six dollars and thirty-five cents for all you can eat.

I pay my admission to the barista behind the counter and contemplate my choices. After pouring a bowl of Lucky Charms, I curl up on one of the couches, flipping the television to cartoons. I'm so distracted by an anvil being dropped on a coyote's head I nearly miss my cell phone vibrating. Catching it on the last ring, I grab it off the side table and answer without bothering to look at the name on the screen.

"Hello?" I say, shoving of spoonful of pastel marshmallows into my mouth.

"You better be kidnapped by Goonies."

And out comes the mouthful of marshmallows.

"Annabelle!" I say, scrambling to put the television on mute. "Hey!"

"Cut the bullshit, Lillie. When were you going to tell me you were in town?"

I bite my lip. "It was a last-minute trip. I got in yesterday."

The sounds of Dallas traffic filter through the phone. From somewhere far off, I can hear the ringing bell of the McKinney Avenue Trolley. I imagine her strolling around Uptown, carrying glossy bags overflowing with linen swatches and stationery samples, phone pressed to her ear as she pops in and out of boutiques.

"You're lucky I love you," she says, then changes the subject with her usual abruptness. "Your fairy godmother,

Sullivan Grace, woke me up at the ass crack of dawn this morning." In Annabelle terms "ass crack of dawn" means any time before ten. Welcome to the cushy life of a wedding and event planner.

"Okay," I say. "And?"

"*And* she knows you're in town," Annabelle says, her voice turning muffled. I hear her shouting at someone in the background.

"Please tell me you're joking," I say, louder than what is appropriate for any indoor space in an attempt to talk over whatever squabble she's having.

Seconds pass of more muffled arguing. Finally she sighs into the phone and says, "Sorry about that. A damn bike messenger nearly decapitated me. Anyway, if you're at the Prickly Pear, you better run and hide while you can. You know how pushy that old woman can be."

As if on cue, a voice as sweet as southern tea drawls my name, emphasizing each syllable. I'd recognize that Charleston accent anywhere.

I cringe. "Annabelle, she's here. I need to call you back."

"Don't worry about it," she says. "We'll catch up later at the committee meeting. Don't be late."

Huh?

Plastering a smile on my face, I set the cereal bowl aside and haul myself up from the couch. Sullivan Grace Hasell—better known as Ms. Bless Your Heart for her uncanny ability to insult the sin out of someone but mask it as a compliment swathed in a little southern flair—stands before me in a floral couture dress. Her caramel-colored hair is styled in an elegant bun that accentuates her long, graceful neck.

"There you are!" She encases me in a hug. I breathe in her perfume, a mix of pears and freesia, the same scent she's worn since forever, as she drawls on, "Where Annabelle said you'd be."

Of course it is.

"Hello, Ms. Hasell," I say with exaggerated cheer.

"I hardly recognized you, dear. You look stressed. Are you stressed?" She cups my face in her hands. "Oh, you know what I think it is? It's the way you're wearing your hair now, all pulled back tight in that ponytail. But never mind about that," she says, peering at me through long, full lashes. "You're looking lovely as ever, even with those fine lines around your eyes, bless your heart. It's nice to see you haven't let those midwesterners pressure you into the Botox craze."

"Actually, I opted for liposuction instead," I deadpan. "Sucked the fat right out of me."

Sullivan Grace ignores me. "Though you really should try a lighter color palette, Lillie. That black sweater makes you look haggard. Not to mention it dulls out the soft blue of your eyes." She collects an imaginary speck of lint between her thumb and pointer finger and discards it to the floor. "Elizabeth would throw a fit if she knew you'd abandoned your apron for those drab pinstripes."

My heart does that dropping-into-my-stomach thing again as anger swirls inside me. I rub my temples in slow, precise circles as I battle the headache forming from the mere mention of my mother's name.

Sullivan Grace was my mother's college roommate and closest friend before my mother went out for butter on my third birthday and never came back. But that didn't stop Sullivan Grace from sticking around. Growing up, I think she saw me as some kind of charity case. Or maybe she was worried that since I no longer had a female figure in my life, I'd end up shaving my head and joining the circus. Or perhaps, in some convoluted way, she felt like she owed it to my mother to make sure I turned out on the right side of normal. Whatever the case, Sullivan Grace has always been there, lingering in the background, pushing my buttons with her veiled reprimands and meddling ways.

"Oh well, it's not important now. It's marvelous to see you," she says, gushing like a shaken soda can. "Jackson said you're moving home."

"Actually, I'm only here for a short visit."

"Nonsense," she says, waving me off with a flick of her wrist. "You're needed here."

"That's kind of you, but the diner is better off without me."

"I'm not talking about the diner, dear, though Jackson did make me the most delectable eggs Benedict this morning. He really is the sweetest man," she says, smiling like a coy schoolgirl. It's no secret that Sullivan Grace has always liked my father. "No, no. I'm talking about the Upper Crust."

"Upper *what*?"

"Honestly, Lillie, have you heard nothing I've said? Sometimes I don't know where your head is at," she says, adjusting the strand of heirloom pearls around her neck. "The Upper Crust is Junior League's annual charity baking competition. You'll make Elizabeth's peach cobbler recipe, of course."

Baking competition?

Peach cobbler?

"Are you crazy?" I say, my voice rising. "I'm not doing that."

"Don't be silly, dear," she says. "Jackson already signed you up!"

My mouth drops open and a disbelieving laugh spills out. The jingling bell above the door interrupts my protest. A voice I never thought I'd hear again flitters into the

Prickly Pear. It's a voice I heard nearly every day for twenty years until the night everything broke apart. *Nick's* voice.

The blood drains from my face, and panic bubbles up in my chest, crushing my lungs. My heart pounds a two-beat bass line, so loud I'm sure even the barista can hear it. A roaring, rushing noise fills my ears.

When I left Dallas, he was a second-year resident at Baylor Medical Hospital, sleeping on cots, living in scrubs, and eating cold cafeteria food. All so he could someday call himself a surgeon. Now he's here, in the last place I expected.

Inhaling sharply, I keep my focus on Sullivan Grace's pearl necklace. *Don't look at him.* I peek anyway. I can't help it. He looks exactly as I remember, but older and somehow even more handsome in that striking way I've always found devastating. A hum of electricity runs through me.

He's standing in the doorway chatting with Candy Cotton, a diner regular from my high school days. Hovering at least two heads over her, he nods politely at something she says. Candy must be pushing ninety and almost deaf by now. I watch as she pats his cheeks with gnarled fingers, then pulls him down by an earlobe, yelling something in his face that brings out his signature crooked grin, followed by a laugh.

My breath catches as I gape at him, mesmerized. Somewhere in the background I hear Sullivan Grace droning on, her words a monotone "wah-wah-wah" like Miss Othmar from the *Peanuts* comics. I'm too fascinated by the sound of his laughter to speak. It comes from deep in his chest—full and real.

That laugh was once my favorite thing about him. The warmth of it. How it made the world seem limitless and bright. But like everything else that fell by the wayside once he started medical school, that laugh eventually faded away into silence.

A weight settles on me and I jump, blinking at Sullivan Grace's hand resting on my arm.

"Are you paying attention, dear?"

When I don't answer, she snaps her fingers in front of my nose and scrutinizes me like I've stuck my head inside an oven and turned on the broiler.

Maybe I have. Nothing else makes sense.

Sullivan Grace sighs. "Lillie Claire?"

My name hangs in the air. Nick's gaze shifts in my direction, and the smile disappears from his face. Every alarm in my body sounds.

Before I can run for cover, he's walking over. Then he's in front of me, studying me with those piercing blue eyes that can see right into me. I refuse to look away. Looking away is weakness. Looking him in the eye is a challenge, a silent way of letting him know I'm not the girl I was before, the girl who lost herself.

Then he speaks, steady and controlled. "Hello, Lillie."

My confidence fizzles away. I'm not sure what I expected after . . . everything, but his simple greeting definitely isn't it.

"Hello, Nick." My voice sounds weird and shaky.

His gaze sweeps over me, taking in my clothes, my hair, my face. My heartbeat speeds up as little pinpricks travel up and down my body, vibrating with energy. I hate how he can still affect me like this.

"You look good," he says with a small smile that accentuates his strong cheekbones.

"Thank you." In my nervousness, my response comes out curt and forced. Up close, I notice faint purple crescents underneath his eyes. Stubble lines his jaw. Worn jeans cling to his toned frame, and a threadbare gray T-shirt hugs his sculpted chest and broad shoulders. His shift at the hospital must have recently ended.

Before my mind has a chance to catch up with my mouth, I blurt, "You look tired."

He raises an eyebrow and clears his throat. "I had a late night and an early morning."

"Oh . . . right," I say, glancing at his shoes—black canvas Chuck Taylor All Stars with scuffed toes and dirty laces. I remember shoes like those banging against the kitchen cabinets in my father's house while Nick sat on the counter and taste-tested my recipes. I remember rubber soles squeaking as Nick chased me around the diner. I remember the feel of rough canvas moving up and down my calf while we made out in the backseat of Susanna—a restored 1969 mint-green Mercedes, named after my favorite James Taylor song, that was a gift from his grandfather.

"How have you been?" Nick asks in a way that sounds sincere, though I imagine he's only being polite.

"Fine," I say, biting my lip. "Just . . . tying up some loose ends for my father before I head back."

"I see."

"And you? The hospital?" As soon as the words leave my mouth, I immediately wish there was a way I could pluck them from the air and put them back inside me.

Nick rakes a hand through his dark brown hair. It's the longest I've ever seen it but still just as untamed. "Things at the hospital are good," he says. "Everything's good. My father's head of cardiology now."

"That's . . . great," I say. "Your mother must be so proud."

His lips form a thin line, and a muscle twitches in his jaw. "Something like that."

"Oh! Lillie, dear, haven't you heard?" Sullivan Grace

interjects, pressing a delicate hand to her chest. I forgot she was standing beside me, and from the startled look on Nick's face, I think he did, too. "Everyone's all aflutter about—"

Nick's shoulders stiffen. "It's fine, Ms. Hasell," he says. "Lillie doesn't care about any of that."

He's right. I *don't* care. Not about him and Baylor Medical, not about this Upper Whatever my father has volunteered me for, and not about managing Turner's Greasy Spoons. I left Dallas to get away from all that.

Sullivan Grace blinks, looking momentarily stunned before regaining her composure. "Right, right. Of course," she says, then changes the subject to the god-awful baking competition again, yammering on about sponsor expectations and donation forms and judging guidelines and *blah blah blah.*

"Ms. Hasell," I cut in. "I'm flattered you want me to do this, but I really must be going. My father's expecting me at his attorney's office and—"

"And nothing, dear," she says with a steel-wool smile, deepening the crow's feet around her eyes. "You'll be at Junior League headquarters tomorrow morning. Eleven o'clock. This is for charity, after all. Are you really going to deny a desperate child the opportunity to receive a warm meal?"

She doesn't wait for me to answer.

"Now you're a bit behind the other contestants with practicing," she continues, "but I'm sure you'll catch up in no time. In fact, yesterday I was telling Paulette Bunny . . ."

I tune her out, grateful she's a talker.

As I tuck a hair that's escaped from my ponytail behind my ear, I watch as Nick's eyes lock on my finger. My left ring finger—the one with the sparkling diamond on it. I meant to leave it in my pocket like I did yesterday, only this morning I must have slipped it on out of habit.

Nick furrows his brow and tilts his head, examining the ring as if it's a Magic 8 Ball giving him a clue he doesn't understand. A moment passes and then his expression hardens into an unreadable mask.

My heart hammers in my chest and my insides twist like they're being spun around fork tines. My hand trembles, and the cushion-cut stone dances under the lights, reflecting tiny rainbows onto Nick's shirt.

Could I be a bigger idiot? I think as I shove my left hand into my trouser pocket.

My eyes dart to Sullivan Grace, hoping she hasn't noticed. Thankfully, she seems oblivious. Now she's in the middle of telling a story about last year's Upper Crust baking competition. Something about how an apple turnover beat out French silk pie for Best in Show.

I start to interrupt before Nick ruins everything. The last thing I need is Sullivan Grace gossiping to my father before I have the chance to tell him myself.

But I'm too late. Nick speaks first.

"Congratulations," he says, like it's the most natural thing in the world. Like he never got down on one knee in our secret spot at Montgomery Park and asked me to marry him. "I'm happy for you."

My gaze meets his, and it's as if we're continents apart. I should feel smug, victorious, showing Nick that I've moved on, put our past behind me, but instead I'm overcome with sadness. *It was supposed to be you.* The thought is like a wound that won't heal.

"Thank you," I say. "It . . . happened recently."

Sullivan Grace finally realizes there's another conversation taking place and turns to me and says, "Recently? What happened recently?"

"Oh, um, my new promotion at work," I stammer, my eyes pleading with Nick to *please, for the love of cherry streusel* go along with it. "So you can understand, Ms. Hasell, why I'm not in a position to stay and help with your charity event. You'll need to find someone else, someone *willing*."

Sullivan Grace's mouth drops open but quickly snaps shut. In all my years, I've never seen her rendered speechless.

Nick stares at me with the focus of a sniper. When he finally speaks, his tone is so sharp it could slice through dry ice. "It's probably for the best, anyway," he says to Sullivan Grace, though I know his words are meant for me. "Lillie's still got all those *loose ends* to tie up before she runs back to wherever the hell she's been. May as well let her get on with it." Then he gives me a look, as if *I'm* the bad guy.

A fire ignites in the pit of my stomach. Flames of anger lick through me and burst from my mouth. "You knew where I was."

"Really?" Nick says with a bitter laugh. "How would I know that? You *left*."

I feel a shift inside me, transforming my anger into righteous indignation as I recall all the meals I ate alone. All the times I waited for him to return home after his residency shift ended only to be faced with cold indifference when he finally did pass through the front door. All the conversations I had with myself because I couldn't bear the silence. All the nights I laid curled up in bed longing for a touch that would never come.

He left me first, long before I ever took the final step.

He left me first.

"Go ahead, Nick. Blame me." I take a challenging step forward. "You're right. I did leave, and I don't regret it," I say, then say it again, louder, firmer, grounding the electrical current pulsing through me. Reminding me that nothing has changed between us. Nothing.

Then with long, purposeful strides, I walk away from him and Sullivan Grace, grabbing my things before stepping out into the warm October afternoon.

And like that day five years ago when I boarded a plane to Chicago, I don't look back.

5

THE LAW OFFICES OF STOKES AND INGRAM, LLP ARE located on the forty-fourth floor of the Trammell Crow Center in the Arts District of downtown Dallas.

Bursting into the reception area, I see a group of men in suits and ties lounging in leather wing chairs immersed in today's *New York Times*. I walk past them but stop when I notice they're all stuffing their faces with . . . raspberry oatmeal bars?

Then I hear my father's booming voice say, "Now if I told you that, it wouldn't be a secret ingredient anymore."

I glance at the reception desk, where my father is chatting with a silver-haired woman wearing an afghan for a sweater, her hand deep inside a pastry box. My father is dressed in faded Levi's and scuffed work boots. *At least he threw on a button-down shirt.*

As I make my way over to him, the receptionist slaps my father playfully on the arm and says, "Jack, don't tease an old woman. Give me a little hint. What else is in the filling?"

Is she flirting with him? The ladies have always loved

my father and his sweet-talking ways, so I guess I shouldn't be shocked.

"You signed me up for a baking competition?" I say in a firm voice, interrupting their conversation. My father keeps setting these traps, and like an idiot, I fall right into them. I thought once I entered adulthood I'd have learned my lesson.

Peering over her glasses, the receptionist scrutinizes me like a judge at a beauty pageant.

My father winks at me and grins. "Course I did, baby girl," he says, popping half a raspberry oatmeal bar into his mouth. "I already ironed your mother's apron. It's waiting for you in the office."

"I don't bake anymore. *Remember?*" I try to sound cordial. I don't succeed.

"With my bum knee, you can't expect me to do it."

"Then find someone else."

Wiping crumbs off his jeans, he says, "You know I'd never give anyone who knows jack-diddly-squat about the diner a copy of our family's recipe."

Frustration sweeps through me, cresting in my chest. "Maybe you should have thought about that before——"

The receptionist clears her throat. "Why don't you have a seat, sweetheart? Mr. Stokes is still finishing up with his three o'clock. I'll come get you when he's ready." She motions to the waiting area with a smile wrapped in barbed wire—a southern specialty right up there with Civil War reenactments and fried green tomatoes.

I want to argue, but I don't. When I'm angry, I have a tendency to say things I'll regret. Instead, I sigh and take the only open seat. Picking up the latest issue of *People* magazine, I flip through the glossy pages.

"Baby girl's competing in the Upper Crust, and she's going to win with Elizabeth's peach cobbler," I hear my father proudly say to the receptionist. "Did you know Lillie used to make it at the diner every week? People would line up around the block for it."

His words sink like stones at the bottom of my stomach, dredging up a memory I've tried so hard to bury. And just like that I'm sixteen again, back in my father's *Brady Bunch* kitchen with Nick on the day I first made my mother's peach cobbler.

The scene feels so real it's as though I can touch it.

"What's on the agenda for today?" Nick said, taking the recipe card off the counter and reading it over. "Ernie's Incredible Edible Carrot Cake. Sounds good."

"I hope so. If only I could find the darn grater," I said as I kneeled on the floor and rifled through the pantry, gathering ingredients for my latest project. "I swear I had it in my hand."

A beat later, the grater dangled in front of my nose. I blew wisps of hair away from my face and looked at Nick.

"It was hiding behind the flour canister," he said with a crooked smile.

Standing, I took the grater, set it on the counter, and got busy shredding carrots.

Nick came to stand beside me and slid the grater toward himself. "Why don't you let me give this one a try?"

"Cooking isn't exactly your forte," I said as I remembered the one and only time Nick tried to bake a cake—eleven years old and all lanky limbs and a mouthful of braces and wild hair. He had forgotten to let the layers cool before icing them, so the frosting had trickled down the sides in clumps. I'd commented that it was the best devil's food cake I'd ever tasted, even though Nick accidentally confused the measurements for the sugar and the salt and put four extra eggs into the batter. My nine-year-old heart couldn't bear to tell him I'd gagged down my slice.

"Come on. Making a cake isn't *that* hard," Nick said. "I mix together the ingredients, pour them into a pan, and throw the whole thing in the oven. Voilà. Out comes the best carrot cake in the world."

My "Yeah, right" expression said otherwise. But I let him have his fun anyway, laughing in unabashed amusement as Nick fumbled about the kitchen, baking powder and egg yolks sticking to his skin. I hoped it'd get his mind off the argument he'd had with his parents. Nick was starting at SMU in the fall, where he wanted to pursue a degree in music composition. Charlotte and Dr. Preston had other ideas. Either Nick majored in biology or he would be cut off financially. Medical schools would never consider an applicant with a liberal arts background. He was eighteen, not some foolish child living in a fantasyland, and he needed to be serious, concentrate on his future. No more late nights playing that stupid guitar at the Prickly Pear. No more hanging around Turner's Greasy Spoons with some misfit girl stuck on a dead-end path.

Once the ingredients were dumped into the stand mixer, Nick scraped down the sides of the bowl with a spatula and secured the whisk attachment. He turned on the mixer and flipped it to the fastest whipping speed. Immediately, batter erupted out of the bowl. Springing into action, I grabbed the power cord and yanked it from the outlet before more damage could be done.

Too late.

Batter was splattered everywhere—on the cabinets, the tile backsplash, the stovetop. Large blobs of it dripped off the counter and were landing in soupy puddles on the floor. When my gaze locked on Nick, I burst into giggles. I couldn't help it. He was coated in it.

Nick only stood there, a stunned expression on his face. Finally, he shook his head and said, "That was not supposed to happen." He pulled his polo shirt over his head, revealing a white cotton undershirt, and tossed it into the sink.

I threw a dish towel at his chest. "I told you tripling the recipe was a stupid idea. You should have taken my advice—"

"Your *unsolicited* advice," he interjected as he cleaned himself up.

"Does it matter? At least we would have something to show for it and the kitchen wouldn't look like a scene from *Animal House*," I said, then dipped my finger into one of the lumpy blobs on the counter and smeared it across his cheek.

Nick narrowed his eyes. "Wipe it off."

"Make me," I said with a wicked smile.

"Is that a challenge?"

"Maybe. What are you going to do about it?" I said, reaching up to spread more batter across his other cheek. Nick captured my wrist, his gaze intense, making my pulse race.

Then all at once we crashed together, two hormonal magnets colliding. Our mouths connected, and when our lips parted and tongues grazed against each other, I was gone, consumed by him. Nick pulled my waist against his, then lifted me up and placed me on the counter. My fingers curled into his shirtfront, tugging him even closer so that there was no room for a breath between us.

A car alarm blared somewhere outside, loud and angry, and we broke apart, gasping, our breathing erratic. Nick dropped his head to my shoulder and let out a soft laugh.

I ran my fingers through his hair and said, "I guess that's our cue to clean up this mess and finish the cake before my father comes home."

Wiggling out of his grasp, I hopped off the counter,

readjusted my tank top, and smoothed down my hair. Then I walked over to the counter and found the recipe card so we could get started again.

Nick followed me. "I say we forget it," he said, reclaiming my waist, a mischievous grin on his face. Then he took the card from my hand and flung it over his shoulder.

I tried catching it in midair but was too late. The card fluttered in between the kitchen cabinet and the refrigerator. "Now look what you did," I said, poking his shoulder. "Go get it."

Nick pushed the fridge flush against the wall and extended his arm as far as it would reach, searching around until he pulled out an index card. Using the fridge door handle for support, he hoisted himself up off the floor and handed it to me.

It was a recipe card, but it wasn't for Ernie's Incredible Edible Carrot Cake.

Summer Peach Cobbler was scrawled across the top. The card was covered in dust and grime, the paper yellowed, edges tattered, ink faded. I cleaned off the filth with the hem of my shirt and stared at the elegant script, knowing immediately it had belonged to my mother.

Tracing the outline of her words, I found myself wondering about her. "Your mother needed to fly, baby girl," was all my father would say anytime I asked. He rarely talked about her or their life together. I knew my father still loved her. The framed photo he kept propped up on his nightstand said as much. In it, my mother's face glowed above a single candle placed haphazardly atop a red velvet cupcake, a tiny bundle swaddled in pink cashmere resting snugly against her sweat-stained hospital gown. The blue of her eyes flickered in the soft, yellow light and her smile, wide and bright, consumed the image.

Written on the back in my father's chicken scratch were the words *Elizabeth with Lillie, twenty minutes old.*

A tear tumbled down my cheek and fell onto the recipe card. Then came another. Followed by another. I didn't bother to wipe them away. At the edge of my consciousness, I heard my name being called.

"Lillie, what is it?" Nick said, resting a firm hand on my arm. "What's wrong?"

I peered up at him, my vision blurred. "Can we make this instead?"

His brow knit as he took the card from my hand, smudging the ink when he wiped away my tears. From his unsure expression, I could tell he knew its origin. Nick met my gaze, his eyes concerned.

"Are you sure?" he asked. "I don't want you upset by this."

"I'm not upset," I whispered, smiling through my tears. "Promise."

"Then why are you crying?"

"Because it was hers."

Nick searched my face. Then he absently linked our fingers together, swinging our arms back and forth, and said, "What do you need me to do?"

For the remainder of the afternoon, we stood side-by-side, Nick blanching the peaches in boiling water and peeling away the skin, while I mixed the filling and prepared the drop-biscuit topping. Before long we were sitting at the kitchen table, treating ourselves to a second helping of bubbling, gooey, peachy goodness, the carrot cake long forgotten.

The distant sound of the front door closing jolted us out of our seats. We looked at each other with wide, frantic eyes. But it was too late to do anything. My father was already striding toward us.

"Baby girl, can you move Big Blue? It's block—" My father came to an abrupt halt, eyes bulging as he took in the obliterated kitchen.

"We made peach cobbler," I blurted, thrusting my still-steaming portion at his chest.

My father looked down at the plate in his hand and scrunched his nose. "By the looks of this kitchen, should I be eating this?"

"We had a small episode earlier," I said, casting a wry glance at Nick, who fidgeted like he wished he could eject himself from the situation.

"In my defense, that crazy electrical appliance had no warning label on it," Nick protested. "Had I known it might get violent like that, I would have used a wooden spoon instead."

"Son, not even a tornado could have caused this much damage," my father said.

"Try some, Dad," I said. "It's delicious. Really."

Tentatively my father picked up the fork and speared a peach segment. He popped the bite into his mouth, and to his surprise, his eyes lit up. "You're right. This is darn good, baby girl. Did you use those white peaches I bought at the farmers' market?"

"Yeah," I said. "We didn't have any yellow ones, so I improvised. Hope that's all right."

"Mmm-hmm," my father hummed while he chewed another bite. "It tastes familiar."

"We used Mom's recipe."

My father dropped the fork onto the plate and stared at me, blinking rapidly, before he replied in an oddly strained voice, "Whose recipe?"

"Mom's recipe," I repeated, showing him the index card. "Nick found it on the floor next to the fridge. I made a few adjustments, but it's mostly the same."

Without a word and with shaking hands, my father placed the plate on the counter and bolted from the kitchen, leaving Nick and me standing there, dumbstruck.

We found him outside on the porch, staring blankly into the distance.

"Dad?" I asked, hovering my hand over his shoulder.

After a long moment, my father turned and looked at me with red-rimmed eyes. Tears threatened to cascade down his cheeks, and I held my breath—I'd never seen my father cry before, and I wasn't prepared for how to handle it now.

"Baby girl, I want that recipe added to the diner's weekly dessert Blue Plate Specials, and I want you to make it." He squeezed my arm. "*Promise me* you'll make it."

Before I could respond, he stepped inside the house, the screen door slamming shut behind him in an exclamation point. I promised anyway. *Of course* I promised, spending one afternoon every week preparing my mother's cobbler. And every time a peach slipped in my hand as I peeled away the skin or my back ached from crafting batch after batch, I felt a kinship with her—a connection stronger than DNA.

Once upon a time, I had these dreams of following in my mother's footsteps, of someday taking over Turner's Greasy Spoons and creating dishes of my own that would nourish people's souls the way hers had. But then years later I learned the truth about my mother and why she left. So I gave up those childish dreams.

I haven't made her peach cobbler since.

"Mr. Stokes will see you now," the receptionist says, startling me when she touches my shoulder. Her cheeks are flushed as pink as a Mary Kay Cadillac, probably from her ridiculous attempts at flirting with my father.

She leads us into a corner conference room with

marble floors, a large mahogany table, and floor-to-ceiling windows looking out at the west side of downtown Dallas. Lining the adjacent wall is an antique sideboard with a platter of pastries and a sterling silver coffee urn perched on top. My father places the box of raspberry oatmeal bars next to the bowl filled with sugar cubes and pours himself a cup of coffee. He's midsip when Roger Stokes enters the conference room, wearing what must be a four-thousand-dollar Italian suit.

"Jack, my friend," he says, slapping my father on the back. "Sorry I kept you waiting."

Hot coffee sloshes out of the cup, landing on my father's calloused hands. He winces slightly, but he doesn't yelp or cause a scene. My father has never been one to outwardly display pain or weakness. Instead, he wipes up the mess with his shirtsleeve. It's the nicest shirt he owns, and now it's marred with a stain like every other piece of clothing in his closet. My father says hello to Roger and introduces me.

"Ah, Lillie," Roger says, shaking my hand. "Wonderful to meet you."

I return the greeting and study him. He seems oddly familiar, but I can't quite place him. He's a tall man with reddish-brown hair, wire-rimmed glasses, and a large, round belly that dares the buttons on his starched-white shirt to pop off like corks flying out of champagne bottles.

"Let's sit," Roger says, gesturing at the conference table where a folder is placed in front of three rolling chairs.

I take the seat across from my father and glare at him. He's leaning back in his chair, hands linked behind his head, smiling. He's so at ease, comfortable, as if he's happy watching my life bounce around in uncertainty like the numbered balls in a lottery machine.

"Quit frowning, baby girl," my father says. "This'll feel like home again in no time."

Narrowing my eyes, I mutter that I doubt that very much.

My father pretends he doesn't hear me, which seems to be a pattern lately, and turns to Roger, who is sitting at the head of the table. "I'll let you explain to Lillie. She's running this dog and pony show from now on. I brought the sustenance," he says, gesturing to the raspberry oatmeal bars on the sideboard. "Feel free to help yourself."

I start to tell him that this isn't a joke, that this is my life, but stop myself when I realize there's no point. My father is beyond reasoning with. He's always been this way. When his mind is set on something, there's no persuading him differently.

"Now, before we begin," Roger says, facing me, "I assume Jack's made you aware of his situation?"

"Told Lillie yesterday," my father says. "Took the news like a real sport." He takes a sip of his coffee and sighs, but does it so dramatically that he looks like an actor in a Folgers commercial.

I sit back in my chair and cross my arms, my lips pressed in a thin line. My father has a knack for reducing me to a petulant teenager.

"Great," Roger says. "Now contained in these folders are copies of a legal document. The original was notarized last week and placed on file. Jack already knows the nature of this document, but since you're unfamiliar, Lillie, spend a few minutes reading it over. Once you're finished, I'd be happy to answer any questions you have."

I nod and open the folder, examining the paper inside.

A medical power of attorney?

My father's signature is scrawled at the bottom, followed by two witnesses: Sullivan Grace and—

"*Nick* witnessed this?" I blurt.

Roger shifts in his chair, looking as uncomfortable as I feel, though I'm not sure why. He doesn't even know Nick.

"Sure did," my father says. Like it's no big deal. Like my *ex-fiancé* being a witness on a document that could someday determine my father's existence isn't some messed-up scenario out of *Twin Peaks*.

Maybe there's another explanation, I think. *There has to be another explanation.*

"Nick's not your surgeon, is he?" I say.

My father frowns. "Course not, baby girl."

Roger clears his throat. "And if he was, he wouldn't be eligible to act as a witness on a medical power of attorney."

"Oh." *Then why?*

In all the times I've spoken to my father since leaving Dallas, not once did he mention that he and Nick are still close. Though, if I'm being honest, I can't say I'm surprised. Nick and my father always did have this special bond between them. When I was a little girl, it used to make me green with envy, like maybe my father cared more about Nick than he cared about me. But as I got older, I could see their relationship with more clarity. Nick was a boy desperate for a father's attention, even if it wasn't from his own. It was a known fact the hospital came first in the Preston family. Even when Nick was a child, Dr. Preston's presence in his life was determined by the needs of Baylor Medical.

I clear my throat. "Isn't this a bit overkill?" I say, tapping the document. Once again I have this nagging sense that my father is hiding something.

"You can never be too careful, baby girl. It's still surgery I'm having, and I ain't the age I used to be," my father says. "Remember ol' Dolores Pinkston?"

I sigh and give him a pointed stare, as if to say, *Why would I?*

"You know, she always put cinnamon roll frosting in her coffee instead of creamer?" When I don't respond, he continues. "Well, anyway, two years ago she went in for surgery and ended up in a coma. Never woke up. But she had one of these and it saved her family a lot of trouble. So really this is just a precaution in case I decide being under is more my cup of tea. You'll get to pull the plug, guilt free."

I roll my eyes. "I wouldn't dare do that. You'd haunt me for eternity."

"Only if you make a poor life choice and dash off to that frozen tundra of yours." He says it in that joking way of his, but the uneasy feeling in my stomach has returned.

Before I start to worry, I remind myself that while my father is devious and manipulative, it's almost always what he's hinting at that's the issue. Which leads me right back to the diner, right back to my roots, right back to home.

Or at least where he thinks my home should be.

6

JUST THE SMELL OF CINNAMON GRIDDLE CAKES IS HEALING.

When I was a little girl, my father would whip up a batch anytime I felt sick. He said the pillows of deliciousness had restorative powers, claiming that if chicken noodle soup and his cinnamon griddle cakes were thrown together in a boxing ring, the heady scent of cinnamon would deliver the knockout punch every time.

Even now, as I ladle more batter onto the griddle, the spices tickle my nose, releasing the tension in my neck and back. I already feel more refreshed. Last night, after my father and I parted ways at the attorney's office, I returned to the house to continue sifting through the diner's files. At some point I dozed off on a stack of unpaid supplier invoices. I woke up this morning with a pounding headache, an aching neck, and the FedEx man banging on the front door. When Thomas Brandon said he'd rush documents over for me to review, I expected a folio's worth, not *three boxes.*

I'm not sure what exactly inspired me to rummage through the kitchen for the requisite ingredients, seeing as how I can't remember the last time I cooked a meal—a bad case of regression, perhaps?

Whatever the reason, after I spent several hours sorting through the mound of files from White, Ogden, and Morris, I found myself in my father's kitchen, measuring and mixing and *cooking*. I don't know what's happening to me. I've worked so hard to establish order, structure, control in my life, but being back here is making a mess of all that, smudging the lines I've drawn.

While I wait for the cakes to finish, I study the mansion next door, observing a grounds crew from a landscaping service haul garbage bags and hedge trimmers to their company truck. Even though the Rosenbloom family has been my father's neighbors since Nick's parents sold the house when I was in high school, I can't help but think of them as impostors. I keep expecting to see Charlotte Preston and her country club cronies gossiping on the veranda as they sip Bellinis. Or Dr. Preston pacing in his navy jacket and cuffed khaki dress slacks on the long circular drive as he shouts into his cell phone at some poor soul at Baylor Medical about his recent transplant patient. Or Nick sitting under the large oak tree in the backyard, writing in his Moleskine notebook and strumming pretty songs on—

I push the thought away. *Nick's not that person anymore,* I remind myself, remembering the edge in his voice, his hard stare, the bite in his words: *How would I know that? You left.*

I knew there was a possibility I'd run into him again, but I didn't expect it to be less than a day after showing up in Dallas. I wonder if Wes told him about my arrival or if it truly was a coincidence.

As I'm plating up the last cinnamon cake, the front door swings open and slams against the wall. Spinning around, the batter spoon dangling from my mouth, I find

Annabelle fighting her way through the boxes blocking the entryway. Hunger distracted me from moving them earlier.

"What is all this crap?" she mumbles to herself as the hem of her cardigan catches on a box corner.

A cheek-splitting smile spreads across my face. "Need some help?"

With a hard yank, she tugs herself free and stares at me, blinking once, twice. Then she springs into action.

"Shut up! You hot bitch. Get your ass over here," she says with a squeal, kissing my cheek before hugging me so tight I almost burst. Hugging her makes me think of summer days sunbathing at the pool, trips to the mall followed by sleepovers, frilly dresses and high school dances.

"Hey, kid," she says, her favorite nickname for me. "Sorry for just dropping by."

"I'm glad you did," I say, pulling back and taking her in.

Her once chin-length black hair has been replaced with long, sleek layers that frame her face and fall down her back. Her makeup is more subdued and classic, enhancing her alabaster skin and violet eyes. She's traded in the jeans and flip-flops from our college days for a pale-green, fitted dress and nude peep-toe heels. But above all that, underneath her smile, she seems sadder, harder, like the light that used to radiate from inside her is now a flicker.

There's a prolonged moment of unease when I remember my conversation with Wes, how my best friend has been lying to me for months. For a second, I consider admitting that I know about the demise of their relationship, but stop myself. Shouldn't she be the one to tell me? Instead I say, "You look good, lady."

She hesitates, and I wonder if she can sense that I

already know her secret by the tone of my voice. "I can't believe you're here. I missed the hell out of you."

"Missed you more."

"How'd Old Man Jack convince you to finally come home?"

"He faked an emergency," I say, then fill her in on the details.

Annabelle smiles, but it seems forced.

"You hungry?" I say, gesturing to the steaming stack of cinnamon griddle cakes on the counter. "I was about to eat a late breakfast."

Craning her neck, she first eyes the plate, then the bag of powdered sugar beside it. I swear there's drool in the corner of her mouth, but instead of taking me up on the offer, she says, "There's no time. We can catch up in the car. You're supposed to be at the Upper Crust meeting, remember? Sullivan Grace will break my fingers one by one if I arrive without you. I think she suspects you're going to bail."

Of course I'm going to bail. I told Sullivan Grace yesterday that I couldn't be involved. She obviously chose to ignore that. My father must have rubbed off on her.

I flop down in a kitchen chair. "Did everyone know I was supposed to be participating in this baking competition except for me?"

At least Annabelle tries to look sheepish when she says, "Sullivan Grace and I sit on the planning committee for the event, and Old Man Jack's been talking about it nonstop for the past month. He expects you to claim the title."

"So I've heard."

Annabelle walks over to the towering plate of cinnamon griddle cakes and steals one off the top. Leaning against the counter, she tears off a piece and tilts her head back, dropping it into her mouth. She swallows and says, "You know your dad won two years ago, right?"

"Really?" In truth, I didn't even know he competed.

"It was a total upset. Everyone expected Thelma Wilbanks to win with her sage and blood orange cheese-cake, but your dad showed up with an off-the-cuff grape-fruit jam rugelach and blew everyone away. He raised over eleven thousand dollars for charity and was even featured in *D Magazine*."

That little sneak. I wonder what else he hasn't told me.

"Last year he had to drop out at the last minute and a Granny Smith apple turnover swept the competition," she continues. "I'm pretty sure Old Man Jack will have an aneurism if that happens again."

I roll my eyes. "Only my father would get riled up about a poor, helpless apple taking the grand prize."

Annabelle sighs. "I know this isn't your life anymore— it hasn't been for a long time—but do this for your dad. It would mean everything to him." She pushes off the counter and comes to stand beside me, cinnamon griddle cake in hand. She is quiet for a moment, staring at me with an intensity I don't understand, but finally she says, "The competition is right after Halloween, so you'll still be here anyway. Then you can fly back to Chicago. Everything else, including the diner, will sort itself out." As if her guilt-inducing words aren't enough, she lays it on thick with the puppy-dog eyes.

I feel myself softening like cereal in milk. "I'll *consider* it." Plucking a griddle cake from the stack, I fold it in half and take a dramatic bite. The texture is fluffy, and the subtle sweetness of the vanilla extract blends perfectly with the sharp contrast of the cinnamon. "But I'm not making peach cobbler."

She sucks in her cheeks as if she's battling against a

grin. "Of course not." Her tone is matter-of-fact, but her expression says, *You'll be eating those words.*

THIRTY MINUTES later I'm riding shotgun in Annabelle's Mini Cooper on the way to Junior League headquarters. Signs, cars, and skyscrapers whip past my window as Annabelle speeds across town. Her haphazard lane changes make me feel like I'm a stunt double in an action movie. My feet push against the floorboard and my wrist is sore from using the dashboard to keep me from crashing through the windshield.

"Hey, shouldn't we be going that way?" I say as we pass our exit.

"Quick detour," she says, jerking the steering wheel violently. The car cuts across three lanes of traffic. Horns blare from every direction. A truck barrels past us. The driver yells something out his window and flips us off. Annabelle doesn't seem to notice. "I need to drop off some flyers for an event next week."

What feels like a nanosecond later, the car swings into the parking lot of a strip mall near the SMU campus. Annabelle parks the car in the handicap spot in front of the entrance to the bookstore, leaving the engine idling.

"I'll only be a minute," she says, grabbing a thick manila envelope from the backseat before dashing inside.

While I wait, I turn on the radio, pressing the prepro-grammed buttons until I settle on a station playing a sad country rock song. There's a familiarity about it—the haunting melody, maybe, or the way it speaks of struggling to survive once-requited love—even though I'm sure I've never heard it before.

The song ends, replaced by the radio DJ's voice. "That

was 'August,' the latest single from our own local boys, the Randy Hollis Band.''

I gasp, scrambling to turn up the volume, wishing I'd paid more attention yesterday when I saw them at the Prickly Pear.

"Tickets for their upcoming tour go on sale Saturday," the DJ continues, "and their new record, *Resolution,* hits stores next month. We'll be giving away advance copies all week, so stay tuned—"

Silently promising to order a copy, I adjust the volume and check my watch. Five minutes have passed since Annabelle went inside. I wait for five more. People continue to walk in and out of the bookstore. Still no sign of Annabelle.

Sighing, I turn off the ignition, grab my purse from the backseat, and go inside, glancing around. When I don't see her anywhere, I take a quick stroll along the perimeter, past the literature and young adult sections. From the corner of my eye, I catch a glimpse of her in the college apparel section, but she's not perusing the merchandise. Instead she appears to be in a very tense and awkward conversation with Wes.

His hands are shoved into his pockets, and his eyes are glued to the sign hanging above the entrance to the university textbook area. He's wearing a backward baseball cap, his curly hair sticking out in tufts underneath, and a bitter expression. Annabelle's arms are crossed over her chest. Her cheeks are flushed and wet. From my vantage point, I can see her bottom lip quivering. The way she's standing makes her look small and fragile, as if she's on the verge of crumbling like a cake that doesn't have enough eggs to bind it together.

In an aisle nearby, a group of women point and whisper. I watch as a store employee tiptoes around Wes, straightening a rack of red and blue polo shirts, no doubt hoping to appear invisible.

A beat later, I'm beside Annabelle. For a moment, they both seem confused as to why I'm there.

"Hey, guys," I say, my gaze darting back and forth between them. "Everything okay?"

Wes flinches but stays quiet.

Blinking back tears, Annabelle takes a deep breath and says with false bravado, "Everything's great. We were . . . catching up."

Wes shifts on his feet. "Whatever," he mumbles, his attention focused on the group of women not even trying to hide their eavesdropping. He looks like he wishes the floor would open up and swallow him whole. "This is such bullshit."

"Hey, knock it off with the attitude, Wesley," I say.

I can see a battle being fought behind his eyes, as if he's contemplating whether or not to challenge me. Finally, he shakes his head and says, "I gotta go." Then he glares at Annabelle, and without even a good-bye to me, stalks away.

Annabelle's shoulders slump and her body seems to collapse in on itself.

As I watch him flee the bookstore, I wonder where the old Wesley went, my protective older brother who can consume twenty hard-shell tacos in less than seven minutes and cringes when people use the word "panties." The Wes that gave Annabelle bouquets of irises because they matched her eyes and mouthed lines to her from the front row of the Highland Park High School auditorium when she landed the female lead in *Macbeth*.

This Wesley is bitter, jaded.

When we get back into the car, Annabelle refuses to meet my gaze. She starts the engine and fiddles with the radio, her fingers shaking as she switches from station to station at lightning speed.

I place my hand over hers and wait. After a long moment, she hits the power button. The silence is heavy around us.

"How long have you known?" she says finally.

"A couple of days," I say, hesitant. "I ran into Wes at the diner. He told me—"

"Everything?"

I shake my head. "Only that you guys broke up."

"I thought he would've told you sooner," Annabelle says. "Every time you called I kept expecting you to bring it up, but you never did."

"It's been awhile since Wes and I have talked," I say. "I guess this is why."

She nods. When she doesn't respond, I squeeze her shoulder. "I'm trying to understand why you didn't tell me."

Annabelle tugs on her seat belt and stares out the window, her eyes locked on a plastic shopping bag skittering along the sidewalk. "Because you never asked."

My mouth drops open. That can't be right. I think back to our conversations over the past few months and all the things we talked about—when her event planning company was featured in *InStyle Weddings*, how she adopted a cocker spaniel puppy named Finley, when she signed the papers on a newly built condo in the heart of Uptown.

The truth hits me like a slap across the face. I assumed Wes had been a part of those milestones, but all that time Annabelle had been alone and heartbroken. *And I had never asked.*

"Annabelle," I start, then falter. "I'm . . . I'm so . . ."

"I slept with someone else," she says, her voice breaking. "Only once, but it was enough."

My mind fills with questions. Never in my wildest dreams would I imagine that Annabelle would cheat. On Wes, no less. I want to offer support, but the words dry up in my throat.

She tells me she waited two months to confess, until the lies and the guilt became so unbearable that she spilled the beans one morning in the grocery store, smack dab in the middle of the frozen dinner aisle. Wes simply said nothing. Not when Annabelle cried and begged his forgiveness, right there by the Stouffer's lasagna. Not when he stormed out of the store and drove away, leaving Annabelle to fend for her own ride home. Not even when he showed up at their rental house hours later and emptied his side of the closet into three suitcases and a duffel bag. He loaded his things into the back of his Jeep and left. She's tried to apologize—attempt number eight being only a few moments ago—but Wes still refuses to even look at her.

"Is this why we're at the bookstore?" I ask.

Annabelle rests her forehead against the steering wheel. "No. Him being here was the universe fucking with me."

"Do you want to tell me why?"

Sighing, she straightens up and says, "We'd been fighting for a while . . . it's just . . . what kind of couple that's been together since they were kids isn't married by now?" She sees me flinch and says, "Shit, sorry. You and Nick aside. I only meant that I'm thirty. It's normal for me to want a husband and kids. Hell, most people already have both of those things by our age."

"And what did Wes want?"

"Not that." She shakes her head as if dislodging a memory. "He's been dating a bit. I think he's trying to punish me. I can't blame him, but it still hurts so damn much, Lillie. When does it stop hurting?"

A lump forms in my stomach as I recall the fateful

night five years ago when I stumbled off the plane in Chicago with my heart shattered into so many pieces I was sure I'd never be able to put it together again. How despite my best efforts to move forward and hold my head high, around every corner and down every street, Nick's ghost haunted me, refusing to let me forget all we had and then lost.

I remember once when I was walking down Michigan Avenue on my way home from taking a final exam, I swore I saw Nick standing outside Crate & Barrel, in front of a window display outfitted with glittery ornaments and signs advertising Christmas sales. His cheeks were red and his breath escaped in clouds in the bitter cold and falling snow. Resting in his gloved hands was a steaming cup. As I crossed the street to approach him, I remember thinking how free he looked—so different from the man who ran his life like he conducted his operating room, with controlled, steady precision—and for a moment, I allowed myself to hope. That maybe he came to apologize, to confess how much he loved me and that he was a fool to let me go. That we could return to that cherished place where we were still two kids, counting the licks to the center of a Tootsie Pop. But before I could reach him, he was gone. A figment of my imagination.

"I don't know when the hurt goes away," I say, unsure if it ever does. Maybe the pain just scabs over until a memory, a chance encounter, a conversation causes it to crack open and spill out. My mind drifts to Nick in the Prickly Pear, the sound of his laughter, those piercing blue eyes, the expression on his face when he saw my engagement ring and the overwhelming sadness I felt. "But sometimes, if you're lucky, you get a second chance."

"Is that what Drew is for you?"

I bite my lip, unsure of what to say. Drew isn't a second

chance. He's the bandage that made everything okay again. He's easiness and warmth and comfort.

"Loving Wes has filled my whole life," Annabelle says when I don't respond. "I don't *want* to let him go, but I don't have it in me to fight for this anymore."

I'm struck by an eerie sense of déjà vu, remembering how I uttered similar words to Annabelle one dreary afternoon five years ago. How I looked her in the eye and finally admitted aloud what we'd all already known—Nick and I had become strangers. Nothing like the foolish teenagers who used to crave each other in a crazy, addictive kind of way that is sacred to first love, back when our world was new and full of possibility and I still believed in magic.

But Wes and Annabelle aren't us. They play hard and love harder. They're scoreboard lights and packed-tight bleachers, Wes running down the football field and Annabelle cheering from the sidelines. They're karaoke competitions, belly flops during Fourth of July pool parties, and coordinating Halloween costumes. Two people deserving of a different ending—a better ending—than the one I had with Nick.

"I think you still have some fight left in you," I say, tucking a flyaway hair behind her ear. "Wes will come around. Give him time."

Annabelle sighs. "Forgiveness isn't supposed to come with strings. Or retribution."

No, forgiveness is to be given freely. Unapologetically.

But does it ever work that way?

7

Junior League headquarters is housed in a sprawling Classical Revival estate known as Hasell House, named after Sullivan Grace's grandmother, former League president Harper Dell Hasell and the original Ms. Bless Your Heart, for her generous bequest to the charitable organization. With its soaring white columns, winged porticos, and Old Carolina redbrick siding, the Hasell House is where the ladies of Dallas's social elite go to be seen.

I follow Annabelle through the wrought-iron gate and stroll along the paved path to the entrance. On the far side of the grounds, positioned under a cluster of trees, is a bronzed fountain with birds taking a bath. On the covered porch, rocking chairs creak slowly in the breeze as soft sounds from a piano float out the stately windows.

Inside headquarters, the late-morning sun fills the foyer, frothing up the walls like champagne and spilling onto the grand, sweeping staircase. On my right, in a floral wallpapered room, a group of League members chat around an oval table while working in an assembly line, folding papers and stuffing envelopes. A sitting room adorned with ornamental crown moldings, tapestries, and antique furniture opens to the left. Ahead lies a massive ballroom featuring an equally massive crystal chandelier.

Annabelle leads me past the staircase toward the tearoom, where League volunteers set tables with silver flatware and fine bone china in preparation for the afternoon service. Even though the committee meeting started fifteen minutes ago, Annabelle insists on dropping by the kitchen to grab some finger sandwiches, pimento cheese dip, and lemon poppy seed scones.

"If we walk in with snacks, Sullivan Grace is less likely to whip us for being late," she says as we climb the staircase, a tray propped on her hip. "But stay away from the scones if you value your life."

We stop in front of large wooden double doors with a sign that reads: MEETING IN SESSION, RING BELL FOR ADMITTANCE. Never one for convention, Annabelle uses the toe of her stiletto to give the doors two swift kicks.

"A simple knock would have sufficed," I say, nudging her with my elbow.

"Too easy." She winks.

A moment later, the doors crack open and a woman with hair more processed and yellow than American cheese appears in front of me.

"Who are you?" she asks with a southern drawl, dissecting my simple gray blouse and black pants, her nose wrinkled and lips puckered like a goldfish. I may have been offended if her expression weren't so laughable. First my father, then Sullivan Grace, and now her? Apparently people in Dallas think I should be dressed for a debutante ball at all times.

Before I can respond, her gaze swings to Annabelle and the tray of goodies. Her face lights up like a child discovering a pot of gold at the end of a rainbow. "Why, Annabelle, aren't you the sweetest thing, bringing us treats and everything," she says, opening the doors completely and ushering us inside.

Annabelle doesn't even have time to place the tray on the sideboard before the woman attacks the pimento cheese, stuffing her mouth with crackers as she gabs on about the latest Junior League rumor circulating around town.

"Jesus, Bernice," Annabelle mutters. "You're allowed to take a breath between bites."

"Bernice Rimes?" I say in surprise. "You look . . . older." Shorter. Rounder. As in, nothing like the first runner-up to America's Junior Miss pageant I remember from high school.

Bernice blinks, a finger sandwich hovering inches from her face, and finally her fish lips stop blabbing. Obviously Sullivan Grace didn't tell her I was coming to this meeting or else she wouldn't be staring at me like I'm a stranger. Then it hits her. "Oh my word, is that really you, Lillie Turner? I didn't recognize you without all those bacon grease stains you used to wear."

I force a smile and remember that Bernice has the IQ of a rubber spatula. Not even her father, with all his money and connections, could get her accepted to SMU. "Guess we both grew up," I say, then grab some cucumber sandwiches before she inhales them all.

Bernice makes a *pffft* noise, then fusses with arranging the scones.

A throat clears behind me. An ominous silence settles over the room. Annabelle and I glance at each other and cringe—we know we're in for it. We spin to face Sullivan Grace.

"Ladies, what do I always say about interrupting?" Sullivan Grace says in an imperious tone. "And about being punctual?"

Annabelle and I glance at each other again and grin. "Only the Devil's allowed to be late," we recite at the same time, then break into a fit of giggles.

Despite her pleasant smile, Sullivan Grace doesn't seem amused. She eyes us up and down, shaking her perfectly coiffed head in admonishment. Around her neck are the heirloom pearls she never takes off, unless she's using them to strangle someone. Like Annabelle and me in about two seconds. Before she has the chance, we slink away like scolded children.

Annabelle takes a seat at the far end of the table, while I sit in an open chair at the other end next to Paulette Bunny—Sullivan Grace's closest friend and, as it so happens, a country club acquaintance of Nick's mother. Time has been kind to her, though I suspect that is more a result of her marrying a plastic surgeon than genetics.

We exchange hellos and make small talk, which equates to Paulette bombarding me with questions: *What have I been up to? Is there a man in my life? How do I like living in Chicago?* I respond with short, vague answers. Finally she pats my hand and says, "I'm so thrilled to see you, sugar. Chicago has definitely agreed with you." She leaves to refill her tea.

Glancing around the table, I spot an empty seat next to Bernice, who is wiping cracker crumbs off her wool dress. Annabelle catches my gaze, nods at Sullivan Grace spreading raspberry preserves on a scone, and mouths to me, *Told ya.* I smile.

As if she knows we're talking about her, Sullivan Grace

blots her mouth with a linen napkin and says, "Now that Lillie has decided to join us, let's begin."

I notice she doesn't include Annabelle in that comment, like it's my fault we're late. Never mind that I didn't agree to come to this meeting in the first place or that I have more pressing matters to deal with.

"Why is Lillie here, anyway?" Bernice pipes up, her southern accent sounding more pronounced. "She's not on the planning committee. She's not even in the League."

"She's here because she missed all the information sessions and needs to figure out what the hell is going on," Annabelle says.

Bernice sits up straighter in her chair and says with a hint of condescension, "Well, I'm not sure her being here is appropriate. Committee meetings are supposed to be closed to nonmembers."

"Would you give it a rest already?" Annabelle snaps. "Once Lillie's had a chance to review her entrant packet, she'll be excused and the meeting will continue on as planned. Happy?"

Bernice sets her jaw and looks away, shaking her head.

Sullivan Grace ignores the entire exchange and takes a sip of tea before launching right in. "Lillie, everyone here at the Junior League so appreciates your willingness to participate in this year's Upper Crust competition, especially given the short notice."

Annabelle snorts and mumbles under her breath, "Willing my ass."

"Language, sugar," Paulette says, tapping Annabelle on the shoulder as she passes by before reclaiming the seat beside me.

Across the table, Bernice snickers, a satisfied expression on her face. Annabelle opens her mouth to say something, but Sullivan Grace cuts her off.

"Ladies, may I finish?" Smoothing her pristine cardigan, her fingernails painted to pale-pink perfection, she continues, "As I was saying, Lillie, if only more people understood the importance of giving back to the community. All of us could learn from your example."

I shift in my seat. "Thank you, but—"

"And we think it's wonderful how *accommodating* you are to honor Jackson's request to make Elizabeth's summer peach cobbler recipe," Sullivan Grace says, her voice escalating in pitch, as if she thinks using polite words to speak over me will somehow prevent an argument. "I know he is simply *thrilled* about it."

Taking a deep breath, I square my shoulders and find my center. "About that, Ms. Hasell. Like I said before, I'm flattered you want me to do this, but I don't bake anymore."

"You were this morning," Annabelle says, an eyebrow arched.

I shoot her a look that could rival my father's, but Annabelle's expression doesn't waver.

I sigh and turn to Sullivan Grace. "*Assuming* I agree to participate, I'd prefer to create my own recipe," I say, thinking about all the amateur baking competitions I entered, all the medals hanging in my childhood room. How I developed every winning recipe in my father's kitchen. Never once did I consider competing with any of my mother's recipes. They were too private, pieces of her that never belonged to me.

After a pregnant pause where Sullivan Grace tugs at the strand of pearls around her neck, she says, "Lillie, dear, your insistence to try something new is admirable . . ." *Bless my heart.* "However, I'm afraid the date to change an entry has passed."

I lean forward. "Surely you can make an exception since—"

Sullivan Grace only peers at me.

"Why?" I ask. "Why the insistence for me to do this?"

"Because that's what Old Man Jack wants," Annabelle says with a shrug, as though that explains it.

I shake my head. "Not good enough."

"Apart from last year, Jackson has been a part of the Upper Crust since its inception five years ago," Sullivan Grace says. "His medical situation prevents him from competing this year, so he hopes that you will continue the tradition."

"Fine. I get that," I say. "But not with the peach cobbler." Just because my father prefers to live in a reality where my mother didn't disappear doesn't mean I'm going to do the same.

"Lillie, this isn't about your mother. Stop complicating things. Old Man Jack selected that recipe. He's no longer able to make said recipe, and like Sullivan Grace said, the date to change an entry has passed."

I sit back in my chair, stunned. Annabelle has always been direct, but this time her tone is different. Almost angry. The room goes quiet. Bernice and Paulette have been silent this whole time, and now they're both studying the table like it's the most mesmerizing thing in the world.

Sullivan Grace clears her throat. A tightness settles around her eyes that doesn't match the smile still plastered on her face. "Right, right. Excellent. Now here are your entry forms, dear," she says, extending a stack of papers in front of me. "Please pay special attention to the competition guidelines and rules. A disqualification wouldn't suit."

I pick up the packet my father so graciously filled out for me. While I flip through it, Sullivan Grace explains the rules.

I want to tell her not to bother. Instead, I keep my mouth shut, listening to Sullivan Grace prattle on about how each entry will be judged on taste, appearance, and creativity by a panel of industry experts and how the winning recipe of each category will be eligible for best in show and showcased in the *Junior League of Dallas Park Cities Cookbook*. The ultimate winner will earn a feature in *D Magazine*.

She finishes by saying, "You'll be competing in the fruit desserts category. And you're in luck because Jackson has already raised *and* exceeded the donation requirements for the event, so all you have to worry about is perfecting Elizabeth's recipe. And winning of course."

"Oh, is that all?" I question sarcastically.

Sullivan Grace presses her lips in a thin line. "Yes, well—"

Without warning, the heavy double doors burst open, followed by someone uttering apologies. My stomach drops as I place the voice and realize why my father's attorney, Roger Stokes, seemed so familiar yesterday. His daughter has arrived.

Margaret Ann Stokes sweeps into the room without a care for anyone else. Still gorgeous as ever, with a statuesque body even runway models envy—tall with long, slender legs, red hair that tumbles down her back in waves, and fair skin without a trace of freckles—she's fiery hot candy and knock-you-naked sexiness and the bane of my existence.

"Excuse my tardiness. Traffic is atrocious today," she says, fanning herself. A black ostrich Hermès Kelly bag swings from her forearm. "But here I am."

Here she is.

Margaret moves around the table, kissing everyone lightly on the cheek. When she embraces Annabelle in a full-blown hug complete with an extra squeeze at the end, I nearly choke on a cucumber sandwich. Arching an eyebrow, I give Annabelle a look that says she has some explaining to do. Annabelle only shrugs, as if to say, *Don't blame me. I didn't ask for her to do that.*

Then Margaret's gaze lands on me and she stops in her two-thousand-dollar Christian Louboutin high-heeled tracks. She seems about as happy to see me as if she discovered her Chanel sunglasses are fake.

The feeling is mutual.

I muster up a weak smile and a hello. It's the best I can do.

She doesn't reciprocate. "Why are *you* here?" Her words come out like a hiss. "Shouldn't you be in Chicago proving you're more than where you came from?"

Oh, the nerve of this woman.

Maybe it's how she still can't be cordial, even after all this time. Maybe it's the way she's always flaunted her status and smug superiority, merely tolerating those deemed beneath her. Or maybe it's the hard glint in her gray eyes that shows she's still bitter that someone like me, with my misfit upbringing and grease stains, beat someone like her, prom queen, cheerleading captain, president of Kappa Kappa Gamma. That even though she was never in the running in the first place, despite her old southern money and family ties, in her warped, jealous, pretentious mind, I stole the one person she wanted most—Nick.

Whatever the reason, I feel like goading her.

I stand. "Haven't you heard?" I say with a smile so phony it would make Sullivan Grace proud. "The committee was filling me in on my duties regarding this year's Upper Crust competition. You see, I've agreed to participate. I figure it's the least I can do since I'll be in town for a while."

Margaret narrows her eyes, her lips pursed. "A while?"

"For several weeks, at least. Isn't that fantastic?" I say, my smile growing bigger. "And if my father gets his way, I'll be back here permanently."

I don't wait to see my words register on her face. With a surge of adrenaline and something close to conviction, I lift my chin, walk out of the room, and descend the grand staircase, wondering what in the name of tangerine marmalade I just got myself into.

8

OUTSIDE AND AWAY FROM THE COMMOTION OF THE meeting, the covered porch is calm and quiet except for the faint rumbling coming from behind me, disturbing the solitude.

I turn to find Nick conked out in a rocking chair in front of the open windows. His head is slumped against his shoulder, lips parted. A small snore escapes each time he inhales. Figures. I should have recognized that sound. A baseball cap is draped over his knee, and his disheveled hair moves gently in the wind. The way his body sags in the chair reminds me of a rumpled dish towel. I notice the purple crescents underneath his eyes are more pronounced than they were at the Prickly Pear, as is the stubble lining his jaw. Another late night at the hospital, I gather.

For a second, I think he's here to see me, to make peace after our confrontation yesterday, but then decide it must be simply coincidence. He's made it clear he blames me for the destruction of our relationship. Perhaps he's running errands for his mother and dozed off, or maybe he's picking someone up. Whatever the reason, in his relaxed, unruly state, he appears out of place napping on Junior League's covered porch in the middle of the day.

Minutes pass while I wait for Annabelle to materialize from the meeting. Nothing. I sigh. I guess I'm going to be here awhile longer, so I may as well make myself comfortable.

Biting my lip, I consider my options. There's the obvious choice of the empty rocking chair next to Nick, though I'd rather not. The sunny grass near the flower beds seems inviting, but it's probably wet and swarming with gnats. Maybe I should go back inside, but another run-in with the Margaret may end in disaster. Or I could wait in the car . . .

What the heck is wrong with me?

With a calm, collected manner, I pull my shoulders back and claim the chair next to Nick. Rocking slowly back and forth, a breeze tickling my arms, I take in my surroundings. Birds cut across the sky and swoop down to the glinting bronze fountain, splashing in the water before soaring up again. On the other side of the wrought-iron fence, two women push strollers as they jog down the side-walk. Peeking over the trees, I see the historical neon sign of the Inwood Theatre in the distance.

Next to me, Nick stirs. His eyes flutter open but quickly close. Within seconds, his breathing is deep and steady again. He looks so peaceful, the way his chest rises and falls in an even rhythm. I can't remember the last time I saw him like this—vulnerable and without life's expectations weighing him down. I wonder if he still listens to the rain forest setting on the sound machine to lull him to sleep after a grueling hospital shift. When I moved to Chicago, it took six months of restless nights before I could sleep soundly without that annoying machine.

Nick stirs again, shifting his body toward mine. The

movement pulls up his T-shirt to expose a flat stomach and a thin line of hair that vanishes into black boxer briefs. My skin prickles, and I have an overwhelming, crazy urge to touch him there, to feel his hard muscles beneath my fingers. The way I used to, only back then my mouth followed everywhere my hands would explore. Warmth spreads through me as I remember the low, smooth rumble of his voice when my lips skimmed across his skin. The hiss that escaped from between his teeth when my tongue slid along the places he craved most.

I shake my head, erasing the memories like an Etch A Sketch, and concentrate on something other than my twitching fingers and the heat pooling in my belly—a garbage truck lumbering down a neighborhood street, dogs barking, the daytime traffic hum.

When I look back, Nick is awake and staring at me with puffy eyes. There's an intensity in them, holding mine captive. A thrum of electricity courses through my veins as his gaze rakes over my face, the length of my body. His eyes flick to my bare finger, where my diamond ring should be. If he's surprised it's not there, he does nothing to indicate it. The air around us feels charged with energy.

"Chicago doesn't have this," I blurt. My mouth has taken on a life of its own. "The openness. The humidity that sticks to your skin. Cheerwine floats at Mr. Vincent's Fountain Shop."

"What does it have?" His voice is raspy from sleep, and a shiver travels down my spine at the sound of it.

Swallowing, I say, "Snow. Lake Michigan. The best Italian beef sandwich you'll ever have."

He's quiet for a moment, his eyes searching mine like he's trying to decipher something in them. He clears his throat and says, "The Upper Crust is right around the corner. You better start practicing now. It may be a competition for charity, but it draws the attendance of some culinary heavy hitters."

"How'd you even know about the Upper Crust?"

A smile pulls up the corners of his mouth. "Jack hasn't shut up about it, among other things."

An ache expands in my chest that fills my empty spaces. Even after everything, how can Nick stay close with my father and discard me? Growing up, Nick practically lived at the diner or at my father's house. He had a designated seat at our kitchen table and his own list of chores. That changed, of course, when Nick started medical school. But still, their relationship remains intact.

"Are you making peach cobbler?" Nick asks.

"I think you already know the answer to that," I say, focusing on the way the sun haloes the trees, how the leaves shimmer in the golden glow.

He studies me, his mouth set in a line. "Is it because it was hers?"

I suck in a breath at his words—the same ones I said to him that day in my father's kitchen a lifetime ago, when I still had my innocence and I believed cooking was a special potion that could fix anything.

Silence stretches between us.

The wind picks up, whipping my hair. "Ouch," I say as something catches in my eye. I blink rapidly, but the object won't budge.

"Let me see." Nick groans when he sits up. The wooden boards creak under his feet as he comes to crouch down in front of me. His knees brush against mine. He's close enough that I can smell his scent—cedar wood and soap and hints of citrus. I hate how good he smells. "Tilt your head back and look up."

I do as he says. He holds my chin in one hand, and with the other, inspects my eye. His calloused fingers feel rough against my skin. Goose bumps pop up on my arms.

"There," he says. Instantly I feel relief. "Is that better?"

Blinking, I nod and wipe the tears from my eye.

"Jack told me about the diner," he says.

I shake my head. "Nick, don't."

"Why?"

"That's not who I am anymore."

Almost instinctively, he tucks a flyaway hair behind my ear, lingering on the spot where my jaw meets my neck. So simple, so natural, as if he touches me every day. "Are you sure?"

"Yes," I say, clenching my hands into fists to keep them from shaking. The electricity is thrashing through me like a live wire.

Nick leans in closer. His eyes are a sky I could fall into, an ocean I could drown in. Images of him peering down at me while he moved over me, inside me, flood my vision. His gaze drops to my mouth, and all at once it's like the missing years between us are gone and I forget why this isn't right or can't be real. My mind has become a haze of *kiss me, kiss me, kiss me.* I squeeze my eyes shut, waiting, wanting. I hear the rustle of his clothes, feel the scratch of his stubble against my cheek, his warm breath on my skin.

"I don't believe you," he whispers in my ear.

"What?" I ask, completely disoriented. My voice sounds strangled. My heart beats in my throat, so fast it hurts.

"I don't believe you," he says, louder and with an edge to it.

The fog in my head clears and I jerk back, my chest heaving. What am I doing? "You don't know me anymore, Nick."

He looks at me long and steady. "Whose fault is that?"

Not this again.

"These past five years are irrelevant," I say as anger builds inside me. "Even when I was here, I was never enough. You're the one who turned me into a stranger. You're the one who locked me out. Or have you forgotten that?"

"I remember. I remember *all* of it," he says, his voice hard, controlled. His eyes are bright with anger of his own. "But you didn't exactly try that hard to fight your way back in." Raking a hand through his hair, he stands and steps away from me. A muscle twitches in his jaw and his body is coiled tight. Finally he sighs and says, "Listen, Lillie—"

The mahogany door swings open. Margaret saunters onto the porch. She looks from me to Nick then back to me. Her gray eyes narrow and harden, as if she's summoning voodoo magic to curse me dead. She struts toward us, her hips swaying seductively. From the corner of my eye, I see Nick notices it, too. Sidling up next to him, Margaret flashes a smile that speaks of something more and hooks her arm through his, her red-lacquered nails digging possessively into his skin.

"Sorry I kept you waiting," she says in a tone too intimate for friendship, gazing at Nick through long, sultry lashes. "I hope I didn't make us late for tonight."

Late for tonight?

It hits me just as Margaret leans in and presses her glossed lips against his.

As if they're alone on the porch and I'm invisible in this rocking chair, she deepens the kiss, her hand tangling into Nick's hair. I swear I hear her moan. The anger drains out of me. My stomach rolls. I'm going to be sick. Still, I can't force my eyes anywhere else, but thankfully Nick breaks away before I lose my breakfast. He considers me warily. Margaret smirks in smug satisfaction, like after all those years of biding her time she finally won the trophy. Only this isn't a game.

"We should probably go," she says to Nick, then with a cool, patronizing stare, says to me, "We've got dinner reservations downtown and tickets to the show later."

"Mags," Nick says, his voice low and serious.

The use of a nickname knocks the air from my lungs. Nick never called her Mags or Maggie or any other endearing form of her given name. It was always Margaret.

"What?" she says, all innocent. She places a hand on his chest, right over his heart.

It's a surprisingly tender gesture for someone as vindictive as Margaret. A vision of what their life together must be like crystallizes in my mind. I imagine Baylor Medical fundraising events, Margaret on Nick's arm in a sparkling dress that costs more than my monthly salary. I imagine Nick and his father yucking it up with their fellow surgeons, while Margaret gossips with Charlotte and the other wives, secure in the knowledge that she will someday be one of them. I imagine five-course tasting menus crafted by Dean Fearing, Junior League charity auctions and society parties, season tickets to the symphony, and Saturday evening dinners at the club.

Aspects of Nick's world I never had any place in.

I avert my gaze, crossing my arms and pressing them tight against me like a shield. The sound of heels click-clacking on the grand staircase gets my attention. Seconds later, Annabelle flies onto the porch like a crazed banshee, her usually sleek black hair flailing in every direction.

"There you are. I've been search—" She skids to a stop and glances around, first at me, then at Nick, then at Margaret. "Oh shit."

"I'd love to stay and chat, but we're already running

behind," she says, flipping her hair over her shoulder and adjusting her five-thousand-dollar purse. "I'll see you next week for lunch, Annabelle."

They're having lunch together? First Nick and now my best friend?

By the triumphant grin on Margaret's face, she knows how much her words have affected me. I want to slap her. Correction, I want to ruin her.

I open my mouth to wipe the smile off her face, but Annabelle interrupts. "Lillie, we're leaving. Now." She grabs my wrist, pulls me to my feet, and drags me away. "I'll explain later," she whispers.

When Annabelle pushes me through the wrought-iron gate, I make the mistake of looking over my shoulder. Margaret is yapping to someone on her cell phone, appearing completely unfazed by what transpired on the porch, but Nick is watching me, his brow furrowed as if he's making sense of something, working it all out.

I wait until we're driving down Lovers Lane before bursting out with it. "How long, Annabelle?"

She shifts gears, the car jerking forward, and keeps her eyes straight ahead. "How long what?"

She knows *exactly* what I'm referring to. Why is she avoiding it?

"All of it. How long have you been keeping your friendship with her a secret from me?"

Annabelle fidgets in her seat. "We're not friends per se. More like casual acquaintances. We're collaborating on a project."

"For Junior League?"

"No, professionally. The event planning side of my company is working with her PR firm."

"Oh," I say, then take a deep breath, gathering courage

to ask what I really want to know. "And Nick? How long have they been involved?"

"Awhile," she hedges. "It's complicated."

"It appeared pretty black and white to me."

"There's a history there. It started after you left. Margaret introduced—"

I hold up a hand. "You know what? Never mind. It's none of my business."

"Lillie, would you—"

"Can we not talk about Nick and Margaret anymore?"

Annabelle shakes her head, muttering something under her breath.

I don't care what Nick does anymore. I've moved on. I have a happy life in Chicago.

So why does my heart feel like it's been pulverized in a garbage disposal?

9

THE FOLLOWING MORNING I'M SITTING AT THE DESK IN MY childhood room trapped on a conference call with Thomas Brandon and the rest of the strategy team.

Kingsbury Enterprises lost a portion of its funding allocated toward the second phase of the product launch, and the company is asking White, Ogden, and Morris to provide Dom Pérignon champagne consulting services on a sparkling cider budget.

As Thomas Brandon outlines the situation, I try hard to be an active participant in the discussion, to offer my opinion and give out-of-the-box solutions. It's what I excel at, why I'm often assigned to the more complicated, high-dollar projects. But today I'm struggling to even follow the conversation.

"Lillie, where are you on compiling those sales forecasts?" Thomas Brandon's nasally voice pierces my ear. "And I still haven't received the market analyses I requested."

I should have completed everything yesterday after Annabelle dropped me off rather than starting an hour ago, but I haven't been able to focus on anything except Junior League and what transpired on the porch. I can still feel Nick's stubble on my cheek, his calloused thumb below my ear. I *wanted* him to kiss me, touch me. Worse, I never even considered Drew. Guilt twists in my chest. But that was a momentary lapse in judgment. Nothing like that will happen again.

Besides, Nick is with Margaret now.

Images of them kissing, the smug look on Margaret's face, the way Nick called her Mags, flash through my mind, but I quickly blot them out.

"Lillie, the items?" Thomas Brandon barks out.

Before I can reply, Ben cuts in, "If she's unable to handle it, I'd be happy to do it." His tone is snide, but I'm sure to Thomas Brandon he sounds helpful, a real go-getter.

I remind myself that Ben is an audible breather with sardine-smelling breath. "Everything will be in your inbox by the close of business today, Mr. Brandon," I say, twirling a lock of hair and peering at the split ends.

Thomas Brandon fires off status questions to the other team members, but after about three minutes, the conversation reverts back to the topics of cost and scheduling, and I find myself once again not paying attention. I spin my engagement ring like a top on the desk, watching it go around and around in a sparkly blur, until finally the conference call ends.

As I put my phone away, I hear the front door open and my father's heavy footsteps, followed by kitchen cabinets banging shut and rummaging in the fridge. He was gone when I woke up, and I wonder if he worked the early shift again.

I walk down the short hallway that connects my child-hood room to my father's, brushing my fingertips along the floral wallpaper adorned with my school photos and tacky watercolor prints of Texas Hill Country, listening to the floorboards creak under my bare feet as I descend the stairs.

"Morning, baby girl," my father says when I enter the living room, his eyes glued to one of those lifestyle food shows on the television. "A little birdie told me you've agreed to participate in the Upper Crust."

He's settled on the couch with his feet propped on the coffee table, a remote in one hand and a half-eaten jelly Danish in the other. I notice some of the raspberry filling has stuck to his cookie duster—my father's nickname for a mustache. His hair is a little mussed. He's wearing his usual uniform of a plaid button-down and faded jeans. Taking up space on the cushion next to him is a box of grocery-store-brand doughnuts.

I lean on the arm of the couch. "Let me guess. You spoke with Sullivan Grace."

"Sure did. I knew you'd come around."

"You didn't give me much of a choice," I say as my father polishes off the jelly Danish. "Not exactly a balanced diet, Dad."

"Nonsense. Sugar and trans fats, the breakfast of champions." He rubs his stomach. "Frosted, glazed, or powdered?" he says, offering the box to me.

"None of the above." I place the doughnuts on the side table, next to a glass of milk using a fishing magazine for a coaster, and flop down beside him. "I fixed myself some toast earlier."

"Fair enough."

"Were you at the diner?"

"For a bit," he says. "Then out running errands."

"Maybe you should cut back on your hours," I say,

studying him, taking in his droopy mustache, baggy eyes, creased skin. "You're looking really run down."

"Don't I know it? Why else do you think you're taking over the Spoons?" He smiles and the grooves around his mouth deepen. "Doc says me and my bum knee need a nap and one of those therapeutic massager chairs."

I nudge his side. "Maybe one will show up under the Christmas tree this year. But don't get any ideas. You know I'm only here temporarily."

"We'll see about that, baby girl." He pats my shoulder. "We'll see."

He turns up the volume on the television and drapes an arm across my shoulders. I snuggle up next to him and rest my head on his chest, the outline of his bones sharp against my cheek. We watch in comfortable silence as the show's host travels around New England, eating his way through local mom-and-pop joints.

Even with the television blasting, the room feels quiet, relaxed. Nothing like Chicago, where my office phone rings nonstop and the incessant sound of honking seeps through the windows at all hours. And though I would never admit this to my father, I miss Dallas and the way I can be in the middle of downtown and smell fresh air. Five years in Chicago and I still haven't gotten used to the stink of exhaust that permeates the streets, or how in summer the wind off the lake blows the odor of dead fish, or the scent of garbage that piles up during an epic snowstorm.

At one point during the show, the host is at a deli in Boston, attempting an extra-large bite of a meatball sub, but instead of a mouthful of Italian deliciousness, he gets nothing but sourdough bread and marinara sauce because all of the meatballs have fallen out the sides and rolled down his shirt. My father laughs as if this is the funniest thing he's ever seen, but soon his laughing morphs into a loud and mucousy coughing fit.

Worry clenches my stomach. I rub his back until the coughing subsides. My father takes a deep breath and gulps down the rest of the milk. Then he relaxes into the couch cushions and puts an arm back around me, as if nothing happened.

"Are you all right?" I keep my voice calm. "That sounded really bad."

He peers down at me and smooths the hair away from my forehead. "I know it does, baby girl. And yes, before you ask, I've been to the doctor. He's treating it."

"When was your last appointment? And when is your next one?" Given my father's aversion to showing weakness, it's probably been months since he visited the doctor and instead he's "treating" his cough with Robitussin and Mucinex.

"You've got no faith in me," he says with a frown. "I see Doc every few weeks. He checks me out, adjusts my meds. But at my age a cough can be a pesky nag that never goes away—a bit like you." He winks and smiles.

I roll my eyes. "Fine. But I'm coming to your next appointment. If I'm being cast as a nag, I want to nag effectively."

He chuckles and says, "All right, all right. Next one is on Halloween."

The rooster clock on the wall crows. My father sighs and kisses the top of my head. "Well, I'd better quit lolly-gagging around." He groans as he stands up and stretches his back. "You should think about visiting the Spoons sometime today. Freshen up on how we do things around there and get some practice time in. You only have a few weeks until the Upper Crust, and I won't have no goddamn *apple turnover* winning again."

Leave it to my father to act like I should be training for this charity event as though it's some kind of Olympic sport. Too bad my plan of attack is to show up and wing it. I almost tell him this just to see him get all bent out of shape. Instead I grab the box of doughnuts and follow him into the kitchen.

"I need to do some work for my actual job. You know, the one in Chicago that I get paid for? I'm being slated to be a partner." Then I remember the binders and stacks of papers I stole from the diner that are still a disorganized mess and say, "But maybe I'll drop by after I finish up."

He takes the doughnut box from my hand and places it on the counter. "I bought extra cobbler ingredients for you to use."

"Dad, I'm not competing with that recipe. I'm going to prepare something of my own."

He turns to face me so abruptly his shoulder knocks into mine, and I stumble a bit. "You ain't doin' no such thing."

"Why is this so important to you?" I ask, but what I really want to know is how he can pretend that my mother didn't throw away our family, how he can pretend she didn't throw *me* away.

My father grumbles something under his breath before he clears his throat and says, "Because it's a darn good recipe, and we're in this to win, baby girl. That's all there is to it."

I sigh. My head is starting to ache.

"Oh, I almost forgot," my father says, rifling around in his pocket. "I've got a present for you." He drops a set of tarnished gold keys in my hand that belong to my old Ford truck.

"When did you get it back?" I say, puzzled, remembering how I abandoned the clunker in an airport economy parking lot the day I boarded a plane to Chicago.

"That's not important. You didn't honestly think I'd let you ditch that dinosaur, did you? Big Blue's a part of our family."

I shrug, closing my fingers around the keys and squeezing so hard the teeth bite into the soft flesh of my palm. "I suppose not."

"Think of this as your homecoming gift," he says with a wink. "She's got a rebuilt engine, new tires, and a clean bill of health. Picked her up from the shop this morning."

"Thanks for rescuing her for me. It saves me from spending a fortune on the rental. I'll call to make arrangements for it to be picked up."

My father's mustache twitches, and a funny expression flits over his face.

"What?"

He crosses his arms and leans against the counter. "You've been cooped up in this house since yesterday afternoon, haven't you?"

"Yeah, so?"

"Well, you might want to take a gander out front before you do anything else." He opens the cabinet under the sink and removes the trash bin. "And you might want to consider bringing this with you."

I look dumbly at him, then at the trash bin, then back at him. "Okay. Why?"

"Does that prank you and Annabelle pulled on Wes that one summer ring any bells?"

"No . . ."

Then it clicks.

No. No freaking way.

"Dad, you can't be serious right now," I exclaim as I

frantically look outside. He couldn't possibly be implying what I think he is.

Only my father doesn't need to say anything more because I finally spot it. My eyes bulge out and my mouth drops open as I absorb that my rental has been hazed worse than a pledge during initiation week. The car has been covered in so many rolls of cling wrap I can't discern the black paint underneath. Hundreds of fudge cookies are glued to the plastic, melting in the sun. Colored balls like the ones in the pit I used to jump into at the local family entertainment center are bursting out of the sunroof—the only part of the car still exposed.

Wes better run, at lightning speed and far, far away, because when I find him I'm going to rake him over a hot bed of coals.

10

I PARK MY TRUCK ON THE STREET AND STARE AT THE building adorned with gaudy neon letters and blue awnings that was once a sanctuary for me.

Every Blue Plate Special and candid photograph on the wall holds reminders of a childhood that has drifted away. Turner's Greasy Spoons is where we congregated—Nick, Wes, Annabelle, and me—on Friday nights after the Highland Park High School football game. It's where Nick tried, and failed, to teach me to drive a stick shift; where my father caught Wes and Annabelle making out in the stockroom after-hours; where the four of us ran around the vinyl booths and laminate tables as children, playing tag and hide-and-seek.

Ghosts of me. Ghosts of them.

I sigh and climb out of the truck, my legs sticking to the cracked leather seat.

Despite the odd afternoon hour, the diner is bustling with activity, though I notice it's mostly an older crowd taking advantage of the early bird dinner menu. At a booth near the windows, a group of ladies with silver hair play spades, cackling louder than necessary, probably a result of the hearing aids they all wear.

I catch a glimpse of Wes sitting at the counter devouring a double portion of cowboy casserole, today's Blue Plate Special, that's like a shepherd's pie but with Tater Tots instead of mashed potatoes and a down-home country flair. It's another recipe inspired by one of my high school newspaper columns that paid homage to the potato, the king of root vegetables.

"Don't you work?" I say, flicking Wes's ear.

Swatting my hand away, he looks at me, then over his shoulder toward the front windows, then back to me. "Fueling up before practice," he says through a mouthful of food, the words garbled. "Homecoming game's coming up."

Through the kitchen window, my father grins and waves. He's sporting an apron with dancing clams on it, though it obviously failed to perform its most basic function because the right side of his Rangers T-shirt is splattered with yellow splotches. There's a faint lipstick mark on his cheek, and I wonder when Sullivan Grace stopped by for her daily diner visit.

On the prep counter in front of him is a four-quart storage bin filled to the brim with ground spices. I watch as he leans the container on a corner edge and measures out a palmful before dumping the spices onto some hamburger meat browning on the stove. Standing next to him, Ernie sautés onion and garlic in a cast-iron skillet.

I hop onto the stainless steel counter and steal the forkful of casserole hovering inches from Wes's awaiting mouth.

"If you value your life, you'll surrender the utensil," he says at the same time my father shouts, "Baby girl, get off of there. People gotta eat."

I roll my eyes, jump off the counter, and hand the fork back to Wes. He swallows the bite without chewing and moves the plate away from my reach.

A moment later, another plate of cowboy casserole, fresh from the oven, the cheese still bubbling, appears in the kitchen window. The vivid scents of cumin and chili powder hit my nose. My stomach grumbles. Ernie gives me a knowing smile and nods, touching his forehead as if tipping a hat.

Grabbing the steaming dish and some silverware, I take a seat on the stool next to Wes. We eat in silence, which is fine by me because the casserole is so delicious I'm shoveling it down as though I haven't eaten in a week.

From the corner of my eye, I notice Wes's shoulders are slouched and there's an uncomfortable expression on his face. I wonder if he's thinking about what happened at the bookstore, if he regrets the way he acted, his harsh words. Then I remember Annabelle's confession, that he was the one betrayed, and I wonder how much Wes is hurting, how lost and angry he must feel.

The silence stretches so long that when Wes finally speaks, I nearly fling my fork across the counter in surprise. "It's nice to see you driving Big Blue again." The mischief in his voice is unmistakable. "It suits you. Better than that ridiculous thing you were driving."

"It's funny you should mention that." I glance at him sideways. "An interesting thing happened last night."

"Really? What's that?" Wes says, tossing a wadded-up napkin on his empty plate, looking everywhere but at me.

"Yeah. Apparently the Keebler Elves have a vendetta against me." I spin on the stool to face him. "They covered my rental car in Saran Wrap and used spray adhesive to stick E.L. Fudge cookies all over it. You can imagine the mess I discovered this morning, especially since the chocolate centers had melted."

Wes twists his lips, as though he's suppressing a smile. "That's rough, Jelly Bean."

I sigh, long and overdramatic. "It took me four hours, two garbage bags, a vacuum cleaner, and a trip to the auto detailing place to get the car looking like new again."

A laugh bursts from his mouth, the sound like the pop of a can of crescent rolls. "I hope you catch those little guys. I hear they're fast."

"Actually, I was thinking you could help me." I put my elbows on the counter and rest my chin in my hands. "That's a pretty extreme prank, if you ask me. Almost like it was payback for something. I mean, those elves spend their days baking cookies in a tree. Can you think of why they may have done this?"

"Nope," Wes says with a toothy grin. "But whatever you did, it must have really pissed them off."

"Hmm. Do you remember that teeny-tiny, completely harmless joke involving a tub of Vaseline and some cereal?"

"You mean when you and Annabelle mutilated my Jeep?"

"Oh please. We didn't ruin anything. It was those cute little gnomes, Snap, Crackle, and Pop. You offended them with your pathetic attempts at making Rice Krispy treats for Annabelle's birthday," I say, trying to keep a straight face as I remember how protective Wes had been over that car. "Anyway, that's beside the point. If I remember correctly, you were out for blood after that."

"Jelly Bean, you pulled pranks on everyone around here, not just me. Any one of those people could have done it. Like Mr. Oswald over there," Wes says, pointing to a frail, elderly man with a big nose and even bigger ears fighting with a packet of sugar. "He's held a grudge against you for years after you TP'd his house by mistake."

"Uh-huh. I'm sure it was him. You should warn him I plan on getting revenge," I say as my cell phone buzzes in my pocket. I pull it out to see Drew's name lighting up the screen. I cringe, but before I can silence it, Wes says, "How's the boyfriend?"

"Fine," I say quickly. Too quickly. I shove the phone back into my pocket.

Of course Wes notices my tone, and of course he won't let it go. "Just fine?"

"He's great," I say. "Better than great actually."

"Very convincing, Pinocchio," he says, tapping the tip of my nose. There's a curious twinkle in his eyes. "Your cheeks are doing that flushed thing they do when you get uncomfortable. I've got a hunch there's something else going on."

My stomach sinks as I realize he may already know about my engagement to Drew if Nick tattled on me, but as I study Wes's face, searching for a sign, something about his expression tells me he is still in the dark. Nick hasn't mentioned it. And why would he? I no longer register anywhere on his importance radar.

"So did you two finally move in together or what?" Wes asks.

"It's possible," I say. It's been two months since Drew bowed out of the lease on his apartment and was added to mine. We've even discussed adopting a puppy from a rescue shelter, but with my demanding work schedule I barely have time to feed myself let alone care for an animal. It's why I have plants.

"I'm happy for you, Jelly Bean. It's about time you found someone who could tolerate your cup habit," he says with a smile, referring to my tendency to leave near-empty glasses scattered around for days rather than putting them directly into the dishwasher when I'm done with them.

"Hey!" I punch his shoulder. "I've gotten better about that." Kind of.

"I'm joking," he says, ducking out of the way before I can hit him again.

"If you two are done being Chatty Cathys, you might want to think about making yourselves useful. I need an extra set of hands around here," my father calls from the kitchen.

"No can do, boss." Wes rises from the stool and tosses some cash on the counter. "I've got a hot date with some future NFLers and a football field." He turns to me, squeezes my arm, and says, "It's all you, Jelly Bean." He starts to leave, but pauses. He meets my gaze and looks at me like he wants to say something else but can't find the right words, so we stand there for a moment in silence. Finally, he says, "Annabelle wanted to get engaged." His voice sounds bitter, almost angry, so different from the Wes who was laughing minutes ago. "She's wanted to for a few years, actually."

"And you didn't." It's a statement, though it should be a question.

"I *couldn't*," he clarifies. "I wanted to give her that. Hell, I wanted it for myself, but I . . . couldn't."

"Why not?"

Rubbing his eyes with the palms of his hands, he sighs and says, "I've seen how marriage can destroy a family. I've seen two people who once promised to love each other for the rest of their lives now only communicate through lawyers and email. I've seen parents force their child to take sides and then get upset when the kid chooses the wrong one—or worse, when he refuses to pick at all." Wes sighs again, heavier this time, so heavy I feel the weight of it. "I've seen the worst, Jelly Bean, and I won't repeat my parents' mistakes. I guess Annabelle thought that my hang-ups gave her permission to do what she did."

I stare at him, struggling to make sense of his words. "Wes, you know it wasn't like that for her. It's obvious you both still care. Why don't you talk to her?"

"Because . . ." He trails off, shaking his head. "Because."

Growing up, I knew he carried the burden of his parents' divorce on his shoulders like an albatross, but until now, I never realized how much it had affected him—how it still affects him—and how his relationship with Annabelle has suffered because of it.

"I guess love makes you chickenshit sometimes, huh?" Wes says, ripping me from my thoughts.

I shrug and give him a small smile. I want to tell him that love can also make you brave. That it has the power to heal as well as destroy. That you can build a world of dreams around it.

But I can't say any of that.

———

I HUG Wes good-bye with the promise to see him later at the Tipsy Teakettle for trivia night and step into the empty hallway that connects the two bathrooms, where more of my framed newspaper columns stare back at me.

I take out my phone and dial Drew's office number. He picks up on the third ring.

"There you are," he says, warm and sincere. "I called you a bit ago."

A rush of guilt surges through me. About the way I purposely screened his call. About seeing Nick again, how his presence has me twisted into tiny knots. About how I've kept that part of my past a secret from Drew.

"I know. I'm sorry." I bite my lip. "I was chatting with an old friend."

"How are things going there?" There's a creaking sound, and I picture Drew leaning back in his desk chair, gazing out his office window that overlooks Lake Shore Drive. "I haven't heard back from you."

Drew's tone is concerned, not at all angry, and the guilt flares up full force again. We usually email or talk at least once throughout the day, exchanging take-out dinner ideas, stories about annoying coworkers, and gripes about the stresses of our jobs. But since returning to Dallas, I haven't been able to find the right words to respond to his messages. How am I supposed to explain Wes and Annabelle and all they've been through, all that we've been through together? How am I supposed to explain Nick and everything we meant to each other before we meant nothing at all?

How do I explain any of that?

Instead I say, "Everything's about as expected. My father's up to his old tricks as usual." I tell him of my plan to manage the diner's back-of-house operations from Chicago.

"That's a great solution," Drew says. "Is your father okay with it?"

"I'm not giving him an option," I say. "Kingsbury Enterprises has asked for me personally to lead the next phase of their product launch, and Thomas Brandon has guaranteed my promotion if it's successful."

"That's fantastic, babe," he says. "Congratulations."

"Thank you," I say. "It's a huge opportunity for me. For us."

As I fill him in on the details, the casual, easy way we are with one another slips back into place.

"So listen," Drew says after I'm finished. "Since your dad will still be in recovery mode, maybe we can spend Thanksgiving in Dallas this year."

An anxious feeling churns in my stomach. I clear my throat and try hard to keep the warble out of my voice as I say, "What about Madison in the fall?" Drew's parents relocated to Wisconsin a few years back to be closer to his maternal grandparents, an adorable couple who recently celebrated their sixtieth wedding anniversary. We haven't seen them since the move, but Drew keeps them apprised of the happenings in our lives, engagement included.

"You've already met my family. It's time I meet yours," Drew says. "We did things a little backward, so I can't ask your dad for permission, but this way I can still ask for his blessing. Properly."

"Okay," I say, reminding myself that it's not Drew's fault I've kept my past and present separate. "We'll celebrate Thanksgiving in Dallas with my father."

"Good, because I've got something to tell you."

"What?"

"Remember when you looked into getting married at the Shedd, but they were booked solid for the next year?"

He's talking so fast I don't have an opportunity to answer.

"Well, yesterday after work, some of the other associates and I went to this networking event hosted at the aquarium," Drew says. "After all the accountants cleared out, I got to talking with one of the aquarium's event managers. I told her about us, that we're newly engaged, and how we want to get married at the Shedd but there aren't any openings. And it was fate, Lillie, because she told me they had a cancellation for the third

Saturday in February and asked if we wanted that spot, so I took it."

My heart is pounding, echoing in my ears. I can't speak, can't move, can't do anything but stand there in the hallway by the bathrooms, frozen like a ghost crab caught under a flashlight. He decided on a wedding date without consulting with me first? I mean, I know we had to pick a date eventually, but it seemed like something we would decide together, when the time was right, not on a whim because a particular date at a particular venue became available. I should feel thrilled we got that slot at all. And I *am*. Really. I'm just shocked, too. I guess I assumed there would be more time to prepare—February isn't that far away.

"We can discuss the logistics with your dad over Thanksgiving. I know he refuses to come here, but we're getting married, so I know he'll make an exception," Drew says.

Since I've been living in Chicago, my father has visited twice. Once for my first Christmas in the city and the second for my MBA graduation. Both times Drew and I weren't dating yet. My father chose to drive the thousand miles because he refuses to board an airplane—"I ain't gettin' on no contraption that can fall outta the sky"—and when he returned to Dallas from the last trip he swore he'd never do the grueling trek again. So far he's kept his word, and I doubt even my wedding will change his mind, especially since Drew isn't exactly my father's pick for my ideal husband. But maybe meeting Drew will show my father just how easy we fit together.

"So what do you think?" Drew says tentatively, all traces of his earlier elation gone.

He's so sincere, so hopeful. I imagine Drew rubbing his earlobe as his leg bounces three times in quick succession

—his telltale sign that he's nervous—and I realize how foolish I'm being. Drew wants to marry me, not someday when his parents approve or the stars align or when he can carve out some time in his busy schedule, but soon.

My mind drifts to the evening Nick proposed. Dressed in gray slacks and a striped collared dress shirt, he took me to our secret spot at Montgomery Park. Under the canopy of oak trees, sun spilled like honey through pockets in the dense cover. Leaf shadows patterned Nick's face. A checkered blanket was spread out on the ground, candles securing the edges. Nick guided me into the center and bent down on one knee, pulling a ring from his pocket. Taking my left hand in his, he looked me in the eye and asked me to marry him, promising to cherish me forever.

As Nick drove us to a celebratory dinner afterward, our fingers intertwined, my ring sparkling in the light of the setting sun, I thought of all the happy, hopeful moments in store for us: exchanging vows among family and friends, waking up beside each other every day for the rest of our lives, growing old together. Buying our first house, then filling it with all those things that would make it a home. Blocking out the world as we touched and kissed and lost ourselves in each other. I thought of the mundane things— grocery shopping, fighting the daily grind, arguments about replacing the toilet paper roll or taking out the trash —we would share as we settled into married life.

I should have known then that I was living in a fantasy-land. Between Nick's rigorous med school classes, the insane hours and late nights spent with his nose buried in a textbook, and juggling to complete my own undergraduate coursework and my job at the diner, our paths rarely crossed. And when we actually did see each other, Nick was often short-tempered and stressed, the responsibility of someday holding a person's life in his hands heavy on his shoulders.

How could I have possibly thought being engaged would change all that? I'd heard the warnings about how many couples didn't survive medical school, let alone residency, with their relationships intact. There had even been a session during Nick's medical school orientation devoted to partners and spouses of med students in which it was emphasized how tough the upcoming years would be on Nick—the demands on his time and energy, the mounting pressure to perform and surpass expectations—and how much patience and understanding were needed from family and friends.

Yet I still believed we could beat the odds, make it out on the other side, battle weary, sure, but also stronger. Only Nick's medical school graduation came and went, as did his first two years of surgical residency, and still no wedding date was set.

Maybe that's the danger in loving someone too much: you're so blinded by it that you can't see what's already over until one side of the bed is empty and cold.

"Lillie, are you there?" Drew's hesitant voice breaks me from my thoughts. "If you're worried about your dad's knee, he should be healed enough by then to walk you down the aisle."

I take a deep breath and the tight, pinching sensation in my chest relaxes. Drew can give me a sense of peace and not make me feel as if I'm unraveling.

Finally I find my voice and say, "I think a February wedding at the aquarium will be beautiful."

11

I DISCONNECT THE CALL WITH DREW AS THE DOOR TO THE men's restroom opens. Two boys dart out, knocking into my legs as they run toward the dining room. My shoulder bumps against the wall. Frames wobble and a metal diner sign proclaiming: *Buy one helping of meat loaf for double the price and receive a second helping of meat loaf on the house!* comes off its nail and falls into my hands. I fumble around like I'm playing a game of hot potato until I finally get a grip on it.

"Baby girl, when I said I could use some assistance, I wasn't referring to fondling the decor."

"You're hilarious, Dad," I say, hanging the sign back on the wall.

"I'm aware of this. There's no need to flatter me. My head will swell up like a melon," my father says, wiping his hands on his apron. "Now are you purposely hiding from me or were you on the phone with that boyfriend of yours?"

"His name is Drew, and he's more than just my boyfriend," I say as he comes to stand beside me.

My father folds his arms across his chest and twists his

mouth so that his mustache whiskers stick out. "Getting serious are you?"

I almost tell my father about the engagement, but stop myself. Drew said he wanted to ask for my father's blessing personally. I don't want to ruin that conversation for him or give my father the chance to stew over it.

"Serious enough," I say. "We've decided to celebrate Thanksgiving in Dallas this year with you. I'd really love for you to meet him, get to know him. He's important to me."

"That so?" my father says in his signature Jackson Turner voice of doubt. "He still a Cubs fan?"

"What?"

"I ain't eating no turkey dinner with a Cubs fan. So if he plans on sitting at the big-kid table with the rest of the adults, he should consider adopting new team loyalties." That's my father, always needing to get his digs in when he doesn't approve of something or someone. "Are you going to dawdle in this hallway all afternoon or make yourself useful?"

"You know, if you're so swamped that you need an extra set of hands, why don't you prepare some menu items ahead of time and freeze them?" I say. "Given that your surgery is coming up, it makes sense."

My father squints and tilts his head as if he doesn't recognize me. "You know what standards are? Well, around here we got 'em. This ain't no chain restaurant. We believe in real, fresh food. You best be remembering that when you—"

"All right, all right. I get it," I say, holding up my hands in surrender. "It was only a suggestion."

"A damn terrible one. Now do your old man a favor and help me get some food prepped." With a skip in his step, he strolls back into the dining room.

If I stay focused, move diligently, I can prep the food for tomorrow and still make it in time to meet Wes for trivia night.

"Hey, baby girl," my father yells as I pass by the kitchen window. "Catch."

I turn my head but not fast enough. My mother's old apron sideswipes me across the face. Rotating on my heel, I scowl out at him, then keep walking.

When I enter the back room, a feeling of dread settles over me. Littering the length of the prep counter is everything needed to make my mother's peach cobbler: bags of thawed, flash-frozen white peach halves, ingredients both wet and dry, baking dishes, measuring spoons, rubber spatulas, and her handwritten recipe card.

As I stand there looking at the items, an idea sparks in my mind. Cobbler is simply a fruit-based filling that is arranged in a deep dish with no bottom crust and a drop-biscuit or batter topping. But what if I put my own unique spin on it? Something like a sweet cheese and peach mixture topped with a light, flaky phyllo dough would do the trick. Okay, maybe my idea is more like a deconstructed strudel—and sure, it has an Austrian flair to it—but with a little imagination, it could be interpreted as a type of American cobbler. Then I wouldn't be violating any competition rules, so the judges would have to accept my submission. Not to mention, nowhere on my entrant packet does it say I have to use my mother's recipe specifically. Only that I have to make a dessert called summer peach cobbler. Which this strudel-in-disguise definitely qualifies as. My whole idea is brilliant, actually.

I toss the apron onto the floor next to the wall, wash my hands, and swap out the ingredients on the counter with the requisite ones needed to make the new recipe. Lucky for me, I notice my father has premade phyllo dough for baklava already in the fridge. I dampen a clean dish towel to keep the dough moist and begin whipping up the first batch. After all, my father did say I should practice.

I set up an assembly line and get to work. The strudel filling comes together quickly. The smooth ricotta, sweetened with honey, provides the perfect balance to the ripe, juicy peaches and the crunchy, tart pomegranate seeds. I spoon the mixture into greased baking dishes and top each one with layers of phyllo dough, brushing butter liberally between the sheets. The scent makes my mouth water.

Ernie walks into the room as I'm covering the dishes with aluminum foil. He looks at my deconstructed strudel, whistles, and slowly retreats. If Ernie knows what's good for him, he'll stay mum about what he saw. The last thing I need is my father storming in here, hollering and causing a scene.

I rifle among the kitchen utensils for a marker to scribble cooking instructions on the foil. My stomach plummets to the ground when I see a faded newspaper clipping peeking out from under a whisk. With shaking hands, I pull it out. Five years ago, I left this article for Nick to find. *So why does my father have it?* I think as anger careens its way through me, the paper crinkling in my fist. Then my tangled thoughts wrap around an even bigger question. *Why would he keep it?*

The memory comes so harsh and fast I have to grip the prep counter.

I was sitting on a bench at Montgomery Park, eating a turkey sandwich while flipping through the style section of the *New York Times* when I saw it. A story about The Maple Door, Greenwich Village's newest upscale-dining hot spot. In that moment, everything inside me froze. Because staring back at me from a grainy black-and-white photograph was my mother, dressed in a crisp white chef's jacket. I knew it was her without question. She had that same glowing smile, those same almond-shaped eyes, the same platinum-blond hair that shined like glaze on a doughnut that I recognized from the picture propped up on my father's bedroom nightstand.

With my heart thumping in my ears, I quickly scanned the article, leapfrogging over phrases like "refined farm-to-table cooking that will make your taste buds do a break dance" and "an unassuming atmosphere with quirky sophistication" and "delectable, old-fashioned desserts brimming with youthful enthusiasm." But then my eyes landed on the sentence that would change me forever:

EXECUTIVE CHEF ELIZABETH KLEIN, WHO RESIDES IN NEW YORK CITY'S UPPER EAST SIDE WITH HER HUSBAND, FELLOW JAMES BEARD AWARD–WINNING CHEF AND RESTAURATEUR PATRICK BAILEY, AND THEIR TWIN DAUGHTERS, MISSY AND MATILDA, ALSO SHOWCASES HER TALENTS AT THE THEATER DISTRICT'S NATIONALLY ACCLAIMED FOUNDRY BISTRO.

In a blind panic, I tore out the article and rushed to my truck, my lunch forgotten. Minutes later I parked in front of the diner and raced inside. I spotted my father leaning against the counter, chatting with Sullivan Grace as he spun a tray on his finger.

Striding over to him, I slapped the paper down on the stainless steel surface. "Did you know?"

Sullivan Grace jumped, a delicate hand pressed to her chest. "Lillie, dear, please soften your tone."

Ignoring her, I kept my focus on my father and asked again, punctuating each syllable.

My father must have realized I was teetering on the

edge of a breakdown, because a worried expression settled on his face. He put the tray aside, then slowly, cautiously, picked up the article, mouthing the words as he read. I studied his features, searching for something that told me he had no idea of my mother's whereabouts. That he was as clueless as me about her glamorous new life, her glamorous new *family*. But then he met my gaze, and the pain and guilt in his eyes confirmed my fears.

"How could you have hidden this from me?" I asked, my voice splintering. Heat flooded my cheeks and tears welled in my eyes.

He looked at Sullivan Grace, who appeared as lost as my father. A silent conversation passed between them. Sullivan Grace nodded, her chin bobbing ever so slightly, and squeezed my father's hand, as if in encouragement.

My father turned to me, and I had never seen him look so nervous. "Baby girl, I wanted to—" He stopped, cleared his throat, and tried again. "I did it to protect you."

I stared at him, waiting for a better explanation. When it was obvious he wasn't going to elaborate further, I rested a hand on his arm and said, "Please, Dad. I *need* to know the truth." The tears spilled over, tumbling down my cheeks.

"Lillie's right, Jackson. It's time," Sullivan Grace said, her voice gentle. "I'll leave you two alone to talk." She patted my hand, stood, and walked out of the diner.

My father rubbed his eyes, smoothing out the wrinkles underneath them. The words poured out of him. "After you were born, your mother got real depressed. She wouldn't rock you or feed you or play with you . . . I thought with time she'd let go of whatever demons were haunting her, but she only got worse."

"Why didn't you get her help?" I asked as more tears flowed down my face. I didn't wipe them away.

"I tried, baby girl—every day I tried—but your mother wouldn't hear of it. She'd just lay in bed, staring at the ceiling. I knew the banks were gonna come knocking on our door soon, so I quit my job at the plant to prevent the Spoons from going under. Then one morning, on your third birthday, she woke up happy. Like a light had been switched on. She was smiling, and there was this fire in her eyes—the same one I'd seen the night I met her."

My father swallowed, his shoulders hunched, and continued, "She wanted to make you some of her peach cobbler, but we didn't have any butter, so your mother insisted on running to the store. Only she never came home. Not that day, or the one after that, or the one after that. And I knew, I could feel it in my gut, baby girl, that those demons had beaten her."

"Did you search for her?"

"Course I did. I filed a missing persons report with the police, visited every hospital, every homeless shelter, every halfway house. For months I searched, but your mother didn't want to be found."

His expression turned grave, and I knew that whatever he was about to tell me was bad. He reached out and touched my hand. "The divorce papers arrived a year later. Your mother had signed over everything to me—Greasy Spoons, the house . . ."

"And me?" I whispered.

For a moment, my father stared at me, his eyes glassy. When he spoke, his voice broke. "Your mother included a letter with the papers. She said that even though she'd finally gotten help, dealt with her problems, she couldn't return to her old life. It'd be too painful for her. She needed a fresh start . . . without us."

Then for only the second time in my life, I watched as

my father began to cry. Tears streamed down his face, falling onto the counter in rhythm with my own.

I left the diner in a haze, the world a gray smudge. Somehow I made it to the brownstone, a medical school graduation gift from Nick's parents that we'd been living in for the past two years. For the remainder of the day, I lay curled up on the couch in the dark, staring at an untouched plate of rocky road fudge bars in the center of the coffee table, until moonlight spilled through the arched windows.

In the foyer, the antique grandfather clock played another round of Westminster chimes. Dim yellow headlights rounded the street corner and swept over the living room. I poured another glass of wine, polishing off the bottle, and gulped it down. Standing, I walked over to the windows and peered out. Nick parked his car at the curb. He made no move to get out and come inside. Instead he sat there, elbows resting on the steering wheel, fingers laced behind his head. This wasn't the first time I'd caught him like that, avoiding me and the stone walls of this place as though they were a prison.

I returned to the couch and waited. My engagement ring weighed down my finger, heavy as a cast-iron skillet. Five minutes passed before the front door opened and footsteps shuffled on the parquet floor. Nick entered the living room without a glance in my direction and tossed his keys into the bowl perched on the console table.

I cleared my throat.

Nick jumped and flipped on the light, the sudden brightness momentarily blinding me. "Lillie? You scared the shit out of me. Why aren't you in bed?"

"I couldn't sleep," I said, tucking a strand of hair behind my ear. "Where have you been?"

He shrugged off his coat and flung it onto a chair. "Out."

"I tried calling you, but it went straight to voicemail," I said, imagining him at some bar, drowning whatever troubles he wasn't sharing with me in bourbon—a habit he'd developed since starting his surgical residency.

Nick didn't respond. Instead, his gaze scanned over me as though I were a cart full of groceries at a checkout counter. I wasn't sure if his cold indifference was a result of exhaustion or if it was merely all that was left between us.

Tears stung my eyes at the harsh realization. The room smeared together in a swirl of colors as I remembered, once again, the crumpled newspaper clipping in my jean pocket.

"Nick, can we talk?" I asked, looking at him, trying to hide the potholes in my voice. We hadn't seen or spoken to each other in almost a week. I only knew he'd been home at all by the dirty dishes he had piled in the sink for me to wash.

He rubbed his eyes, bloodshot and ringed with dark circles. "It's late, and I have to be back at the hospital soon."

"Please. It's important." My hands shook. I clutched the couch cushion to steady them.

A hardness settled over his features. "Lillie."

"What?"

"I don't have the energy to do this right now."

"Then when?" I asked as tears soaked into my shirt.

He clenched his jaw, covered with several days of growth, and stared at me as though I were a child who had asked him for the eighth time to go to Chuck E. Cheese's after he repeatedly told me no. "How about once I get a vacation from gluing people's bodies back together? Is that a specific enough time frame for you?"

Silence stretched between us. The air grew thick and charged, the moment before thunder cracked.

I knew I was goading him, pushing him past the point of no return, but everything inside me told me that it was now or never. That the outcome of this moment would forever shape our future, for better or worse.

"Something happened today," I said finally. "I found something."

The storm broke. Nick crossed the room and hovered above me, nostrils flaring.

"Lillie, do you know what my day was like?" he asked, his voice rising to a shout. But then just as quickly as the anger came, it dissipated. He shook his head, sighed, the sound settling across him like a blanket of weariness that bowed his back and slumped his shoulders. "No, you couldn't understand. You serve people pie all day, fill their coffee cups, toss around jokes with them. You have it so easy, so *safe*. So excuse me if I don't see why this conversation can't wait until I've had some rest."

I wiped the wetness from my cheeks. "That's not fair."

"Fair? Who the hell said anything about being fair?" Nick laughed, but it lacked all warmth, a hollow echo of what it used to be. Then with a cold, hard glare, he turned and disappeared upstairs.

While Nick slept, I wandered through the house, taking it all in. The monogrammed hand towels folded neatly in the guest bathroom. The ornate mahogany cabinet in the dining room that showcased Nick's great-grandmother's gold-trimmed bone china. The Persian rug adorning the entryway, greeting visitors into our farce of a home. All of it picked out with Charlotte Preston's approval, all of it meant to illustrate the kind of life Nick was expected to have.

None of it me.

I was like tapioca in a caviar family, desperately trying to blend in but failing miserably. There wasn't even a framed photograph of us together. Nothing from the time before we became shards of who we once were. Those people had been reduced to a box in the small storage closet on the third floor, collecting dust along with the unframed diploma granting me a bachelor's degree in business administration and my father's abandoned Taylor acoustic guitar.

But then, who was I really?

My whole life I had imagined countless scenarios about why my mother had left: she was a woman with a Gypsy heart who couldn't bear the responsibility of being a wife and a mother; she broke the law and was serving a life sentence in prison; she was diagnosed with cancer and passed away when I was a toddler and my father had been too devastated to confess the truth.

Not even in my worst nightmares did I ever consider that she had abandoned my father and me so she could escape to New York City, become a famous chef, and find herself a shiny new family. All this time, while I'd been crafting batch after batch of her beloved recipes, actually *believing* I could feel a connection with her—that I'd *mattered* —she'd been attending culinary school and opening restaurants and kissing her husband good night and driving my *half-sisters* to ballet recitals. And my father had never said a word about any of it. *Your mother needed to fly, baby girl,* he'd said. Only that had been a lie. All of it.

The realization ripped open something deep and feral inside of me, a raw feeling that surged through my whole body, leaving in its wake a crippling pain. Though there was something underneath it, too, a small voice chanting in my ear, urging me to *go*. It grew stronger and stronger, until I had no choice but to listen.

That night I left the crumpled newspaper clipping on the kitchen counter for Nick to find and packed a suitcase.

Hours later I was gone.

The memory fades. Breathing in deep, the tightness in my chest relaxes and I straighten up. My father is standing in the doorway, staring at me with heavy, sad eyes.

"Why did you keep this?" I ask, the newspaper clipping still clenched in my fist.

"It's a reminder, baby girl."

"Of what?"

He crosses the room and puts a hand on my shoulder, gently squeezing. "That every choice has a cost."

12

THE WEIGHT OF THE MEMORY IS STILL HEAVY ON MY CHEST
when I arrive at the Tipsy Teakettle. Celtic music barrels
out of the door.

As I step inside, I notice the decor hasn't changed
much. Teapots from around the world are still mounted on
every available inch of wall and ceiling space. Chandeliers
adorned with cups and saucers illuminate the room in a
soft glow. A long, mahogany bar flanks one side, perfect for
elbow resting while enjoying a Belgian ale on tap or a rich,
hearty porter.

Dangling from hooks in the ceiling above the stage, a
black letter board showcases the trivia Wall of Champions.
As my eyes scan the list, my breath catches. Nick's name
stares back at me from the number-one slot with my name
butting up against it. Throughout high school and college,
Nick and I participated in trivia night religiously, often as
solo acts but sometimes as a tag team. Either way, one of
us would end the night victorious. All that came to an
abrupt halt once anatomy and biochemistry became Nick's
top priority, so how are we still tied for the most trivia

games won? Surely someone's come close to stealing our records since then.

Across the bar, I see Wes straddling a chair at the head of a rectangular table, pint glasses and beer bottles littering the surface, chatting and laughing with two guys I recognize immediately as half of the Randy Hollis Band. At the other end, Nick and another band member are hunched over what appears to be a Moleskine notebook, deep in discussion.

I can only stand there and stare, my feet bolted to the floor. Nick is *here*, at the Tipsy Teakettle on trivia night, hanging out with the Randy Hollis Band? None of this makes sense.

As if he can sense my gaze on him, Nick looks up, straight at me, and shoves the notebook into his back pocket. His expression is unreadable, but his blue eyes lure me in, seize hold of me. The intensity in them feels as though he's scooping me out from the inside like a pumpkin. My heart stutters. Sweat pricks up on my palms and I wipe them on my jeans.

"Jelly Bean is in the house!"

The hollering jerks my attention to Wes, who is pumping a fist in the air and whooping. The anxiety buzzing through me eases up, and a big, goofy smile spreads across my face. Wes has always been a doofus in that inherent way that can't be taught or mimicked. I dare anyone not to find it calming or comforting.

By the time I force my way through the crowd and make it to the table, the final member of the Randy Hollis Band has returned and stolen what was the empty spot beside Wes, leaving me with no other choice but to take the only remaining seat, smack-dab next to Nick. He stares at me for a moment before he turns away, bringing a beer bottle to his lips and taking a long pull.

Wes springs up from his seat. "Jelly Bean, get over here. I'll introduce you to everyone." He grabs me by the elbow and guides me over to his end of the table, while I pretend Nick's presence doesn't unnerve me.

I meet guitarist Karl Randy and lead singer Matt Hollis, followed by drummer Jason Douglas and bassist Tim Oliver. Shaking their hands, I expect to feel starstruck, given that their songs are blasting all over country radio, but they all seem so . . . normal, if not a little rugged with their torn jeans, stubbled faces, tattoos, and piercings.

For a few minutes we make small talk. The band tells me about the radio appearances they've done to promote their new record, some smaller venues they've played like the Prickly Pear and Billy Bob's Texas, how they are preparing to travel the country and live in a bus for six months while on tour, and their upcoming album release party for *Resolution* at the House of Blues.

As I settle into my seat, Jason slides a cold beer into my waiting fingers. I nod in thanks and swallow a few sips, savoring the hoppy notes and citrus overtones.

Tim taps a rhythm on his pint glass, condensation trickling down the Shiner Bock logo. Studying me, he says, "So, Lillie, you're the pretty girl who—"

"Don't," Nick interrupts, his voice sharp as ice crackling. With a slight shake of his head, he mouths something I can't make out.

Tim regards Nick with a quizzical expression, while Wes and the rest of the band exchange uncomfortable glances. My gaze bounces from face to face, hoping to gather a clue as to what everyone else knows but won't say. Only I glean nothing from them. We sit there in silence, sipping our beers and avoiding eye contact.

Thankfully, Wes breaks the awkwardness by chucking a

bottle cap at my head. "Ready to defend your title, Jelly Bean?"

"Guess we'll find out." I hurl the bottle cap back at him, but Wes ducks out of the way before it hits him. "Why is my name still up there anyway?"

"The owners never bothered to remove it," Nick cuts in, though something about the edge in his tone indicates there's more he's not saying. "But don't think your record hasn't been demolished."

"It's true. You've got some stiff competition to contend with, Jelly Bean. Nick's like the next Alex Trebek with all this trivia mumbo jumbo." Wes fishes an ice cube out of a water glass with a straw and pops it into his mouth, chewing gleefully.

"You've been playing again?" I say to Nick.

He lifts a shoulder in a lazy shrug. "Occasionally."

"He's a liar," Wes interjects. "Don't let him fool you. He's still the reigning champ around here. He's dominated the last thirteen weeks in a row. Everyone's out for his blood."

Nick stares pointedly at Wes. "It's not my fault no one else can name all eleven tracks off the tenth studio album from Hall & Oates."

"I wouldn't be so sure of that," I say a little too smugly, then count off each song one by one. "My favorite happens to be the title track, 'Private Eyes.' "

For a second the table is quiet as they sit there, slack-jawed. All at once they're shouting over one another.

"I call dibs on Lillie for my team," Karl says, thrusting a trivia scorecard across the table.

Jason intercepts the paper before it reaches me and says, "No way. That's cheating."

"Not if she agrees to it," Matt says, then pushes his

own scorecard and a pen at me. "Just jot your name down right there on that blank line."

"Fellas, hold up," Wes says. "If she's playing on anyone's team, it's mine."

Their arguing fades into white noise when Nick brushes his arm against mine. My skin tingles. He leans over and whispers, "Show-off."

My stomach dips as one side of his mouth curves higher than the other. I hate how devastatingly sexy I find that grin, how sexy I've always found it. It's the smile that charmed the pants right off me in the back of his vintage Mercedes when we were in high school. The one that had been private to only me right before his touch brought me to life.

Quit it, I think as I'm reminded how Nick used to say that people don't change. They only manipulate what you see. Which means that hiding behind that penetrating gaze and crooked grin capable of transforming my insides into a puddle is the same Nick as before, skilled at hurting me in ways only he can. I need to remember that. I can't ever let myself forget it.

"Tell me about Chicago."

I jolt in my seat. Nick has shifted his body closer to mine, so close that I inhale his natural scent and feel the heat radiating off his body. Too close.

I finish off my beer, then say, steady and strong, "What do you want to know?"

"Anything." His eyes roam over my face. "I want to hear about your life now."

"Why?" I say. "You willingly gave up the right to know those details."

Sighing, he says, "Lillie, come on. Stop being combative. I only want to talk."

"We're not kids anymore, Nick. We stopped talking to each other a long time ago."

He doesn't respond, probably because he knows I'm right. What else is there to say, anyway? I stand to head for the bar, but Nick grabs my wrist. A current of energy pulses through me. He looks at me in that piercing way that makes me feel exposed.

"Stay," he says, his voice low and deep. That one word stirs something inside me. I need to move away from him, create some distance, but my body betrays me. I sit back down, my heart racing too fast for me to speak. I hate that there's still this pull toward him, a thread that won't sever. Nick drops my wrist, but the impression of his fingers lingers on my skin.

"I'll get the next round. Trivia should be starting soon," he says, then stands and goes to the bar.

"Jelly Bean," Wes says as he lowers himself into the chair Nick occupied. "He's trying to make peace with you. Let him."

As if the Fates are conspiring, Annabelle appears in the Tipsy Teakettle's doorway. "You first," I say, jutting my chin in her direction.

Wes furrows his brow, comprehension dawning too late, since Annabelle is walking toward us. When Wes notices her, his lips press into a thin line. He turns to me and, to my surprise, gives a faint, almost imperceptible nod of his head.

"I'll go borrow a chair from another table," he says, patting my shoulder. "Be right back."

As Wes disappears, I watch Annabelle's face collapse. She must think Wes dashed out the emergency exit when he noticed her. Tossing her purse onto the ground by my feet, she circles the table, embracing everyone in a hug. Clearly she's friends with the band. When Annabelle reaches me, she kisses my cheek and says, "Hey, kid. Thanks for the invite."

"No problem," I say. "Glad you got my message."

"I'd never miss an opportunity to witness you kick Nick down a few notches." Her eyes dart around, and I wonder if she's searching for Wes when, out of nowhere, he reappears like Houdini.

"Hi, Annabelle," he says, gripping a chair, his knuckles white. The way he says her name makes it sound like he's devouring his first bite of food after a long fast. "This one's for you." With me in it, he scoots my chair over and places the one he swiped beside it.

Annabelle blinks, momentarily stunned before regaining her composure. "Thank you." Her voice is hesitant, so different from the confident, assured demeanor she usually portrays.

I wait until Wes has reclaimed his seat at the other end of the table and Annabelle has gotten comfortable in hers before pouncing. "Do you want to explain to me how y'all know the Randy Hollis Band?"

"That's what I was trying to tell you in my car, if you would have let me," she says. "We all met when—"

"When I threw a spiral at Karl's head and knocked him out at a Baylor Medical charity football tournament," Nick pipes up, setting a shot glass filled with red liquid in front of me. He settles in the seat across from me, a Fat Tire in hand.

Annabelle shoots Nick a curious glance. She opens her mouth to say something but quickly closes it, as if thinking better of it.

Frowning, I look around at the band. "You guys play football?"

Karl takes a swig of his Guinness, inspecting a teapot glued to the ceiling like it's the most fascinating thing he's ever seen, while Tim and Matt burst into laughter and Jason says with a wink, "We attempted to play football for the sake of supporting youth cancer research, but obviously that didn't work out so well. We stick to music now."

"Lucky for us," Wes and Annabelle say in unison. They grin at each other for a beat too long before averting their gazes in opposite directions.

"What is this?" Tim says, his nose scrunched up as he sniffs the shot glass. "It smells disgusting."

Nick links his fingers behind his head and leans back in his chair. The movement pulls the shirt tight across the broad expanse of his chest. I pretend not to notice, but my traitorous hands twitch, desperate to feel the hard muscles in his shoulders and biceps.

"A Loopy Ladybug," Nick says. "Lillie's favorite."

Annabelle snorts, jabbing me in the ribs, and Wes cackles so hard his body convulses. I know they're remembering my twenty-first birthday party when I got wasted off three of those deadly shots, then proceeded to perform a striptease for everyone in the middle of Nick's apartment. Only instead of removing the shirt seductively over my head, it got stuck, and I ended up face-planting on the carpet, where I fell asleep.

I scowl at them. "Excuse me. I'll have you know that despite everyone's insistence to the contrary, I *can* drink a ladybug under the table. Heck, I can even take on a hippo given the chance." To prove my point, I slam the shot back, squeezing my eyes shut as the liquor burns my throat, and wave a server over, ordering another.

"Easy there, Jelly Bean," Wes says, wiping wetness from his cheeks. "Maybe you should have ordered something a little less potent."

"Like a chocolate cocktail, perhaps," Nick says, a ghost

of a smile flickering across his face. "We all know how much you adore those E.L. Fudge cookies."

Puzzle pieces whirl in the air around me, but since I'm already feeling a buzz, it takes a moment before they click into place. I whip my head back and forth between Wes and Nick, my eyes growing wider than the saucers decorating the chandeliers overhead.

Gibberish sputters out of my mouth. "You're the one who pranked my rental car? You? It took me all morning to clean up that mess!"

"Pure speculation," Nick says with a sly smirk. "There's no proof of my involvement." He's so cheeky, thinking he got the last laugh.

"The payback you're in for—" I stop. Out of the corner of my eye, I see Wes miming an explosion. Annabelle fidgets beside me. Tim nudges Nick's side, signaling discreetly at something over my shoulder.

Like a five-tier wedding cake toppling over, I watch it happen in slow motion: Margaret sauntering into view, hips swaying and red hair cascading over her shoulders, greeting Nick with a long, sensual kiss.

I down my second Loopy Ladybug.

13

My buzz fizzles, dull dread filling its place.

Margaret pulls back and gives Nick a long, seductive look. My throat constricts, and there's a pinching in my chest. She makes the rounds, greeting everyone with an air kiss. I can feel the pressure of Nick's gaze on me like a hot touch, but I refuse to meet his eyes.

"Oh, Lillie, you're still here," she says when she reaches me. "How wonderful."

Sure it is.

"Mags," Nick says, a warning.

She glances at him, then refocuses her attention on me. With a spiteful smile, she says, "Some people can be such hemorrhoids, don't you think, Lillie? They never seem to go away."

"Is that the reason you walk the way you do?" I say, flashing a grin that rivals hers. "I assumed it was because of the silver spoon stuck up your ass, but a quick trip to the pharmacy for Preparation H can cure that for you."

Margaret narrows her eyes. "Charming as always."

"Likewise," I say, my voice so chipper it hurts my ears.

Nick scrubs his hands over his face. Annabelle snickers. Wes whistles, a nervous habit, while members of the band murmur to each other about an upcoming radio interview and their tour schedule.

Appearing unfazed by the tension swirling around the table, Margaret steals a chair from a nearby group of women dressed in identical T-shirts and wedges it beside Nick. She settles into the seat, crossing her legs so that her pencil skirt rides up, and possessively loops an arm around his.

"So, Lillie," she says, as if we're friends. "What have you been doing these past five years? I hear you graduated from Northwestern with an MBA. Is that true?"

Be cordial, I remind myself. "That's correct. With a dual concentration in finance and strategy," I say. I envision strangling whoever is sharing personal details of my life with her.

Nick studies me, turning a beer bottle slowly in his hand. Annabelle and Wes are tellingly silent, and I wonder which one of them I'll be murdering first.

"I imagine that was quite an accomplishment for you," she continues.

"What's that supposed to mean?" I ask.

"Nothing, really," she says, tracing a manicured nail up and down Nick's arm. "Just that you've spent the majority of your life in a diner, never challenging yourself. I would think that living in a new city while tackling the demands of graduate school would be a large mental hurdle for you to overcome."

"Margaret, that's enough," Nick snaps. He shrugs her off and rakes his fingers through his hair.

For a second I gape at her, hating that her words have burrowed under my skin, but quickly recover. Squaring my shoulders, I say, "I'm sure it was no more difficult than when you completed the Texas dip without landing on your face at your debutante ball."

Margaret glowers at me from across the table.

Wes slaps his knee and says, "Who needs a drink? I could sure go for a stiff one right about now." He stands, looking at Annabelle for a lingering moment before stalking off to the bar.

"I should help him," Nick says, then he's gone, too, following after him.

At the other end of the table, the band is lost in a conversation of their own, abandoning Annabelle and me with Margaret. As I turn toward Annabelle, Margaret calls my name and leans forward so her cleavage is on full display. "There's one last thing," she says. "You'll never get what it is that you came back here for."

"Excuse me?" I say.

"Allow me to be direct, so that you don't misunderstand. You had your time with Nick, but we're together now." Her voice is low and restrained, her tone steely. "He's moved on. Forgotten you. I suggest you remember that."

"Whoa, Margaret, that's—" Annabelle starts.

I hold up a hand, quieting her. Because it's *my* turn to talk, and I've had enough of Margaret and her underhanded comments.

Rising from my chair, I match Margaret's hard stare. "Listen, you self-righteous, Botox-crazed, armpit-licking hag," I say, balling my hands into fists. "You're obviously threatened by me. But I have news for you. I'm *engaged* to someone else. His name is Drew Harrington, and he's amazing. So the next time you feel the need to fling your insecurities in my face, perhaps you should remember that."

I drop back into my seat and inhale a breath.

Annabelle kicks my shin and gives me a loaded look that says we need to talk later. Margaret opens her mouth to respond, but she's cut off by a microphone squealing.

"All right, folks. It's trivia time," the emcee says from the stage set up near the bar. He has a stack of cards in one hand and a lager in the other. Servers deliver a bell to each table.

Nick and Wes return with another round of drinks. Passing a Shiner Bock to me and a glass of red wine to Margaret, Nick glimpses between us and frowns. Margaret is shooting daggers at me, her jaw clenched. I imagine she's accustomed to having the final word. Too bad.

"The rules are simple," the emcee continues. "I'll read a question. The first person or team to ring the bell and answer correctly earns a point. Fifteen points wins the game. Anyone using a cell phone to cheat will be disqualified. Now y'all will be happy to know that Nick Preston is in attendance tonight. Let's find out if he can remain victorious for another week."

A collective groan erupts around the room. Nick waves, a smug expression on his face.

"It's going to be such a shame when I destroy your streak, Preston," I say.

Nick crosses his arms and raises an eyebrow. "Those are some big words coming from someone who hasn't played in an eternity."

"Wait and see," I say. He's right, of course. College was the last time I participated in trivia night, but I won't admit that to Nick. I once considered taking Drew to a bar that hosts various games, but our relationship doesn't operate like that; it doesn't feed off competition.

Nick dangles a scorecard in front of my face. "It's not too late for you to back out. Save yourself the embarrassment."

"You scared?" I say, swiping it from him and writing my name at the top.

He cocks his head and smirks at me. "Do I need to remind you of the Wall of Champions?"

"Just how serious are you two about this sort of thing?" Jason pipes up from the other end of the table.

"Very," Wes and Annabelle say at the same time. They both laugh before trailing off into silence.

Margaret only glares at me.

The emcee announces the game is officially beginning, and I sit up straighter. "Question number one," he says. "What was Oscar the Grouch's original color before Jim Henson decided on green?"

Blue? No. Red?

Crap. I'm rustier than I thought.

"By all means, ladies first." Nick gestures to the bell. His eyes are full of challenge, and my stomach tightens. He knows I'm clueless about the answer. I could try to fake it, but that would only give him more ammunition if I'm wrong.

Nick reaches for the bell but someone at another table beats him to it. "Orange," the person declares, which the emcee deems correct.

"You just cost me a point," Nick says.

I shrug. "Every point you lose is still a point for me."

The emcee calls out, "Famous singer-songwriter Carly Simon's father cofounded which company?"

Nick rings the bell so fast I don't have time to process the question. "Simon & Schuster," he proclaims when prompted for the answer. More groaning fills the room.

"So much for destroying my winning streak, Turner," he says, and puts a mark on his scorecard, that lopsided grin spreading across his face. "Sure you still want to keep going?"

Snatching away his beer, I take several long sips and say, "Worry about yourself. You and your fragile ego have enough to contend with."

"Like what? Your oh-so-impressive knowledge of Back-street Boys songs?" Nick seizes the bottle hovering inches away from my mouth and polishes it off.

Annabelle snorts. Wes chats with the band, none of them even attempting to play. Margaret mutters something about Nick and me behaving like playground enemies.

The emcee's voice booms over the noise. "What happens to a jellyfish left in the sun too long?"

I steal the bell away from Nick and shake it. "They'll evaporate," I yell louder than necessary. Score one point for me. "What were you droning on about again, Preston?" I say with a smug smile of my own.

"Lucky guess."

"Keep lying to yourself."

Huffing in exasperation, Margaret slings her purse over her shoulder and marches toward the door. Nick doesn't seem to notice her departure, his attention laser-focused on the game.

The next two questions stump us, but then we're back on track in a cutthroat battle with each other. Nick earns the next three points, but I jump in, replying, "Forty," when he falters on "What number has all its letters in alphabetical order?" Then I nail the answer on the only planet in our solar system that rotates clockwise (Venus).

The game continues on like a Ping-Pong match—Nick scores a point, then I score one right back. Occasionally, someone else slides in with a correct answer, but still no one comes close to catching us.

As our taunts grow heated, Wes takes on the role of sportscaster. "The mood is tense here at the Tipsy Teakettle as these two rivals vie for trivia dominance."

Annabelle remains firmly on my side, while the band watches from the sidelines, offering neutral high fives and nods of support. It's not long before Nick and I are tied with fourteen points, one answer away from winning.

We're both on our feet and grabbing the bell when the emcee calls out, "What is the only U.S. state whose name is a single syllable?"

"Drop it," I say, tightening my grip on the handle.

"Not a chance, Turner."

"You know I had it first."

Nick places a palm on the table and leans forward, his eyes blazing. "Bullshit."

I mimic his stance. "You just can't admit when you're wrong."

"Oh, that's rich coming from you," he says, his voice dripping with innuendo.

"Hey, guys, take it down a level," Wes says, placing a hand on both our shoulders. "It's only a game." We ignore him, staring at each other from across the table in a silent standoff, both unwilling to concede.

There's a clanging sound on the other side of the bar, followed by someone shouting, "Maine."

We release our hold on the bell, and it's as if the atmosphere between us has shifted.

"All right, folks. This next one may end the game," the emcee announces. "What is the only essential vitamin not found in the white potato?"

The question breaks something open inside me. A memory rushes in of the time Nick and I received that exact question years ago, here at the Tipsy Teakettle, on a night much like this one. Only back then we'd played as a team. I remember how we huddled together, ticking off various nutrients as choices, when suddenly I recalled a fact I had researched about the starchy root vegetable for my newspaper column. That night had been the beginning of our streak as trivia champions.

My heart pushes painfully against my chest. We had loved each other beyond reason. How could we let ourselves stray so far from that? How could we start fighting against each other instead of for each other?

I peer at Nick, wondering if he's remembering the same things. He makes no move for the bell in the center of the table, even though I'm certain he knows the answer. His eyes are steady on mine, imploring, as if he's waiting for something. When he remains motionless, I pick up the bell and ring it.

"Vitamin A," I declare, though it sounds hollow.

"We have a new winner!" the emcee hollers into the microphone in an awful Bob Barker impersonation. Cheers and applause pierce my ears. Annabelle hugs me. Wes claps me on the back. The band does . . . something. I drown it all out.

Nick let me win.

I look at him. There's a stillness to him, but his gaze flickers with an emotion so fierce and raw a knot forms in my stomach.

I need air, some space from . . . all this.

Pushing through the crowd, I step outside. A light drizzle falls from the night sky, shrouding the area in a cool mist. The colors of the Tipsy Teakettle's neon sign reflect onto the slick asphalt, bleeding together like food coloring in frosting.

When I get to my truck, I rest my forehead against the door and practice inhaling and exhaling.

"Lillie."

My breath catches at the way Nick says my name—fast and certain and hoarse—the way he used to, the moment before he'd claim me as his. I turn to face him. He crosses the pavement and traps me between him and the truck. I can feel the cool metal through my shirt. He stares at me, consuming me with those blue eyes. My body is coiled as tight as an electrical wire.

Then he tugs me flush against him, and his mouth is on mine, hungry, desperate. It's as if a charge has been set off inside me; my feet nearly come off the pavement. The kiss is deep, so strong, and I gasp. *Oh, I missed this.* My whole body is humming, telling me this is right.

He runs his hands along my sides, down the back of my thighs, lifting me slightly, destroying every rational thought in my mind. Everywhere he touches is fire.

Nick groans, his teeth nipping at my jaw, my neck, the exposed skin along my collarbone.

I dip my fingers under his shirt, sliding over his hard lines and corded muscles, even more defined than before. His skin is hot and so smooth. Some part of my brain knows this is stupid, irresponsible, but I can't stop.

A moan escapes me as he wraps my legs around his waist and presses me into the truck. "Fuck, you feel good." His voice is so low I have to strain to hear it, a hoarse whisper in my ear.

As I register his words, sobering reality washes over me. I jerk back and disentangle out of his grasp, nearly tripping as I step away from him and reach for the door handle. "We shouldn't be doing this," I say, my chest heaving.

He catches my elbow. "Lillie, wait."

"I need to go."

"No. You don't get to run away from me this time."

Shaking my head, I say, "That kiss was *a mistake*, Nick. Something that never should have happened."

For a moment, he stands there, studying me. Silence stretches between us, the sounds of traffic and the wind filling the void. Finally he drops my arm.

"I still jog the trail around Montgomery Park every morning, break of dawn," he says. "It'd be nice to have a partner sometime." Then he retreats back into the Tipsy Teakettle, and I'm all alone.

It feels too familiar.

14

LATE THE NEXT MORNING, I SQUINT MY EYES OPEN, BLEARY from sleep, to see a figure hovering over me. I scream and fall backward out of bed, landing with a thud on the hardwood floor, my limbs tangled up in the sheets. My heart drums loudly in my chest. I know I should be racing to dial the police, but my head is hazy—probably from one too many drinks—so instead all I can do is curl up into a ball and hope the intruder disappears.

"Are the theatrics necessary, dear?"

Brushing hair out of my mouth, I look up to find Sullivan Grace peering down at me, arms crossed.

"Ms. Hasell!" I scramble to my feet only to realize I'm standing in the middle of my childhood room dressed in nothing but a tank top and lace underwear. Snatching a pillow off the bed, I use it to shield myself. "You scared me."

"Yes, well, that much is obvious." Eyeing me up and down, Sullivan Grace clears her throat and says, "Now, please make yourself presentable and meet me downstairs.

We need to have a chat." Then she's gone, the door clicking shut behind her.

How did she even get in here? A horrible, disgusting thought enters my mind: *What if my father gave Sullivan Grace a key to the house because she spends the night often?* I groan, burying my face into the pillow.

Twenty minutes later I stroll into the kitchen, where Sullivan Grace sits at the table, preparing a cup of Earl Grey tea as though she's at a royal palace. She adds a dash of milk, stirring in small arches back and forth, never allowing the teaspoon to touch the sides or rim of the cup. She removes the spoon and gently places it on the saucer. Her lips purse when she notices me, no doubt judging my simple dress and damp hair. What does she expect after barging in on me like that? She didn't exactly give me much time or warning. I'm sure any moment now she'll flatter me with one of her backhanded compliments.

Sure enough, lifting the teacup to her mouth, she takes a small sip and says, "Lillie, I have always admired secure women like yourself who can flutter about town without giving a second thought to their appearance. Such a lovely trait." *Bless my heart.*

Ignoring her, I open the fridge and reach for the eggs, but stop short when I recognize the baking dish crowding the top shelf, one of many that should contain my mother's peach cobbler but instead is filled with the deconstructed strudel I created yesterday. I wonder why my father brought it home.

"I guess someone discovered my version of today's Blue Plate Special," I say, glancing over my shoulder at Sullivan Grace.

"Have a seat, dear," she says, tapping a chair like she's patting out dough for scones.

I roll my eyes, grab a yogurt, and kick the fridge door closed before dropping into the spot next to her.

"So, how angry is he?" I say, peeling back the foil lid, careful not to tear it. I mold it into a U-shape, creating a makeshift spoon. It's easier than dirtying a utensil. Plus it's economical. And maybe there's a teeny-tiny part of me that wants to goad Sullivan Grace with my poor table manners.

"What were you thinking, Lillie?" she says, adjusting the Rolex adorning her slender wrist. "Jackson is beside himself. I haven't seen him this upset since—" She cuts herself off, the words she didn't say—*since your mother left*—floating between us.

Stifling a grin, I imagine my father huffing around the diner, the vein popping out of his forehead, hollering about how I'm grounded to a month of potato-peeling duty for this stunt. "I don't understand why this is such a big deal. It's still a dessert with peaches in it," I say, then scoop some yogurt into my mouth.

Sullivan Grace presses her lips in a thin line and tugs at her pearl necklace as she watches me slurp down my breakfast. Even when she's angry, she's still a picture of poise and grace. "That isn't what this is about, dear. You know how particular Jackson is about his Blue Plate Specials. You can't change something that important without discussing it with him first. The regulars plan their week around those dishes. Several patrons even walked out this morning when they discovered there wasn't any cobbler."

"Did anyone even taste the strudel? People may like it better," I ask, licking off a strawberry chunk stuck to the foil spoon.

Sighing, Sullivan Grace shakes her head, her expertly blown-out hair swishing with the movement. "I understand you have some . . . reservations about the diner and the Upper Crust," she says, crossing her legs at the ankle, "but I think it would be in everyone's best interest to resolve those lingering issues as soon as possible. Your disrespectful behavior simply won't suit. All this added stress is bad for Jackson's well-being."

My chest tightens. "I would never intentionally hurt my father or do anything that would threaten his health. *Never.* I'm aware that he's getting older, that he's sick," I say, recalling the harsh sound of his cough, his run-down appearance, the limp in his step. "But you know what my mother did, how she just tossed aside her family as if we were nothing. Why would you or my father want me to compete with her peach cobbler recipe? How could you both be so cruel as to expect that? Because it doesn't make sense to me." There it is—the crux of the issue. What I desperately need explained.

I cut my gaze away, out the kitchen window. At the house across the street a little girl is learning how to ride a bicycle. Straddling the rear wheel, an older man with white hair and bushy eyebrows slowly guides her forward until she gains enough momentum to pedal on her own.

When I look back at Sullivan Grace, her eyes have softened. A sad kind of smile flits across her face. She squeezes my hand, and to my surprise, there's a tenderness in her touch I've never felt before. A lump forms in my throat.

"You really haven't figured it out yet have you, dear?" Her voice is sincere but also cautious. "I thought by now you'd realize this isn't about Elizabeth. It's about *you*, your life, the choices you're making. Jackson only wants what's best for you, and it's time you accept—"

She's interrupted by my cell phone vibrating on the table between us. Thomas Brandon's name flashes across the screen. Crap. With all the insanity that happened yesterday I didn't send him the sales forecasts and market analyses I promised.

"I'm sorry, Ms. Hasell, but I need to take this call. It's important." Swiping the phone off the table, I rush out of the kitchen. "Hello, Mr. Brandon," I say, the stairs moaning under my feet as I climb them two at a time.

"My inbox is still empty," he barks, once again jumping over basic pleasantries.

Always one to state the obvious.

"Yes, I know. I apologize," I say, stealing into my room and booting up my laptop. "There were several circumstances beyond my control that prevented me from submitting the information you requested in a timely fashion. You'll have everything by close of business today."

"I'll be frank. Your recent mishaps are not instilling much confidence," he says in his normal no-nonsense voice. "I'm rather concerned about your dedication to this project, and if you're treating it with the seriousness that it deserves."

Irritation floods through me. After everything I've sacrificed for this job—the long hours and late nights I've spent at the office, the weekends and holidays I've given up—the least he could do is grant me an iota of leeway. I'm well aware I haven't been putting forth the effort required to successfully execute the Kingsbury Enterprises account, but it's not as if I've been purposely slacking. Since arriving in Dallas everything has been all twisted around. Sure, I could have returned to my father's house after leaving the diner yesterday to complete the items for the product launch instead of attending trivia night, but I think I'm allowed a break every once in a while, a night off to hang out with friends I haven't seen in five years.

"I assure you, Mr. Brandon, that isn't the case," I say in

my most professional tone. "The Kingsbury Enterprises account is my number-one priority."

Except, even as the words leave my mouth, I know they're a lie. Already my mind is spinning with thoughts of my father and his surgery, Sullivan Grace and the Upper Crust, Nick and all our history and . . . well, Nick—really, what the heck was that kiss at the Tipsy Teakettle? I shiver as I remember his hoarse voice in my ear: *Fuck, you feel good.* I shake my head. We'd been caught up in the moment and the memories. That's all.

"You're one of my top performers, Lillie, which is the only reason I'm not ripping you off this project right now. If something like this happens again, you're done and Ben will take over. I've told you what's at stake for you and the firm. You've been warned." Thomas Brandon says this in a way I assume is meant to sound threatening, but rather, reminds me of everything I've been striving toward, everything I have to lose. "Now in addition to the items you owe me, I need you to prepare a presentation outlining the various branding strategies we've developed."

I spout off a string of "Yes, sir" and "I understand" and "I'll get it all to you right away," as I tell myself that I've worked too hard to jeopardize my career now. Yet after the call ends and I start on the various tasks, the usual thrill and drive I feel when tackling a project are strangely absent.

It doesn't bother me as much as it should.

———

"Baby girl, what's this I hear about you makin' a mess of my pretty office?" My father pokes his head around the doorway, eyes wide as they bounce around the tiny room.

Papers litter the floor. Crowding a corner are cardboard boxes overflowing with three-ring binders that have seen better days, ripped file folders, and grimy office supplies. The rusted, olive-green filing cabinets that used to flank the matching desk have been emptied and thrown in the Dumpster. Standing in their place are the replacements I purchased at Office Depot this afternoon after I sent off the items I owed to Thomas Brandon, along with everything needed to finally organize the diner's files. I've delayed it long enough.

"I'm not making a mess of anything," I say, crawling over to a dry-foods catalog and flinging it onto a pile. "I'm categorizing."

"What's the purpose of all them dots?" he says, pointing to the stickers beside my feet.

"I'm developing a color-coded filing system for you," I say. "Yellow dots are for daily sales figures. Green dots are for purchase orders. Red dots are for employee payroll information. Black dots are for distributor and supplier invoices. Blue dots—"

"Now hold your horses, baby girl," my father says, stepping into the office. "There ain't nothing wrong with my old system."

Blowing strands of hair out of my face, I sit back on my heels and stare incredulously at him.

"Everything was how I liked it before. How am I ever goin' to find—"

He breaks into another coughing fit, as loud and wet as before, his whole body hunched over. I rush to his side, the spark of worry now a full-fledged flame. He grabs on to me, using my weight to keep his balance, until finally he draws in a ragged breath and the hacking stops.

I wrap an arm around his waist to hold him up. "Dad, that sounds like it's not getting any better."

"It's okay. I'm fine now," he says, his voice raspy and

weak. My father pats my shoulder and straightens his back. "Some episodes are worse than others. This was a bad one."

"How long have you had that cough?"

He twists his mustache, and wrinkles line his forehead. "I dunno. About five months, I guess."

"Why didn't you tell me?"

My father scratches his jaw and says, "It's only become bothersome recently. Plus I knew you'd be coming home for the surgery. No need to worry your pretty little head unnecessarily. I promise I'll discuss it with Doc, ask if he can adjust my meds again."

I study him, noticing he seems more rested today, despite the cough. Still, I don't want to take any chances. "Maybe you should visit the emergency clinic before it shifts into something more serious. There's one not far from here."

"I ain't goin' there," he says. "The people at those places don't know their ass from their elbows. I'm waiting for my appointment on Halloween and that's that. Now, as I was saying before, how am I ever goin' to find anything with you messing up my organization?"

I sigh. Always so stubborn.

"How about this," I say, clearing some space on the floor. "Why don't you let Ernie deal with the dinner crowd and join me instead? That way after I'm back in Chicago you'll know where everything is."

I expect him to tell me no, that his bum knee can't handle the strain and I'm crazy for even contemplating something other than managing the diner. To my surprise, my father unties the apron, cracks his knuckles, and says, "All righty then. Show me what that one-hundred-thousand-dollar MBA bought you."

"That's it? No complaints about my job or Chicago?"

It's weird. I thought I'd be happy about him not challenging me. Maybe it's that I've waited so long for him to accept my life in Chicago, show genuine interest, that now his acquiescence feels underwhelming.

"Baby girl, when are you gonna learn that sometimes it's easier to placate you than listen to your nagging." He pinches my nose as if I'm four years old, inviting him to be a guest at my cupcake party.

Rolling my eyes, I slide a stack of purchase orders over to him. For the next few hours we work in tandem, sorting papers and recycling others, marking folders with dot stickers, then filing everything away. I discover that while the diner's records are disordered and, in some cases, incomplete, it's not as bad as I originally suspected.

"Dad, can I ask you something?"

"Course you can," he says, fighting with the plastic on a new package of dot stickers. "You know you can always ask me anything."

"You used to be so meticulous about everything, the diner, the house, almost to a fault. Now it's all so . . . rundown." I gesture to a patch on the wall where paint is peeling away. "What happened?"

My father blows out a breath and says, "I ain't a spring chicken anymore, baby girl. It's getting harder for me to keep up with everything, is all. That's why you're here, to set me straight as spaghetti."

A knot forms in the pit of my stomach. I wish he would've told me all this sooner. I could have arranged help for him, ensured he slowed down and didn't work such long hours slaving in the kitchen.

"Do your old man a favor and help me with this, will you?" He tosses me the now-mangled package of stickers. "It's the least you can do after that phyllo and peach whatchamacallit disaster."

"It wasn't a *disaster,*" I say, walking over to the desk and rifling around in the drawers for a pair of scissors. "In fact I thought the dessert tasted delicious, even with my bias." While I finished my tasks for Thomas Brandon, I baked the dish in the fridge and ate several portions of the strudel.

My father grumbles something about how it's still no peach cobbler.

"So you served it?" I say as I cut through the plastic and hand him back the stickers.

Peeling off a yellow dot, he places it on a folder with last week's sales figures and says, "Course I did. You left me without much choice after that stunt you pulled. Gotta give the guests something to satisfy their sweet tooth."

"And they loved it." I say it as a statement rather than a question, because I know it to be true. "Which is great news, because I'm competing with it for the Upper Crust." There. It's out in the open now so it doesn't surprise him on the day of the event.

My father frowns, the creases around his eyes deepening. "Well, baby girl, I know it's a dessert that's got peaches in it, but you've always had this talent for creating something from scratch, something that's uniquely yours. So I don't know why you'd submit a dish derived from a superior recipe, but that's your decision, I guess."

That's what my father doesn't understand. Under the confines of the competition guidelines, the deconstructed strudel *is* something uniquely mine.

It has to be good enough.

15

THE FOLLOWING AFTERNOON, I PUSH OPEN THE SHINY black door to B is for Beholden, Annabelle's wedding and event planning company. As I step inside, I'm immediately greeted by decadence. A pair of wing chairs and a sofa adorned with Ikat throw pillows welcome clients, and a chevron rug and a faux bamboo coffee table anchor the space.

In an alcove off the main area, Annabelle sits at a white-lacquered desk, stacks of papers, sticky notes, and Red Bull cans cluttering the top. Framing her on each side are two identical desks, though they're much tidier. They must belong to her assistants, Nora and Ruthie. A phone is propped between Annabelle's ear and shoulder as her fingers fly across a computer keyboard. She smiles when she sees me holding up a large paper bag from her favorite Tex-Mex joint and motions that she'll only be a couple more minutes.

While she finishes her conversation, I roam around. Framed accolades from local and national publications hang on walls painted silver sage. Built-in white book-shelves lined with magazines, invitation sample books, and fine-art wedding albums from past events flank a tall doorway that leads to a room brimming with party decor ideas and linens in various textures and patterns.

By the time Annabelle joins me in the main area, I have set up a picnic on the floor using a checkered table-cloth I borrowed from one of the racks.

"Holy hell," she says, kicking off her heels before flop-ping down beside me, legs stretched out in front of her. "I'm so hungry I swear the caterer could hear my stomach rumbling through the phone." Grabbing one of the Styro-foam containers, she opens the lid and inhales the spicy scent of barbacoa tacos. "Thank heavens for chipotle peppers in adobo." She takes a giant bite as chunks of shredded beef fall out of the corn tortilla.

I laugh as I doctor up my tacos with jicama-mango slaw and guacamole. "I can't believe how much your place has grown," I say through a mouthful of food. "It really looks fantastic."

When Annabelle entered the industry out of college, she worked for Simon Ross, a slave driver who had a wedding planning show on TLC and whose clientele consisted exclusively of Dallas's most elite, until she gained enough money and experience to break out on her own. At first, she operated the business out of her rental house. But after landing a few high-profile clients and earning a feature in *Martha Stewart Weddings*, her reputation soared and she was able to make the leap to the Dallas Design District, where she firmly established herself. Now she's one of the most sought-after wedding and event planners in the area.

"Thanks," she says, licking her fingers. "We expanded

last year, but it's still too cozy. We're drowning in clients. I really need to hire another assistant."

While we eat, we chat about inconsequential things—what we should do for Halloween and the new deep-fried desserts that are all the rage at this year's Texas State Fair. I fill her in on the big promotion I'm in line for at work. She tells me about how her company is organizing the album release party and private concert at the House of Blues for the Randy Hollis Band and that, of course, I'm invited and must come, no excuses.

I'm scooping some black beans and rice into my mouth when Annabelle catches me off guard and says, "So you and Drew are engaged."

My stomach drops as the realization sinks in that I accidentally let that bit of news slip during my tirade against Margaret.

"Which is rather interesting," she continues with a pointed stare, "because the last I heard you weren't ready for the relationship to progress to that stage."

I cringe. It sounds so much worse when she puts it like that, especially after what happened with Nick at the Tipsy Teakettle. My mind floods with images of his mouth on mine, my legs wrapped around his waist, his hips pressing me into the truck while my hands explored. I shake my head, dislodging the memory.

"Well I'm ready now." My voice is so strained I barely recognize it. I clear my throat. "And you never mentioned your breakup with Wes. That isn't an excuse or a reason for not confiding in you sooner, but I'm not the only person who hid things."

Annabelle sighs. "So that somehow makes it better?"

"No," I say, shuffling mango pieces around with the plastic fork. "Of course it doesn't."

"When did we start keeping secrets from each other, Lil?" she asks. Not accusatory or mad. Just . . . sad.

"I don't know." I bite my lip. "When life got bigger than the both of us, I guess."

"Maybe, but no more secrets, okay?"

I nod. "Promise."

For a moment, we're both quiet, lost in thought. Then the confession tumbles out of me.

"I kissed Nick," I blurt. "In the parking lot after trivia ended."

Annabelle freezes in the midst of pouring tomatillo salsa on her tacos. "You did *what?*"

"Obviously it was a mistake," I say quickly. "A result of the alcohol and the thrill of the game and . . . a stupid moment of weakness."

She snorts. "Right. A mistake."

"It was," I insist, wondering if wanting to believe my words and deep-down believing them can be the same thing.

"Have you told Drew?"

"It was a onetime thing that didn't mean anything. What would be the point?" Even to my ears the excuse sounds flimsy, but kissing Nick *was* a one-time occurrence.

"Did you and Nick talk about it after?" Annabelle asks. "Or at least get some things straightened out?"

I look at her, my silence a resounding no.

She sets her food container aside. "You two are ridiculous."

"What does it matter? I have Drew, and Nick's with Margaret now," I say, careful to conceal the bitterness creeping into my voice. "After everything, she's finally sunk her claws into Nick."

"It's not like that. Margaret can be a bitch, for sure, but her intentions are good."

I choke on a laugh. "You're joking, right? Her intentions have never been good," I say. "More like manipulative and vindictive. Or have you forgotten all those times she showed a blatant disregard for my relationship with Nick?"

"I haven't forgotten," Annabelle says, shifting her legs beneath her. "I just don't think it's relevant anymore."

Not relevant? Is she kidding?

"Are you on her side now?" I ask.

"This isn't about picking sides," she says. "All I'm saying is that Margaret does care about Nick."

"Whatever," I mutter.

"No, not 'whatever.' Whether you like it or not, you need to hear this. Margaret's been a real friend to Nick these past few years and supported him when he desperately needed someone there. He was a mess after you left, Lil. Destructive . . ." Annabelle presses her eyes shut, as if trying to erase a painful memory. She clears her throat. "After a while of getting nowhere, Wes and I . . . we had to let Nick fail, learn his own lessons, but Margaret refused to do that. During his parents' divorce—"

"Charlotte and Dr. Preston are divorced?" I say, my mind spinning. I never thought that would happen. While I'm certain Nick's parents haven't been in love since their wedding day, they always presented a united front to the outside world, especially in regards to family matters. "When?"

"Three years ago. It was ugly, too. Roger Stokes's firm handled Dr. Preston's side of the case. Nick and Margaret grew close in the process."

"What happened?" I ask.

"That's something you'll need to discuss with Nick," she says, tucking a strand of hair behind her ear. "It's not my story to tell."

I shake my head. "You know I can't do that, Annabelle."

"No, you *won't* do that."

"Does it make a difference?"

She sighs. "Lillie, you're my best friend, so *please* feel free to take this the wrong way. You're a first-rate idiot."

"Excuse me. I resent—"

She holds up a hand, cutting me off. "I'm not done. Listen, I know how rough those last few years were for you and Nick. How angry and depressed you were—hell, how angry and depressed you both were—but you gave up on each other. You gave up on yourself."

I pull my shoulders back, resolve straightening my posture. "I never gave up on myself."

"No?" Annabelle says. "Tell me the last recipe you created."

"What does that have to do with anything?"

"You used to live your life through a kitchen," she says. "When you needed a space to think, a space to *be*, that's where you went. Now you're a strategy consultant? How does that make sense?"

"You know it's more complicated than that."

"No, it's really not," Annabelle says. "Your mother did a shitty thing, Lil. I'm not arguing against that. But you've allowed something that's about her to cause you to turn your back on everything important to *you*." She pauses, as if searching for the right words. "You're in a job that dictates your existence but is in no way fulfilling. And Drew . . . he provides you with a safe little world without any challenges."

"You say that like it's a bad thing. Like stability and genuine affection and comfort are worth less than passion and heat. They're not."

Ignoring me, Annabelle rises onto her knees and continues. "What about friendships outside of Drew? Not once have you ever mentioned grabbing drinks with girl-friends after work or eating out with other couples on a Friday night. I could maybe get on board with all of this if you were truly happy in Chicago, but instead you're just kind of floating."

My body tenses. "You have no idea how hard it was for me to leave, how tough it was to start over."

She nods, as if granting me that point, but then says, "That doesn't mean you settle. You claim you love Drew, that you're ready to *marry* him, but someone in a committed relationship doesn't hide something like that from her closest family and friends. And she definitely doesn't kiss her ex-fiancé. I would know, given my experience on the topic."

"Don't compare us," I say, rising onto my knees to match her. "Me kissing Nick is nowhere near the same as you sleeping with someone else."

Annabelle arches an eyebrow and plants her hands on her hips. "Careful in that glass house, Lil. It may be new to you, but it still breaks."

Wadding up a napkin and tossing it into the brown paper bag, I stand and say, "You don't know *anything*." I move around her toward the door, but her voice stops me cold.

"Go ahead, Lillie. Run away again when things get hard."

"That's not fair," I say as I turn to face her. "You act as if this whole thing between Nick and me is my fault. I wasn't in that relationship by myself." Though as I say the words, I'm struck by how true they felt at the time.

She gets to her feet and takes a deep breath, the way

she does when she's trying to tamp her frustration. "You're right. Nick's far from blameless. I know he hurt you, that he became an entirely different person once he started medical school, that he abandoned you when you needed him most, but you're not blameless either. What did you do to fix your relationship? Or to prevent it from failing?"

"Are you serious?" I say, my voice escalating. "What could I have done, Annabelle? Beg him to acknowledge me? Pretend Nick made me happy and that everything was great when it wasn't? Somehow force him to change his attitude and become his old self again?"

"Yes!" she says, exasperated, throwing her arms up. "Anything would have been more than what you actually did—more than what you are doing—which is *nothing*."

"How was I supposed to do that? Nick wouldn't even talk to me, let alone look at me. He shut me out." I'm shouting now, my voice trembling.

"That is such bullshit, Lillie. You didn't even *try*." Fierceness blazes in her eyes. "Quit playing the victim and recognize the truth for what it is—you tucked your tail between your legs and *ran away*. From Nick, but more importantly, from yourself."

Heat races through me as tears prick my eyes. How dare she insinuate that I'm some kind of coward who so easily surrendered. Annabelle's not the one who felt powerless witnessing her world crumble into dust. She's not the one who cried herself to sleep so often that her eyes became permanently swollen and bloodshot. I had to get out. I couldn't keep living like that.

"It wasn't that simple, Annabelle. I didn't just quit," I say as I turn and continue on my path to the door.

"Funny. I'll bet your mother said the same thing when she left," she says, a knife in my back.

My hand freezes on the knob as something inside me

snaps. Venomous words rise like bile from my stomach, the taste sour and foreign on my tongue. Spinning on my heel, I meet her hard gaze. "Fuck you, Annabelle. At least I found someone who *wants* to marry me."

Because unlike her, I have the decency to stab her in the front.

16

My fight with Annabelle is still replaying itself on an endless loop in my head when I wake early the next morning. Clad in sneakers, workout shorts, and an old SMU Pi Phi T-shirt I dug out of the package of clothes Drew sent from Chicago, I sit on a wrought-iron bench at the entrance to the dirt path in Montgomery Park, gearing up for a run. The sky is laced with pinks and lavenders, and the rain from the past several days has cooled the air, making me shiver. Or perhaps it's my nerves getting the better of me. Now that I'm actually here, about to take Nick up on his offer, I'm not entirely convinced this isn't a giant mistake, but I refuse to prove Annabelle right. I'm not my mother. I'm not a coward.

Tires crunch on gravel as headlights sweep across the small parking lot. A shiny black Mercedes pulls into the spot next to my Ford truck, which sits there resembling moldy leftovers.

Nick steps out of the car, apprehension on his face. "Lillie?"

"You got rid of Susanna," I say, grabbing my phone off the bench and walking over.

"Her engine couldn't survive the summers anymore," he says, leaning his elbows against the open driver's side door. "This one's named Kelly."

"After 'Machine Gun Kelly'?" I ask, referring to his favorite James Taylor song.

Nick nods, then gives me a small, rueful smile. "I'm glad you came. I didn't think you would."

I shrug and bite my lip, having nothing to say.

"You still run?" he asks, yanking the sweatshirt over his head and throwing it onto his passenger seat. The outline of his pecs is visible beneath the fabric of his T-shirt. My mouth dries a little.

"Not as much as I'd like to," I say. "My job keeps me pretty busy, so it's been awhile."

I touch my toes, and my hamstrings cry in protest. I right myself as Nick is pulling his foot back, stretching his quads, the muscles bunching and flexing in his legs. I follow the lean, hard lines of his body—his toned arms, his sculpted shoulders, his smooth, tan neck that leads to his stubbled jaw.

Nick takes a swig of water and says, "We'll start off easy."

Scrolling through the music library on my phone, I select the nineties pop playlist before taking off down the trail, leaving Nick scrambling to catch up. He gains on me quickly, his strides in rhythm with mine. Nudging my elbow, he motions to my earbuds. I put the Paula Abdul track on pause and look at him.

"You good with turning around after crossing Bower's Bridge?" he asks.

I nod again, resuming the song, and keep my eyes

trained ahead. Bower's Bridge is where I broke my ankle tripping over a loose plank during a game of capture the flag. Even in the eighth grade, the doctor in Nick crafted a splint using a few scraggly sticks and his shirt until my father arrived and drove me to the hospital for a plaster cast.

Sighing, I lean my head back and soak up the sun filtering through the overhang of branches, thinking of all the times Nick patched me up when I was hurt. Even now, the faded scars and slight imperfections covering my body tell secret stories of all the knife cuts he bandaged, the oven burns he soothed, the sore backs and throbbing feet he massaged after grueling diner shifts.

But then, he's also the one who shattered my heart into so many pieces it shocked my soul into silence.

We jog along the quiet trail. Our shoes pound against hard dirt as we run past a stone waterfall, navigate through a tunnel littered with dead leaves and water puddles, and skirt around a group of picnic benches where my father taught Nick how to play the guitar when he was nine.

So much has changed between us since then. Yet here I am, back in the place where life was simple, just a boy and a girl and a childhood love.

Overwhelming sadness rushes through me. For those kids we used to be, so full of hopeful innocence, clueless about the jagged, rocky cliff looming ahead in their future. For straying so far from where we started. For all we have lost.

As we run, my whole body tingles. A cramp stabs at my right side. Peering over at Nick, I notice his breathing is steady and that he's barely breaking a sweat, while I'm wheezing like a cow is sitting on my chest and my skin is slick with moisture. He's obviously slowed his pace so I can keep up with him. His arms are relaxed at his waist, and I can't help but stare at the way his body moves in beat with his strides—perfect runner's form.

Our sneakers slap against the warped, weathered planks of Bower's Bridge. As we cross over, I wonder what would happen if instead of turning around on the other side like we agreed, we let our legs carry us to the secluded canopy of oak trees a hundred yards beyond. The home to so many of our memories. Nick glances at me, and I swear by the flicker in his eyes he's wondering the same thing. Something deep inside me aches.

We don't allow ourselves to find out. When we reach the other side of the bridge, we jog in a sweeping circle before crossing back over and following the same path until we hit the parking lot. Resting my elbows on my knees, I take large, gasping breaths. Pain eddies through me, and my legs wobble. Sweat drips from my hair into my eyes, stinging and blurring my vision. Ordinarily I'd be embarrassed at how out of shape I am, but right now I can only concentrate on not collapsing.

"Move around," Nick says. "It'll help flush out the lactic acid in your system."

I nod, too exhausted to reply, and walk back and forth with my fingers linked behind my head. A breeze washes over my face, cooling me, but still my lungs are screaming. I can't seem to suck in enough air.

Nick strides over to me. "You want your breathing to come from deep in your diaphragm. Right here," he says, placing one hand on the curve of my back and the other just below my rib cage, applying pressure. "Can you feel that?" His gaze rakes over my face, painfully slow, as though he's afraid to miss something.

Is he kidding? His palms are burning holes in my shirt, making me dizzy, and he wants to know if I can feel that? Suddenly I go from barely being able to retain oxygen in my lungs to a total inability to breathe at all. I should be shocked that after all this time a simple touch from him has the power to steal my breath, but after what happened between us at the Tipsy Teakettle, nothing surprises me anymore.

Stepping away, I pick up the water bottle lying on the ground by his feet and gulp some down, the liquid sloshing around in my stomach.

"Drink it slowly. Otherwise you'll throw up," he says, tugging on my ponytail. My heart trips in my chest at the way his voice dips with his playful scolding. Sticking out my tongue, I squirt some water at him and stretch my aching muscles. Nick does his own form of postrun recovery, which involves some strange yoga poses mixed with light strength exercises. I squeeze my eyes shut when I hear him groan, the sound similar to those he once murmured during sex.

After he's done, he uses the hem of his T-shirt to wipe his neck and forehead. His chest expands and retracts with his breathing, his skin glistening. I swallow thickly, watching a bead of sweat travel down the length of his torso and absorb into his mesh shorts. Everything about Nick is corded muscle and hard, chiseled angles and lines. My eyes drop to his hands resting on his hips, and I have an overwhelming urge to feel them on me. My whole body clenches as I remember *exactly* what those fingers are capable of.

A dog barks, snapping me out of my haze. I focus on the college-age guy playing fetch with a golden retriever across the park and wait for my heart rate to return to normal.

"It's okay, you know."

"What is?" I ask.

"To check me out," Nick says, smug and without shame. "Don't think I didn't notice your little eye dance."

I balk. "I wasn't checking you out. You were doing those weird poses, and I was curious."

He laughs, deep and sexy, erasing all of my common sense. His soles scuff against the gravel as he saunters toward me. He stops and stands so close I can feel the heat radiating off his body and see the faint scar above his left eyebrow—a casualty from back in my diner days when I accidentally opened the freezer door into his face.

When he speaks, his words send a shiver down my spine. "You forget, Lillie, I know your blush."

My breath hitches, and his smile grows into that destructive grin that's always been deadly to me. I force my eyes away, over to the other side of the parking lot where a woman is adjusting a set of ankle weights, back to the guy still tossing a tennis ball with his dog, down at my grungy shoelaces, anywhere other than at him.

"At least I used to," Nick says, low and hoarse. "Before . . ."

He settles a hand on the crook of my neck, his thumb ghosting along my collarbone, and everything inside me ignites, alive and volatile. I look at him, and the intensity in his stare causes a fresh wave of heat to rush through me. I lean toward him, pulled by invisible fingers. His gaze flicks to my mouth, and as if on their own volition, my lips part. My breath comes in shallow gasps, my body humming in antici-pation, waiting for him to pin me against my truck and kiss me the way he did at the Tipsy Teakettle. The way he used to.

Nick blinks, then blinks again. His expression darkens, and before I have the opportunity to process what it means, he backs away from me, the imprint of his touch branded on my skin. Without his nearness, the fog in my head clears, even as my heart continues to pound a frantic rhythm against my chest.

Silence stretches between us.

Then I hear myself say, "Except we're different people now, leading separate lives." My voice sounds distant, as if it doesn't belong to me.

An emotion I can't describe flashes across his features. Nick opens his mouth to reply but quickly closes it. Shaking his head, he turns away.

"It wasn't supposed to be this way," I blurt. Just like that, without gathering my bearings first, without practicing it a hundred times in my mind beforehand.

Nick faces me. His gaze is probing, as though I'm an onion whose layers he's peeling off one by one. Long seconds pass before he says, "Maybe this is exactly how it's supposed to be." The quiet confidence in his voice seizes my heart.

I want to tell him he's wrong, that we were supposed to be each other's forever, but at this moment, I can't listen to him tell me why I wasn't worth the sacrifice. Why it took me moving a thousand miles away for him to find happiness. Why he was able to unfurl his fingers and let our relationship go so easily after we'd spent our whole lives clinging desperately to each other. This time I know once the wound I so carefully stitched together all those years ago is ripped open again, the sharp, searing pain that follows will devour me.

We stare at each other in silence, his words hanging in the space between us, loud and ominous. Finally, Nick rakes a hand through his hair, the roots slightly damp with sweat, and says, "Lillie . . . about the other night. . . . You're right . . . I shouldn't have kissed you like that. I was out of line."

Drawing in the gravel with the tip of my sneaker, I say,

"I guess old habits die hard." I try to make it sound like a quip, but my tone is all wrong—too high-pitched, forced.

"Tell that to Bruce Willis," he says, returning my awful attempt at a joke with a pun of his own, breaking the tension between us. I'm glad for it.

I look at him. "You seem happier, Nick."

"I am."

"What changed?"

He studies me carefully, as if searching for something. "Everything, Lillie," he says. "Everything."

I wait for Nick to elaborate further, but he offers nothing.

"Annabelle mentioned your parents got divorced," I say after awhile. "What happened? They always appeared so solid."

Nick stares at me with a fierceness in his eyes that makes my throat constrict. "I think we both know the facade is more believable than the reality it hides."

The implication in his tone isn't lost on me—the end of our relationship was nothing more than a massive charade. I nod and ask him again about what happened.

Nick rubs the back of his neck. "After you left, everything kind of . . . disintegrated. My parents were arguing constantly. Then it all fell apart . . ." His vague response reminds me of all those times I'd ask him about how his medical school classes or clinical rotations were going. Except before I could even finish my question, he would cut me off with something curt like, *Everything's fine.* Or, *If I wanted to talk about it, I'd say so.* Or his personal favorite, *Leave it alone, Lillie.*

This time I don't let him off the hook but keep staring until he sighs and says, "I told my mother I was contemplating quitting my surgical residency. She refused to even entertain the idea, reminding me in her steadfast way that there're six generations of surgeons in our family. That it's a badge of honor worn by all Preston men."

My stomach twists. Nick considered abandoning his residency?

"What about your father?" I ask, knowing Dr. Preston's approval has always mattered most to Nick.

"He was disappointed but understood . . . said he'd support me in whatever decision I chose." Nick pauses, glances toward the sky, and then looks at me again. "I think my mother saw my father's response as a kind of betrayal, like he was giving me permission to disown my birthright. They couldn't keep it together after that. My mother hired an attorney out of New York and moved back to North Carolina shortly after the divorce was finalized. We're not . . . we don't communicate anymore."

"That must have been difficult for you," I say, imagining the emotional strain the whole experience put on him. "I know how close you were to them."

"It was difficult," he says. "Sometimes it still is."

"So you quit then?" I ask. "Your surgical residency?"

He nods and says with a chuckle, "I opted for something not quite as rigorous or stressful and that doesn't require me to be on call all hours of the day."

"That's good," I say, picturing him in his element as a general practitioner, healing people.

Nick steps close to me again. "What about you?"

"What about me?" My reply comes out as a whisper.

"Are you happier?" he clarifies. "Is this the life you wanted?"

I don't know how to answer his question. My life now isn't a happiness I ever imagined. I was supposed to marry Nick and take over the diner and live my happily ever after, but that all changed the day I found the article about my mother. It forced me down a foreign road, a different

course, to a new city, a new career, a new me. While it's not
what I wanted or even dreamed of, maybe it's where I'm
meant to be.

Maybe it's enough.

"I'm happy," I say, and I wonder if he notices I didn't
say "happier." I wonder if he believes me.

"You deserve that."

Annabelle's words echo in my mind. *You gave up on each
other, Lillie. You gave up on yourself.*

Is she right? Could our relationship have been saved if
only I had fought harder? I think back to all the times Nick
would crawl into bed after a brutal shift at the hospital,
when we would both lay there in the dark, pretending to be
asleep. I remember hoping he would pull me close, bury
his face into my neck, whisper that he loved me, only to be
shredded when he remained firmly on his side. What if I'd
been the one to roll over, wrap an arm around him, hold
him tight? Could a small gesture like that have mended the
brokenness between us? Could we be happier now,
together? Would Chicago be nothing more than a city we
visited on a last-minute weekend getaway and not the place
where I permanently rest my head at night?

An ache seizes my chest, more consuming than guilt,
more devastating than regret.

I let Nick slip away, and I did nothing to stop it.

I'm equally to blame, I think as the pressure in my chest
continues to build.

As though the truth is suffocating me.

17

THAT AFTERNOON I SPRAWL OUT ON MY BED, MY HEAD resting on a pillow, my bare feet pressed against the headboard. I stare at the glow-in-the-dark plastic stars stuck to the ceiling that lost their magic years ago, listening to the familiar creaks and groans of my father's house settling as it adjusts to the warm October air.

The ache in my chest is still there. Snapshots flash through my mind. A ruined dinner because Nick and I are too busy fondling each other on the couch like the horny teenagers we used to be. The two of us traveling along the highway on a road trip to Austin City Limits with the radio blasting and windows down, hand-surfing the wind currents. A rainy Saturday, thunder booming outside, where we remain under the covers all day, tangled up in each other. Moments that may have been if only I had stayed, swallowed my pride, rebuilt the bridge between us.

Rolling onto my stomach, I wiggle out the thumbtack wedged into the windowsill and spin it between my fingers, thinking about our soup-can phones. Nick threw his away when the yarn broke, but I still have mine buried in an old shoebox hidden in the back of my closet. Besides a few photographs, it's the only memento I brought with me to Chicago.

My secret piece of Nick.

I shake my head. What am I doing?

Annabelle's right, I can't separate my actions from hers. I have to tell Drew. Grabbing my cell phone off the floor, I dial him at the office. He picks up immediately.

"Hey, there," Drew says in his warm, familiar tone. "I thought maybe you got kidnapped by a cowboy."

I bite my lip. "Not exactly. Things have been crazy here." I wonder if he can detect the uneasiness in my voice. "Are you upset?"

"With you? Never." I picture him with his feet propped up on his desk, tie thrown over his shoulder, a pen tucked behind his ear. "I'm only worried about you, babe."

I breathe in deep, gathering my bearings. "Drew, I . . . I need to tell you something."

There's a creaking sound on the other end and the soft click of a door closing. "What is it?"

My mouth feels dry as I say, "I kissed someone here . . . an ex . . . I'm so sorry." Then I stammer a brief explanation about Nick and our history, how we bumped into each other again recently, that things spiraled out of control during a trivia game and we kissed. Confessing to Drew brings my disloyalty into sharp focus.

Drew's quiet for a moment. My stomach twists into knots as I brace myself, awaiting his backlash. Finally he clears his throat and says, "It's okay, Lillie. I know you didn't mean for it to happen. We can move past it." His voice is steady, collected, as if I told him I requested a tax extension.

His response is meant to reassure me, I know this, but for some reason it has the opposite effect. I want him to feel angry, hurt, or at the very least, disappointed. How can he not be mad that I kissed another man? Is he so secure in our relationship that he doesn't think news like this warrants a strong reaction?

Then again that's not Drew's style. He's kind, sensible, earnest. Not the type of person who resorts to slamming doors, name-calling, or shouting to solve a problem. In fact, in the two years we've been together, we've never had a disagreement about anything more serious than who forgot to empty the dishwasher or fold the laundry. Even then, no voices were raised or tears shed. Which means that we have never engaged in mind-blowing makeup sex either.

Not like that's a deal breaker. There's more to a solid relationship than intense physical intimacy and a Tilt-A-Whirl of emotions. Like companionship, stability, mutual respect—everything I have with Drew.

Still it would be nice if on occasion he showed a little passion, stopped being so dang agreeable bordering on perfect.

"Why are you so calm about this?" I ask, certain if our roles were reversed I'd be far from rational. In fact I'd be irate.

"I know it was a mistake," he says matter-of-factly, which only adds to my annoyance. "I understand how overwhelmed you've been juggling all these different responsibilities."

"I'm not that overwhelmed!" I snap, clenching my hand, the sharp point of the thumbtack piercing my skin. I squeeze tighter.

"See? This is what I'm talking about, babe. You don't sound like yourself," he says, still without a trace of anything other than concern.

I get up from the bed and pace the room, my frustration bubbling over. "Of course I don't sound like myself. You're acting as if I told you I forgot the dry cleaning."

He sighs, and I hear papers shuffling. "Lillie, I'm at a loss here . . . How would you prefer I behave?"

The fire inside me burns out, and I sink onto the desk chair. I want that possession, that flare of passion. Unfurling my fingers, I watch as a few drops of blood pool in my palm. "I need to know that this matters, Drew. That it *bothers* you."

"Of course I'm not happy about it," he says, though by his tone he could have fooled me. "But we've both invested too much into this relationship to allow something like this to affect it. Let's put it behind us."

What if I can't do that? I think. "So that's it then? It's a nonissue?"

"Lillie, I don't know what it is you want me to say . . ."

I tug at a loose thread on my shorts. "Neither do I, which is why we both need to step back, give each other some space. I think we should take a break, figure out if this is really what we want," I say, knowing there's so much more I need to figure out—where I belong, my feelings for Nick, how best to help my father.

"Maybe that's a good idea, given all the stress you're under. Take the time you need. Once you're back in Chicago, things will return to normal. You'll see." Drew says all this with a confidence I don't reciprocate.

For the first time in five years, I'm not sure normal is what I want anymore.

———

I SPEND the remainder of the day combing through files of data in order to create a life-cycle cost analysis to aid Kingsbury Enterprises with its product launch. It's tedious and draining, and I wonder how I ever enjoyed this.

After I email the completed model to Thomas Brandon, I curl up on the couch and zone out to *Beverly Hills, 90210* reruns. I like to think I'm merely getting in touch with my nostalgic side, reliving my teenage years when Annabelle and I would lounge on the floor in front of the television, tucked into our sleeping bags, watching taped episodes of our favorite show and arguing over Dylan McKay's true soul mate. I feel a pang in my stomach as I remember those days, wishing Annabelle were here with me right now. We still haven't spoken, probably because we're both in uncharted territory.

I switch off the television and stare at the ceiling. Before I can process my actions or talk myself out of it, I steal up to the second floor and climb the pull-down staircase that leads to the attic. I find the box with the extra party supplies and lug it down the ladder, hitting every rung on the way.

My father comes out of his room, rubbing sleep from his eyes. "Baby girl, what are you doin' out here makin' such a ruckus? Don't you know your old man's gotta get his beauty rest?" He glances at the box in my arms, shakes his head, and mutters something about how I'm begging for trouble. He's back in his room with the door closed before I can respond.

I carry the box to the kitchen, grab a few more items from the pantry, and stuff everything I need into a duffel bag. I hop into my truck and speed over to Annabelle's condo, dialing her cell on the way. No answer. I call again. She picks up on the fourth ring.

"Do you have a death wish?" she says, her voice raspy.

"Get ready. I'll be downstairs in the parking garage."

There's a shuffle on the other end. "Lillie, it's three thirty in the morning—"

"I don't care. Do it." I hang up.

Ten minutes later, Annabelle climbs into my truck. She's dressed in yoga pants, a fitted cotton shirt, and sneakers. Her sleek black hair has been pulled into a ponytail. We look like twins in our matching outfits. For a moment, it feels as if we are fifteen again, sneaking out of my father's house after curfew to play night games at Montgomery Park with Wes and Nick. Like no time has passed at all.

Annabelle yawns and slumps against the passenger door. "You want to tell me what this is about?"

"Drew and I are on a break."

She sits up straight and looks at me.

"You were right," I say, tossing her the duffel. She unzips it and rummages through the contents. Then she meets my gaze, a twinkle in her eyes and a devious expression on her face.

"I'll show you the way," she says, her voice almost giddy.

I smile. And just like that, I know that while our argument isn't forgotten, we've both forgiven.

We cruise across town in comfortable silence. When we turn onto Nick's street, I cut off the headlights, shift into neutral, and coast the remainder of the way to his house. My fingers clench the steering wheel as I stare at the charming, Craftsman-style bungalow with its gabled roof, ganged windows, and wide, columned front porch. So different from the three-story brownstone we once occupied. I wonder why he decided to downgrade. Then again, maybe he wasn't given a choice if the brownstone had been sold as part of his parents' divorce settlement. Another possibility enters my mind: maybe he wanted to start over and bought the bungalow with Margaret. Maybe they are in bed together right now, at this very moment, satiated and in a state of postcoital bliss. How did I not consider that scenario before I acted on this harebrained idea? A lump forms in my throat.

"Margaret's not here," Annabelle says, as though reading my thoughts.

I shift in my seat. "How do you know?"

"Do you see her car?"

"You mean they don't . . ." Live together? Have naked sleepovers?

"No," she says, her features silhouetted in shadow. "Now, come on. We've got a job to do." She throws the duffel over her shoulder and motions for me to follow.

We race across the lawn, up the porch steps, and to the front door, so quiet it's as if the soles of our sneakers are made of air. Annabelle taps my arm and points to a window. Shaking my head, I run my hand along the sill of the door. My fingers bump against something metal. Bingo! A key tumbles onto the welcome mat with a soft clank. Annabelle arches an eyebrow. I shrug, pick up the spare, and unlock the door. It swings open with a whisper.

Inside, the house smells like laundry detergent and citrus wood polish. Moonlight streams into a small living room, illuminating it in a silvery glow. I peer around. None of the furniture looks familiar. The decor has a rustic vibe to it, though I notice feminine touches are littered here and there—a vase perched on the fireplace mantel, patterned throw pillows adorning an overstuffed couch, a stained-glass floor lamp wedged between a pair of cigar chairs. Margaret may not permanently inhabit this space, but her presence lingers.

As we tiptoe through the house, my eyes roam. A jumble of mismatched frames line the walls and book-shelves, scenes and figures dancing in the shadows, the details a blur. A flash of blond hair catches my eye. I gasp, staggering to a halt. Annabelle collides into me, and my hip bangs against the wall. A wooden frame wobbles on its nail. We pause, listening for any sign that Nick is awake. Other than my heart hammering in my ears, I hear nothing.

Annabelle glares at me. *Sorry,* I mouth. She sighs, shaking her head, then continues moving deeper into the house. I trail after her, but my mind has yet to catch up. It's still focused on the memory captured in a photograph, the image fuzzy from condensation on the camera lens. In it, two kids splash in a puddle, mud and dirty water staining the girl's cotton dress and the boy's khaki church pants. I remember that summer. It rained the entire month of August, but that didn't prevent Nick and me from playing in it, drenching ourselves to the bone. I wonder why Nick kept that picture when it seems all other traces of our former life together have been erased.

Annabelle stops when we reach a hallway, pressing a finger to her lips. Faint rain forest sounds drift out from under a closed door. A grin spreads across my face. *Such a creature of habit,* I think, as Annabelle cocks her head and guides us to the kitchen. While she dumps the contents of the duffel onto the island—two plastic funnels, a bag of flour, and packages of balloons—I snoop around.

Magnets, a Peanuts calendar, postcards, and more photos clutter the fridge door—snapshots of Nick and the Randy Hollis Band toasting with pints of beer at the Shiner brewery, of Charlotte and Dr. Preston at Nick's White Coat ceremony, of Margaret and Nick at a concert. There are pictures of Wes and Annabelle from college and one of them cheering with foam fingers at a Texas Rangers baseball game. There's even a shot of Nick and my father fishing. *Since when does Nick fish?*

I open the fridge and stare down at a carton of eggs, some rib-eye steaks, rows of bottled water, and a whole shelf overflowing with fruits and vegetables. No leftovers or take-out containers in sight, not like I expected any different from a doctor.

"Lillie, quit gawking and help me!" Annabelle hisses.

"I'm not gawking," I whisper, coming to stand beside her. "I'm investigating."

"Whatever. Now take this," she says, handing me a package of balloons.

We waste no time getting to work, establishing a rhythm as Annabelle siphons flour into the balloons while I inflate and tie them off. The bright colors appear silver in the moonlight. Soon the floor and countertops are awash in balloons and Annabelle is handing me the last one. As I blow it up, it escapes from my grasp, bouncing off the cabinets and sputtering into the sink. I look at Annabelle, then at myself. Flour is splattered all over us. A fit of giggles overtakes me.

"Shhh!" Annabelle slaps my shoulder.

I clamp a hand over my mouth, trying to stifle the laugh, but that only makes it worse. Annabelle rolls her eyes, but then she cracks up, snorting into her palm.

"Okay, okay," she says, careful to keep her voice low. "Let's finish this."

With arms full of balloons, we exit the kitchen and tiptoe down the hallway to Nick's bedroom. Holding my breath, I turn the knob and open the door slowly, praying the hinges don't squeak. Silence. I exhale. We slip into the room and scatter the balloons around. The tranquil noises of waterfalls, birdcalls, and cicadas surround us. Nick lies on his back, legs tangled in sheets, an arm draped across his stomach. I try not to stare at his bare chest. I succeed a little.

It takes us several trips to and from the kitchen, but before long, the room is bursting with balloons. They crowd every available surface and are piled to the ceiling in the walk-in closet and adjoining bathroom. We position the remaining balloons on the bed, then start backing out of the room. Just when I'm sure we're in the clear, my heel connects with a stack of old vinyl records next to the door-frame. I lose my balance, and Annabelle grabs my shirt collar. I have to bite down hard on my tongue to keep from yelping. Nick stirs and mumbles. Everything inside me freezes, waiting for him to snap to attention, catch us red-handed. Miraculously, Nick rolls over and buries his head under a pillow, his knee brushing against a balloon. A beat later, his breathing is steady again, as is his snoring. I relax, and feel Annabelle do the same.

We dart out of the house, not even bothering to return the spare key to its hiding spot, and jump in my truck. When we are a safe enough distance away, I pull into a gas station and shut off the engine.

"So, that was a success," I say.

Annabelle eyes me skeptically.

"Okay, there were some minor hiccups," I admit.

Annabelle shakes her head, suppressing a smile.

"What?" I say.

"Next time your ass is staying in the truck."

The sun is cresting over the horizon by the time I stumble into my childhood room and collapse like a ruined soufflé on the bed. Within seconds, sleep drags me under. I wake up just before lunchtime to discover a folded paper propped against the bedside lamp. Still half asleep and groggy, I unfold it. The note is written in Nick's handwriting, so neat it looks as if it's been typed. My eyes trip over the words: *You throw away the outside and cook the inside. Then you consume the outside and throw away the inside. What did you eat?*

I know I've heard this one before. The answer nags at the back of my mind but never crystallizes.

I'm still contemplating the riddle when a realization slams into me. While I was drooling on a pillow, Nick was *here.* I jolt upright in bed, glancing down at myself, then around the room. Nothing seems out of order or tampered with. *What did he do?*

Whipping the covers off my legs, I head for the door, wondering what kind of retaliation awaits me. I start to ease it open but hesitate when I feel something heavy pressing against the other side. Only it's too late, the strain is too much. The door opens against my will, knocking me on my butt. A trash can falls on top of me. Unsealed containers of cream corn, corn husks, and corncobs spill out, sticking in my hair and soaking into my clothes. A few strands of corn silk have even found their way inside my mouth.

Another note is taped to the lip of the garbage bin, fluttering from the breeze floating through the window. With slimy fingers, I peel it away and read: *You still snore worse than an elephant. I hear a greasy burger can cure that. Interested?*

18

Despite the late-afternoon crowd at Otto's Corner, I spot the rowdy crew crammed into a round booth in the back corner almost immediately. From the bottles littering the table and the volume of their voices, I gather they've been here for a while. Wes and Annabelle are smushed together in the center of the booth, surrounded by members of the Randy Hollis Band. Nick and Margaret sit on chairs pulled up from a nearby table.

It appears our once tight-knit group of four has expanded its membership. Or maybe I've simply been replaced. A pang shoots through me, longing for how things used to be.

I inhale a deep breath and make my way over to them. Tim seems to be the only one who notices me, tipping his cowboy hat in acknowledgment. The others are too absorbed in a story Matt is telling. Something about a crazed fan who broke into his car, filled the trunk with underwear, and snapped racy Polaroid pictures before taping them to the windshield and review mirror. The cops found the woman passed out on Matt's front lawn, stark naked and drooling, using an empty bottle of Jim Beam as a pillow. One of the biggest highlights of his career as a musician so far.

Everyone breaks into laughter. Everyone except Nick, whose gaze is now locked on mine. There's a flicker behind his eyes, something mischievous, though his face remains impassive. My heart speeds up.

I clear my throat and tuck a strand of hair behind my ear. "Hey, guys," I say over their cheerful chatter and the Bonnie Raitt tune playing through the overhead speakers. "Is there space for one more?"

The table turns quiet, eight pairs of eyes on me. Then, all at once, a chorus of hellos ring through the air. Even Margaret offers a thin smile and a wave. That's . . . different. I wonder if her attitude adjustment has something to do with finding out about Drew. Perhaps she no longer views me as a threat. Then again, maybe she's adopted the age-old tactic of keeping your friends close and your enemies closer.

"Jelly Bean! It's about time you got here," Wes hollers, his usually slight southern drawl more pronounced with the addition of alcohol. "What's that you've got there?" He stretches across the table and snatches the foil-covered plate from my grasp.

"Jalapeño and pork tamales," I say. "I had some extra corn husks lying around, so I figured, why not?" My eyes cut to Nick. He's still staring at me, one side of his mouth quirked up.

Wes frowns. "This is all you brought?"

Annabelle snorts. "What are you, pregnant?" she says. "You've already devoured two baskets of fried pickles."

"Those were an *appetizer*. I'm a growing boy who needs constant sustenance," Wes says, patting his stomach.

"Besides, you ate at least half of those pickles, and the chipotle ranch dip."

"Give me a break," Annabelle says with a playful shove to his arm. "I had like three bites."

Wes's mouth twists into a grin. "But they were big bites."

I blink and shake my head, convinced I've been transported to some alternate reality. Their banter is so normal, so reminiscent of how they used to be. Any moment I expect Wes to lean over and plant a kiss on Annabelle's nose, something he did when he thought she was being particularly cute or sassy.

Jason scoots out of the booth, and Karl slides out after him. "Lillie, we were about to order some food," Karl says. "What's your preference?"

"The Labyrinth," Nick, Wes, and Annabelle say at the same time. Though Wes's words come out garbled because of the tamale stuffed into his mouth.

Otto's Corner is the only place in town where every burger on the menu is named after an eighties cult-classic movie. There's The Heather—a half-pound patty stuffed with sharp cheddar and bacon and smothered with chili con carne, onions, and hot dog pieces. Or The Gremlin— poblano corn relish and pepper jack cheese piled atop a buttermilk fried chicken breast, served on a pretzel bun.

I scoff. "I don't always order The Labyrinth," I say, though my mouth is watering just thinking about that delicious turkey burger with tangy peach barbecue sauce.

"Yes, you do." Once again in unison.

"I got The Toxic Avenger that one time—"

"The curry mayo knocked you on your ass, if I remember," Nick interjects as he stands and taps my nose. "You were sick for a week after."

Margaret huffs and mutters something about people

being like itchy scabs before she saunters off toward the order counter. Soon everyone else is trailing behind her and it's Wes and me at the table. I slide into the booth beside him. Silence settles around us.

Wes drapes an arm over my shoulders and sighs. Sad, wistful. I follow his line of sight, which is focused on Annabelle talking to the poor guy manning the register. From the frustrated expression on the worker's face, I'm guessing Annabelle has changed her burger choice no less than four times. Par for the course, I'm afraid.

"I'm trying, Jelly Bean," Wes says. "Fuck if it doesn't kill me, but I'm trying."

I'm quiet for a moment before I say, "So am I."

My gaze flicks to Nick. He and Margaret have meandered to the area with the dartboards, a beer in his hand and a glass of red wine in hers. I watch as Nick rolls up his sleeves. Margaret unbuttons her fitted suit jacket and tosses it onto a stool. Her emerald-green blouse underneath is a perfect complement to her ruby hair and fair complexion. Nick walks over to her and places a few darts in her open palm, gesturing for her to have the first shot at the board. Standing on tiptoes, Margaret whispers something in his ear, then playfully aligns her hips with his, running a finger along his forearm, as if she's tempting Nick to take a more hands-on approach to the game. Nick shakes his head and steps back. I wish I could read something into the space he puts between them, but it seems clear with the way Margaret laughs over her shoulder, the sound high-pitched like a spoon tapping against a champagne flute, that the only distance between them is friendly competition.

My chest tightens. For a moment, seeing Nick this way —content, relaxed, exactly what I've always hoped for him —it's hard to hold on to my dislike for Margaret when he wears his happiness so well.

I cut my eyes away. Wes still hasn't taken his attention off Annabelle. She's now with Matt and Tim at the bar. They seem to be in a heated discussion about some college football game on TV.

"We met for coffee this morning," Wes says after a while.

"Yeah?" I wonder how Annabelle isn't acting like a zombie right now from lack of sleep after this morning's early shenanigans.

He nods, spinning an empty beer bottle between his palms.

"And?" I ask.

"I'll let you know. For now we're . . . talking. Working things out. We still have a long way to go and mounds of shit to deal with, but it's a start."

"I'm glad, Wes."

"What about you?" He gestures with his chin at Nick.

Jason and Karl have joined him and Margaret at the dartboard and are now teaching Margaret proper dart-throwing techniques. As if Nick can feel the weight of my stare, he meets my gaze, grabs hold of it, and doesn't let go. Then he smiles, reaches into his pocket, and pulls out a deflated pink balloon.

A grin spreads across my face. "I'm working it out, too," I say to Wes as I pick up a tamale wrapped in a corn husk and tilt it toward Nick in a silent toast.

———

LATER, after we've gorged ourselves on burgers, we sit around the table sharing stories. My stomach hurts from laughing so hard. It echoes the ache in my chest. There's so much I've missed, so much I haven't been a part of.

"I'm going to grab another round of refreshments,"

Annabelle says, sliding out of the booth. "Who's in?"

Even though everyone raises their hand except for me, Annabelle insists on counting each one anyway. I stopped drinking hours ago, I'd rather avoid another episode where I end up passed out on the floor.

"I think you're going to need some assistance," Wes says, scooting out after her. "Nobody touch Jelly Bean's tamales, and save the onion rings. Those are for breakfast tomorrow." He spins his baseball cap around so the bill is facing the back, his curly hair sticking out underneath. He and Annabelle move away from the group toward the bar.

I shake my head and smile. Leave it to Wes to consume the most random things at any hour of the day. I glance at Nick, wondering if he remembers when Wes ate nothing but SpaghettiOs for a month. The grin on his face tells me he does.

Karl leans forward. "How about that time Margaret went crowd surfing?" he says, peering at the rest of the band.

My eyes cut to Margaret. She's studying her wine like it's the key to the universe. A faint blush kisses the tops of her cheeks.

Jason and Tim scrunch up their faces like they're confused, but Matt bursts into laughter. "Shit, I forgot about that. Where was that?" he asks.

"I think it was at that club on Lower Greenville," Karl says. "There were only a handful of people in the audience that night, so she ended up landing on her ass."

"I remember that now," Jason says, putting his elbows on the table. "Didn't she have to be escorted out by a bouncer?"

Tim removes his cowboy hat and rakes a hand through his sandy-blond hair. "Yeah, because she tried to climb the stage lights like some kind of monkey."

"I wasn't escorted out," Margaret says, straightening her posture. "I was calmly and politely shown the exit." She smiles and shrugs.

This gives me pause. I've never seen Margaret be anything other than smugly confident, but now she seems almost shy, if not a little silly. Like the kind of person I would be friends with.

"You tried to climb the stage lights?" I say, picturing her scaling the tall metal structure in three-inch heels before being yanked down by a man double her size and thrown out like a holiday fruitcake on the sidewalk.

"I think one too many glasses of Cabernet may have been involved," she says, brushing a speck of lint off her skirt. "But that type of behavior hasn't occurred since college, when I was allowed to be young and stupid."

Nick rocks back on his chair with an arm bent behind his head. "Oh, it's happened a few times since then."

"Liar," Margaret says. "The last time I was that over-served was at Matt's wedding, and I was still in college so it doesn't count."

"You were in *grad school*," Nick says.

Waving him off, she takes a sip of wine and says, "Same difference."

Matt's wedding?

"How long have you known the band?" I ask.

"Shortly after they started playing together," she says, matter-of-fact, like I'm an idiot for not already knowing this.

"She missed some of our early shows," Matt interjects. "After that, if we had a gig in the area, she was there."

"Really?" I say. "How did you discover them?"

"By chance, actually," she says, tossing her hair over her shoulder. "One of my sorority sisters set me up on this horrific blind date with a guy named Jerry. I called a cab when he went to use the restroom, then left him at the restaurant. I told the driver to pick me up a few blocks over so Jerry wouldn't find me waiting outside. On my way to our meeting point, I passed this hole-in-the-wall bar where the band was playing a small show. I've been a fan ever since."

The Margaret I remember growing up with spent her time at the Dallas Country Club with her other spoiled, rich friends, but this side of her reminds me so much of the way I used to be, when I'd hang out in smelly venues to watch Nick perform the songs he wrote. Maybe we're more alike than I thought.

Wes and Annabelle return with a tray of drinks and reclaim their spots in the booth.

Karl takes a long pull from his Shiner Bock and says, "Margaret's the reason we all met."

"I thought you were introduced at a charity football tournament," I say.

"We were," Jason says. "Margaret's the one who invited us to participate in it."

"My PR firm was responsible for the press and marketing of the event," Margaret says. "I figured they might want to get involved in a good cause."

"Little did we know that Nick would make such a memorable impression," Tim says without a hint of humor. "Or is that a tale for another day?"

Nick shoots him a pointed stare too loaded with meaning to decipher. The table grows quiet, the easy atmosphere dissolving around us. I shift my gaze to Annabelle and Wes, who exchange an uncomfortable glance.

"What am I missing here?" I ask.

"You mean other than the last five years?" Margaret says, touching Nick's knee, her thumb tracing a pattern. "Do you need a manual so you can keep up?"

Just like that any thoughts of friendship I had fall away. Acquaintances will be quite enough.

Nick sighs and shakes his head, but doesn't look at me. Still, it's clear from the way he shifts away from Margaret that he's unhappy.

As if scolded, she removes her hand. "I think it's about time I head home," she says, standing. "I've got an early morning appointment I still need to prepare for."

"I'll walk you to your car," Nick says, helping her into her suit jacket.

Everyone offers their good-byes as Nick ushers Margaret outside. The gang scatters then. Matt, Annabelle, and Wes join a neighboring booth for a Jenga challenge. Jason and Karl go throw darts again.

I'm perched on a bar stool talking with Tim about the band's early days and how they got started when Nick reappears a long while later. His whole demeanor has changed—his jaw now clenched, his shoulders tense as a pulled wire. I wonder if he and Margaret had an argument in the parking lot.

Nick spots me and walks over to the bar, setting a copy of *Resolution* in front of me. My brow furrows. The album isn't released for a few more days.

"Earlier you mentioned you were excited about hearing the whole record," Nick says with an edge in his voice. "Now you can."

"Wow. Thank you." I pick up the album. The cover shows the band smiling as they lounge on a grungy old sofa in someone's garage. Maybe it's a nod to their humble beginnings. The track listing on the back is comprised of fifteen songs, only a few of which I recognize. "You know, I'm tempted to slip out of here right now to listen to it."

That makes Nick crack a smile. "Too bad Big Blue only has a tape deck," he says.

I open the plastic case to scan the various lyrics, but only the glossy cover photo is there and not the CD booklet. "Where are the liner notes?"

Tim clears his throat. "The early advanced copies don't have them, but be sure to check them out. The liner notes are often the best part of a record." He looks at Nick. A message passes between them, even more encoded than the one before. "I'm going to hit the road. I'll see you at the launch party, Lillie." Tim squeezes my shoulder and leaves without a word to Nick.

What's up with them?

Nick settles onto Tim's vacant stool and motions to the bartender for a beer.

"Balloons, huh?" he says after he's squeezed an orange wedge into the glass and taken a few sips. "Not exactly original, but I'll grant you points for getting them into my room without waking me up."

"You always did sleep like the dead," I say, smiling. "Cute riddle. The containers of creamed corn were a nice touch."

A smirk finds its way to his mouth. "I thought so. It's your move, Turner."

I roll my eyes, shaking my head. We lapse into comfortable silence. It's been awhile since I've been content to sit still and enjoy the moment. Around us, Otto's Corner is a swirl of laughter and elevated voices and muffled music. Even though the kitchen is concealed behind a wall with only a small window opening, a thin layer of smoke from the charcoal grill hangs above our heads.

"Why Chicago, Lillie?"

I swivel on the bar stool to face him. "What do you mean?"

"Of all the cities you could have chosen, you decided on that one. Why?"

For a second I can only stare at him until all my pretenses fall away. "Desperation is a powerful motivator, Nick. I was a mess when I got to the airport and not thinking rationally. I asked the agent behind the ticket counter when the next available flight was departing. She said a plane destined for Midway was in the process of boarding, and if I hurried, I'd catch it in time. I made it to the gate right before the doors closed."

His expression turns puzzled, as though he was expecting some kind of compelling reason rather than a decision made out of hopelessness. "You never considered coming home?"

"I didn't think there was a home to come back to." The words seem to echo through the room, despite the noise.

He nods as though he understands, even if I'm not sure I do.

"What was it like?" he asks.

"It was terrifying at first," I say, recalling how I stumbled off the plane and into a cab, begging the driver to take me somewhere, *anywhere*. I ended up at a cheap motel outside downtown Chicago. For days I lay on the lumpy mattress balled up under the scratchy covers. Eventually, though, I got up, put one foot in front of the other, and learned to laugh again.

"It was also exhilarating," I continue. "Freeing. Being in a place where no one knows your name and your past is a mystery. Like my slate had been wiped clean. Since I had almost no money, I rented this run-down, shoebox-size apartment around the corner from a delicatessen that'd been around since the 1960s. They make the best cannoli, the cream filling is so light and fluffy it melts in your mouth. The day I received my acceptance letter to Northwestern, I quit my receptionist job at the dentist's office where I'd been working and proceeded to eat a half dozen by myself in celebration."

"Did you re-create them?" he asks.

Nick must read the confusion on my face because he clarifies, "The cannoli. You know, put your own spin on them?"

My stomach tightens. The girl Nick knew would have done something like that. I remember all the times we'd be out somewhere and I would discover a dish I adored. I barely had time to finish it before I'd rush to my father's kitchen to make my own version. I thought I outgrew that part of myself, but maybe it's still inside me somewhere, buried beneath ugly memories and wishes that didn't come true.

I shake my head. "No. I haven't really cooked anything more complicated than scrambled eggs in years. Not since . . ." I don't have to say the rest. The implication is clear.

"What about the Upper Crust? You've been preparing for that, right?"

I shrug. "Not really. Mostly I've been winging it."

He frowns, his fingers tapping a rhythm against the pint glass.

"What?"

"Nothing." He hesitates. "I guess I'm surprised. It's not like you to wing something as big as a baking competition."

"Things change, Nick."

"Maybe. But not something like that. Not something that's so fundamental to everything you are."

How do you know? I want to ask him, along with a thousand other things on the tip of my tongue. But I don't. I can't.

Silence settles between us. I peel off the Fat Tire label

on my beer bottle. If I keep my hands busy, keep my focus on anything but him, maybe he won't notice that his words have chipped away at something locked inside me.

My eyes drift over to him. "Where'd this come from?" I touch the scar between his ring and pinkie fingers.

Nick glances down and grimaces. He clenches his hand and hides it under the bar top. "I had an unfortunate encounter with Wes's jaw."

I squint at him. "What?"

"The memorable impression Tim was talking about earlier, the one regarding the football tournament?" He pauses. When he speaks again, his voice is low, serious. "I arrived drunk to the event. Blackout drunk, Lillie. That's when I nailed Karl in the head with the spiral and did some other idiotic shit I'm not proud of. I caused quite a scene in front of my father and several other important people who sit on the charity's board of directors. At some point, Wes attempted to shove me in his Jeep to take me home, but I wasn't ready to go yet, so I punched him. Shattered a few bones in my hand. The scar is a result of the operation."

My mind is spinning, his words whipping around like they're in a food processor. Best friends for more than two decades, all that shared history, and Nick *punched* Wes?

"Why?" I say, still not believing it.

"It's not important."

"It is to me," I say, placing a hand on his forearm.

Nick rubs the back of his neck. "I guess you could say I checked out."

"On what?"

"Everything. Me. *Life.*" There's pain in his eyes, a kind so helpless I have no name for it. He's quiet for a moment, his attention focused on the foam residue ringing the inside of his glass. Then he shakes his head, as if dislodging a memory, and says, "I was in a bad place for a long time, Lillie. That day was the wake-up call I needed, though, and got me to admit to my parents that I was unhappy with my surgical residency. Things improved after that."

"When did this happen?"

"About six months after you left," Nick says. "Margaret was the only person who stuck around and didn't coddle me."

"She seems to care about you a great deal."

His shoulders sag as he says, "She's been a good friend to me when I didn't deserve one and helped me through one of the darkest points in my life."

My heart lodges in my throat. I wish so much it'd been me who supported him, but I'm part of the reason he was in that dark place at all.

"She'll also tear down anyone she considers a threat," Nick continues. He takes a sip of beer and sighs. "Listen, Lillie, I know Margaret hasn't been kind to you, and I'm sorry for that. It's me she's angry at but is taking it out on you."

I nod, even though I'm not sure if what he said is entirely accurate. "Still, I'm glad Margaret was there for you in that way," I say, shocked at the truth in my words.

"I wasn't the only one who was hurting, Lillie. You said good-bye to everything when you left." Nick leans in close to me, his gaze roaming over my face. "I've often wondered who was there for *you* while you healed. Who held you up."

My breath catches as a feeling so overwhelming and huge surges through me. Because I alone patched myself back together, by circumstance and necessity.

Maybe that's why the wound won't fully heal—I did such a poor job of it.

19

MY FATHER IS READING THE NEWSPAPER AT THE KITCHEN table when I walk downstairs the next morning. His hand is cupped around a mug of coffee that doesn't seem strong enough for how exhausted he appears.

"Morning, baby girl," my father says as light cuts across his face. The sun is just waking up, kissing the tops of the trees and seeping through the windows in soft streaks. It reminds me of the hollandaise sauce I spent an entire summer perfecting, the way it would ooze between layers of roasted asparagus, a smooth and creamy pale yellow. "Happy Halloween. What time did you get home last night?"

"Way too late. Otto's is regrettably doing karaoke now. Wes sang Richard Marx's 'Should've Known Better' three times in a row. We finally got kicked out when round four began." I pour myself a steaming cup of chicory coffee and grab the seat beside him.

Chuckling, my father gives the newspaper a few shakes and folds it closed. "I'm glad to see you got rid of all that corn business. It was stinkin' up everything."

"Thank you very little for that, by the way. You didn't have to let Nick in the house to prank me." I tuck my knees under an oversized hoodie I've had since college that smells faintly of campfire and rain.

"Don't go blaming me for that. You brought that trouble on yourself," he says, then finishes his coffee with a giant gulp. He places an elbow on the table. I can't help but notice how knobby it is, or the way his chest and shoulder bones show through his shirt.

"How are you feeling?" I ask, adding the decline in my father's appearance to the list of things I plan on discussing with his doctor.

"My left hand's been bothering me a bit and my knee still aches, but otherwise no worse than usual." Standing, he moves to the sink and turns on the faucet.

Joining him, I say, "I told Wes I'd volunteer at Mustang Spook Fest this morning, but I'll meet you here at the house this afternoon to drive you to your appointment." When I was hugging everyone good-bye last night, Wes somehow convinced Annabelle and me to assist with SMU's Halloween carnival for kids and families from around the Dallas community. We're in charge of the creepy crawler games tent, hosted by the football program.

"Sounds good." He squirts some dish soap into the running water and hands me a dish towel. "Now help your old man tidy up."

I collect the dishes stacked on the counter and place them in the sink. Our arms bump against each other as my father cleans and I dry. I remember how Nick and I used to complain about the lack of a dishwasher, but secretly I loved the monotony of washing things by hand and the quiet comfort it afforded.

When the last plate is put away, my father stretches his back and says, "I need to set up the Halloween decorations on the front porch and run by the Spoons before the crowd gets unmanageable, but I'll be back in time for you to take me. Okeydokey?"

"Dad, you shouldn't be lifting heavy stuff by yourself," I say, looking at how the outline of his spine sticks out like a zipper. "I think I should stay here with you."

He coughs and pats my shoulder. "Nonsense, baby girl. I'm perfectly capable of hanging a few bats and spiderwebs on my own. Go help Wesley. I'll see you at home in a few hours. That's an order."

"Will you promise to call me if you need anything?"

My father coughs again and mumbles something about how that won't be necessary before darting out of the kitchen. I sigh. His stubbornness continues to grow worse —thank goodness his appointment is today.

I dig in the attic for my Alice in Wonderland outfit. Wes, Annabelle, and I agreed to dress up in a theme using costumes we already have. After a quick shower, I change and drive to SMU. The parking garages are filled to capacity and cars line the surrounding streets. I get lucky and find an available spot in Snider Plaza, an old-time shopping center nestled across from the law school. Big Blue barely manages to squeeze into the space. I hop out of the cab and head for Bishop Boulevard in the heart of the campus.

A familiar storefront catches my eye. I stop short and check my watch. I'm running fifteen minutes late already, but I don't care. Annabelle and Wes will have to deal with it.

A bell rings as the door opens. I step inside, inhaling the smells of marshmallow fluff and waffle cones. I've visited Mr. Vincent's Fountain Shop hundreds of times, and there's still something whimsical about it. The way it seems to whisk you away to a Willy Wonka–esque edible wonderland. Advertisements from the 1950s hang on walls covered in fruit wallpaper. In the center of the store, bulk candy is bursting out of cupcake-shaped bins. The patterned tin tile ceiling reflects soda-lined shelves filled with nostalgic favorites like Nesbitt's Orange Soda and Dad's Root Beer.

My fingers dance across the glass bottles as I stroll to the fountain counter at the back. I halt in front of a display of Cheerwine. I pick up one of the bottles and rub my thumb across the label. Memories rise and expand as they reach the surface of my mind: Nick challenging Wes to a Cheerwine chugging contest the day Wes made the varsity football team, the two of them burping and laughing so hard burgundy liquid shot out of their noses. Annabelle and me in my bathroom the night before the homecoming dance, using a liter of Cheerwine to dye my hair strawberry blond because it was cheaper than buying the real thing at the drugstore. Nick and me sitting on blue vinyl stools, slurping Cheerwine floats on our first official date, tongues and lips stained red. I remember how after Nick kissed me good night on the front porch, I snuck into my house through my bedroom window so my father wouldn't catch me with fruit punch–colored lips and think I spent the whole night getting frisky with Nick in the backseat of his vintage Mercedes.

"Can I help you, sweetheart?"

Mr. Vincent emerges through a pair of swinging doors. He slides behind the counter, adjusting a soda jerk hat, his thinning, silver hair barely visible underneath. He's worn the same uniform since forever—yellow bow tie, starched white, button-down shirt, black jacket with red polka dots. A banana split in clothing form.

"Um . . ." I bite my lip. "No. That's okay."

He smiles. Wrinkles fold around his eyes. "Never been to a soda shop before?"

I shake my head. "The opposite, actually. I used to come here all the time as a kid."

Mr. Vincent drums his fingers against a stainless steel malt mixing cup. A crease appears between his eyebrows. "I remember you now. You're Jack Turner's daughter. Lillie, right?"

"The one and only," I say, now full-on grinning.

"How's your father doing these days?" Mr. Vincent pulls out a frosted mug from the freezer. "I haven't seen him in a while."

I shrug. "Causing trouble as usual."

"That sounds like Jack. Why don't you give me that bottle you've got in your hand. I'll make you a float, my treat." He picks up an ice cream scoop and dips it in a bucket of steaming water.

"Thank you, but I can't stay. I'm supposed to be at Mustang Spook Fest right now, manning the fuzzy cater-pillar toss."

"In that case, I'll make you one for the road." He winks at me, puts the mug back into the freezer, and grabs a Styrofoam to-go cup next to the register.

As if on cue, my stomach rumbles. I laugh. "I guess there's no harm in eating dessert first." I walk to the counter and hand him the Cheerwine.

While Mr. Vincent prepares my float, I wander around the store, taking in its years of history that mingle with my own. It's amazing the power of memories. The way they touch a sacred place deep inside each of us. How certain ones seem to linger forever, leaving a lasting impression, the full impact of which is often not realized until later.

When I pass by the section of grape-flavored sodas, I swear I can see the giggling childhood version of myself perched on my father's shoulders, reaching for a Fitz's Grape Pop on the top shelf. Like a sort of psychic imprint. For a moment, I'm frozen, seized by the scene in front of me.

An uneasy feeling settles in my stomach, and I have the sudden urge to hug my father, to tell him how much I love him even when he drives me crazy. I fish my cell out of my dress pocket and call him at the house, and when he doesn't answer, at the diner. The phone rings and rings. He's probably still putting up Halloween decorations or dealing with the breakfast rush, but the panic continues to build. I'm nervous about his doctor's appointment, I tell myself. It's nothing.

Mr. Vincent rests a hand on my shoulder, and I jump. "Here's your float, sweetheart."

I force a smile as I thank him, take the Styrofoam cup in his hand, and sip a little. The cool, sweet treat does nothing to quell the sense of foreboding surging through me.

———

WES SHOVES an entire brownie into his mouth. Crumbs tumble down his Mad Hatter jacket.

"You know it's acceptable to take two bites," I say, dropping a prize into a grinning ballerina's oversized pillowcase. She twirls in an unsteady pirouette, then dances over to where a new game of bobbing for eyeballs is about to begin. The uneasy feeling in my stomach has dimmed, but it's there nonetheless. If only my father would pick up the phone.

"Not enough time, Jelly Bean," he says, licking his thumb. "It's my turn to be the creature in the green lagoon." By "green lagoon" he means the dunk tank set up outside the game tent. Someone in the football program came up with the brilliant idea to fill the tank with green slime instead of water. All players and coaches are required to participate.

Annabelle wrinkles her nose, the perfect addition to her Queen of Hearts ensemble. "You better shower after."

"You know I'm going to do the exact opposite because you said that," Wes says, stealing the crown out of her wig, then darting away with such speed that it knocks the top hat off his head. The card reading "10/6" floats to the grass.

"You know what happens when the queen loses her temper," she yells after him, heart wand waving in the air. "Off with your head!"

I roll my eyes. Since last night at Otto's Corner, Annabelle and Wes have been tight-lipped about the current status of their relationship, and I haven't asked. I get the impression they're afraid to jinx what forward progress they've made by talking about it. Maybe there's this unspoken fear, this possibility it could all erode again.

After Wes disappears out of sight, Annabelle straightens her dress and looks at me. "Have you returned Sullivan Grace's calls yet?"

"What do you think?" I say as I rearrange the cups on the fuzzy caterpillar toss board. The pushy woman has already left numerous messages in the hour I've been here. Something about how my presence is needed at an Upper Crust run-through. If only my father could be as persistent.

"You know she won't stop bothering you until you do," Annabelle says as a gap-toothed boy dressed as Superman zooms past us, cape billowing behind him, lollipop in hand.

My phone vibrates and Sullivan Grace's number lights

up the screen. "Speak of the devil," I say. "Can you handle this for a bit? I'll be right back."

I walk out of the tent onto the majestic, tree-lined Bishop Boulevard. All around me are children in costumes and face paint lugging bags bursting with candy, jumping in bounce houses, shielding their eyes as they listen to ghost stories. It appears every family within a one-hundred-mile radius decided to partake in Mustang Spook Fest.

"Hello, Ms. Hasell," I answer, plugging my ear as I cut through a group of kids waiting to enter the haunted house put on by the various fraternities on campus.

"There you are," she says. "I've been trying to reach you for hours. Behavior like this simply won't suit, Lillie. What did I teach you about manners?"

I sigh, imagining her in Junior League headquarters, sipping tea and eating a scone. "I've been a little busy volunteering at—"

"Never mind about that," she continues. "Now, pay attention. You need to arrive at the Ritz Carlton ballroom promptly at . . ."

She prattles on about the logistics of the Upper Crust run-through as though she hasn't explained the same instructions in the many voice messages I've already received. Contestants are to use the time as an opportunity to familiarize themselves with the setup and smooth out any kinks before the big event. *D Magazine* will be in attendance, after all.

"Lillie, dear, are you taking notes?"

No. "Yes, Ms. Hasell," I say with exaggerated cheer as I stroll through the fake cemetery built on the lawn area in SMU's south quad. Plastic skeletons dangle from trees. Cobwebs with hundreds of tiny spiders cover painted foam gravestones.

"I'd also like to remind you that, as stated in the

competition guidelines, no late recipe modifications will be permitted," she says. "The judges will be observing to ensure all contestants are acting in accordance with the rules."

Translation: *Your father will force-feed tofu down your throat if you show up with that deconstructed strudel nonsense.*

"I'll keep that in mind," I say.

She rambles on for another few minutes. I tune her out. After I disconnect the call, I make my way back to Annabelle and Wes but stop when my cell vibrates again. I swear I'm going to strangle Sullivan Grace with her precious heirloom pearls.

"What?" I snap into the phone.

A throat clears on the other end. "Uh, Lillie, this is Ernie." There's a long pause. I can hear him breathing, deep and heavy like his favorite Dutch oven at the diner. "It's your—" He stops, then starts again. When he speaks, his voice shakes. "It's Jack."

The way Ernie says my father's name crashes into me like a storm-driven wave, strong and fierce. My knees buckle, and I sink to the ground, the foreboding feeling like a current pulling me under. Kids and their parents rush around me, a blur of spinning colors and shapes.

"What's wrong?" I whisper.

"He collapsed."

20

I'm floating outside myself. Or watching a stranger. Because the crazy person speeding across town toward Baylor Medical, swerving around cars, blowing red lights, violating all traffic laws, can't possibly be me.

Panic balloons in my chest. I grip the steering wheel, palms slick with sweat, so tight my knuckles have turned white. I swing my truck onto Gaston Avenue. A forest of stone hospital buildings looms ahead. Following the signs to the ER, I whip into a spot in the parking lot, then dash through the glass double doors that lead to the emergency department.

The visitor waiting area feels calm, as if I've entered a Michelin-star restaurant rather than a hospital. I race toward the reception desk where a woman in navy scrubs sits in front of a computer.

"Jackson Turner," I blurt, the words coming out in a breathless jumble. "He should—"

"A moment please," she says, her acrylic nails zipping across the keyboard. She peers up at me, her eyes roaming over my Alice costume. A hint of a smile tugs at the corners of her mouth before it vanishes. Then, as if she's reading the nutrition facts on a microwave dinner, she rattles off information. My father arrived via ambulance twenty minutes ago and was rushed into surgery. Afterward, he will be moved to recovery for monitoring before being transferred to the ICU. "The doctor will meet with you in the OR waiting room to discuss the status of his condition," she says, then hands me a map and directs me to a set of double doors adjacent to the reception desk.

That's it. No further details given. No opportunity to ask questions.

The doors hiss open and dump me into a corridor that cuts down the middle of the emergency room. The smell of disinfectant and body odor surrounds me. My shoes squeak on the floor as I pass a nurses' station teeming with activity. Patient rooms flank me on both sides. An orderly wheels an empty gurney with rumpled linens and life-support equipment piled on top, sending my heart skittering in my chest.

My phone vibrates as I walk through another set of double doors that open onto a bank of elevators and a minilounge. I fumble around in my dress pocket and pull it out to see Thomas Brandon's name lighting up the screen. I silence the call, but before I can put the phone away, it buzzes again. My fingers clench around the unforgiving plastic, itching to hurl it against the vending machines.

I punch the elevator's up button and pace back and forth. A few beats later, the elevator arrives with a whoosh. I dart inside, press the button for the third-floor operating rooms, and collapse against the steel wall. A guy with gauze taped to his forehead stands across from me, fidgeting with the strap of his messenger bag. A mangled bicycle leans against the handrail beside him.

"Hurry up, hurry up, hurry up," I mutter, hitting the

little button over and over again, as if that will somehow make the elevator climb faster.

"Late for a tea party?" the guy asks.

My eyes narrow. "You're hilarious. Did you come up with that one all by yourself?" The elevator comes to a halt and the doors slide open. "Happy Halloween," I toss over my shoulder and step out into the bleach-scented hallway.

In the OR waiting room, I check in with a nurse, who instructs me to take a seat and wait. For how long she doesn't know.

Seconds tick away, yet time in the waiting room seems frozen. When Wes and Annabelle barrel through the doors hours later it feels as if no time has passed. They've changed out of their costumes into regular street clothes.

"Sorry we're so late, Jelly Bean," Wes says, engulfing me in a hug. "Coach can be a real jackass sometimes. We got out of there as soon as we could."

"It's okay," I say as Annabelle butts in and wraps an arm around my neck.

"What happened?" she asks. "What's going on?"

"My father's in surgery right now. That's all the information I have."

For some reason I have an inexplicable urge to see Nick. I peek over Annabelle's shoulder, hoping his face will appear at any moment. Then I realize he's probably dealing with patients himself. I bet he doesn't even know my father is here.

"I brought something for you to change into." Annabelle grabs the bag resting at her feet and yanks out jeans and a T-shirt. I force a tight smile and wonder if it looks as fake as it feels. She must recognize that I don't have the energy to do anything other than bite my cuticles raw, because she crams the clothes back into the bag and says, "Or maybe you should stick with what you're wearing."

My phone vibrates in my hand.

"Who's Thomas Brandon?" Annabelle asks, pointing at the screen.

"My boss. This is the third time he's called."

"Should you answer it?"

I shake my head and let it go to voicemail. Only he doesn't leave a message. Instead he calls back again. If it wouldn't get me escorted out of the building I really would smash my phone into a million pieces. I settle for shutting it off and shoving it into my pocket.

The three of us sink into uncomfortable waiting room chairs, Wes and Annabelle on each side of me, and wait. A sense of exhaustion hangs in the air. Nobody says much except for the hospital staff and an elderly woman fiddling with a container of stirring straws near the complimentary coffee. She chatters away to a man who I assume is her husband. Or maybe she's babbling to the air-conditioning vent in the ceiling. Perhaps keeping her mouth busy is preventing a flood of emotions from bursting out of her.

Annabelle flips through a gossip magazine, mumbling about some celebrity's gaudy million-dollar wedding and how she could have planned a more elegant affair for a fraction of the price, while Wes tears off the lip of a Styrofoam cup, dropping it onto the coffee dregs. My eyes stay glued to the doors that lead to the operating rooms until finally they open. Dr. Preston emerges in his scrubs, and I know that the head of cardiac surgery has come to talk to me. All I can think is: *Please, God, don't let my father be dead.*

Dr. Preston approaches, a heavy expression on his face. Apart from the creases at the corners of his eyes and the gray in his sideburns, he looks the same as he did five years ago, an older, more refined version of Nick. He even has the same blue eyes and tousled hair as his son.

"Wes. Annabelle," Dr. Preston says, nodding. "I'd like to speak with Lillie privately for a moment, if you don't mind."

Wes squeezes my arm, and Annabelle kisses my cheek. "We'll be downstairs in the café if you need us," she says.

Dr. Preston situates himself in the chair beside me, his demeanor stoic—exactly how I remember it. "It's good to see you again, Lillie. Though I am sorry it has to be under these circumstances. How are you doing?"

My insides twist and my fingers curl around the edge of the seat, bracing myself for the worst kind of news. "Please tell me what happened."

Dr. Preston clears his throat "Your father suffered a myocardial infarction, which is the technical term for a heart attack, and underwent bypass surgery. Given the severity of his condition, he came through the procedure better than I anticipated."

I exhale. My father made it through surgery. He's going to be okay. He's going to live. "May I see him?"

"Jack is in recovery right now and needs to be alone, but you can visit him later for a few minutes," Dr. Preston says. "I need you to understand, Lillie, that this is Jack's second episode in a short period of time. The likelihood of him surviving another one is slim."

Second episode?

"What are you talking about?"

His brow furrows. "Last year, Jack was diagnosed with unstable angina, or a mild heart attack. Didn't he tell you?"

"No," I whisper. Of course he didn't.

Dr. Preston sighs. "Don't be too hard on him, Lillie. Sometimes we parents assume to know what's best for our children and the limits they can handle. No matter how good our intentions, we don't always get it right."

I nod, wanting to believe him.

"We were able to treat his condition with medication," he continues. "I warned Jack then, and again recently, that he needed to keep up with his medications, watch his blood pressure and cholesterol levels, exercise several times a week, and adopt a heart-healthy diet to reduce his chances of suffering something more serious in the future. He has chosen to ignore my advice and is now displaying early signs of congestive heart failure."

The room spins, a blur of colors and sounds. A prickling sense of unreality crawls its way through me. I take deep breaths, trying to concentrate on something other than the words "congestive heart failure."

A solid hand rests on my arm. I jump. Dr. Preston has never been one to show me affection, or acknowledgment, really. I was considered a misfit, a distraction for Nick.

I wonder why he is acting so kind toward me now. Maybe his messy divorce somehow softened him, made him more accepting. Or maybe he's simply playing the part of concerned doctor. Either way, I welcome it.

When I finally speak, my voice sounds as brittle as a fortune cookie, the scrap of paper inside a bad omen. "Is it fatal?"

Dr. Preston studies me. "The course of the disease varies with each individual, so it is difficult to determine the long-term prognosis for any given patient," he says. "Though I can tell you that if Jack does not significantly alter his lifestyle and follow the regimented treatment plan I have laid out for him, then his condition will turn life threatening, but we're not going to allow that to happen." The firmness in his gaze makes me trust that maybe my father has a prayer of beating this.

"Does my father know?"

Nodding, he says, "We discussed it during his most recent appointment when we went over his test results and spoke about the logistics of his upcoming bypass operation."

I frown. "My father was scheduled for a bypass operation?"

Dr. Preston gives me a confused look. "Yes, Lillie. An X-ray revealed significant blockages in three of four of his coronary arteries. I advised Jack to undergo surgery as soon as possible, to which he agreed. It was scheduled for a little under two weeks from now, though it seems fate had other plans."

The truth slams into me like another one of my father's sucker-punch pies. The "emergency" phone call. His ridiculous demands about me managing the diner. The meeting with Roger Stokes and the medical power of attorney. My father's tired, unkempt appearance and his loud, mucousy coughs.

The signs have been there, shouting at me that this was never about a knee-replacement procedure. Why didn't I listen better to my instincts?

That's the thing about denial, it's powerful enough to create reality out of an illusion.

Two hours later, a nurse is guiding me down a long corridor that stretches in both directions. It seems to go on forever. The hospital is quiet despite the swarm of people bustling around. Even the sounds of my footfalls absorb into the floor.

"Here we go," the nurse says, pushing open the door to my father's room. "You have ten minutes, sweetheart. Then you can visit again in the morning. Don't even consider sleeping in the waiting room. Dr. Preston gave you specific orders to go home and rest."

Unease churns in my stomach as I step into the sterile, white space. Dr. Preston warned me about what I would encounter when I finally saw my father, but he didn't prepare me for *this*.

My father's skin looks ashen and translucent. Bruises blossom out from the places where tubes enter his body, which appear to be everywhere. There's one in his nose, providing him oxygen. One inserted into a vein in his left wrist, recording his blood pressure. Another in his right, hydrating him. Several on top of his hands, pumping in heaven knows what. There's a larger tube in his neck that disappears inside of him. A pair of wires are taped to his chest, connected to the heart monitor hanging near the bed. The slow, staccato beeps of the EKG line and the drip of the IV are all that reassure me that my father is still here.

I walk to the side of his bed and sit on the edge, my father's leathery hand warm in mine. Brushing feather-light strokes across his palm, I trace over every callus, every scar, every crack.

"Were you ever going to tell me the truth?" My voice is low, steady, even though my insides are roiling. "Or were you going to continue to be evasive and let me think this was all about knee-replacement surgery?" When my father doesn't answer, anger swells in my veins. My fingers itch to shake him awake, to force him to explain himself. Because this involves me, our family, and yet my father has left me standing on the outside—a mere spectator.

They all have, I realize. Otherwise, why would Nick agree to be a witness on the medical power of attorney? Why would Annabelle and Sullivan Grace be so insistent on me participating in this year's Upper Crust competition? Why would Wes be hanging around the diner as much as he does when he should be at practice?

Tears sting my eyes, their betrayal thick in my throat. My legs move on their own volition, out of my father's hospital room, down the hallway, and into the OR waiting room. Annabelle and Wes leap to their feet when they see me approach, worry etched in their features.

"How could you?" I say, glancing between them, the tears finally tumbling over. I swipe them away. "You knew about his condition and purposely kept me in the dark."

I want confusion or surprise to cross their faces, but neither comes. Only guilt, or is that shame? They avoid my question, a fist to my gut.

My gaze locks on Annabelle. "What happened to no more secrets?" My voice shakes. "We promised each other, Annabelle."

She winces, pink coloring her cheeks. Wes looks paralyzed, as if he doesn't know what to do.

I turn on my heel and run.

21

CLOUDS DRIFT OVER THE ORANGE-TINGED MOON. KIDS dressed in costumes rush down the sidewalk, bouncing from lighted front door to lighted front door, shouting, "Trick-or-treat" and accumulating candy in oversized pillowcases, oblivious that my world is crumbling around them.

I sit on the front steps of my father's house veiled in moonlight, an empty plastic bowl shaped like a jack-o'-lantern resting on my lap. Salty tears stream down my face. There's a throbbing in my chest, the pain so crippling I'm sure my heart is about to burst.

I glance at the rows of rooftops lining the street, one after another, contemplating how far my legs would have to carry me before I could drop to my knees, pound my fists into hard earth, and scream at the top of my lungs without anyone being able to hear me.

"I thought this is where you might be," says a familiar voice, startling me.

Wiping the wetness off my cheeks, I peer around until I

spot Nick standing in the driveway. "What are you doing here?" I say.

Closing the space that separates us, he kneels in front of me, regarding me as if I'm a delicate sugar sculpture that may shatter at any moment. His eyes take in my rumpled appearance—the dirt smudges tainting my once pristine blue dress and pinafore, the rips in my knee-high stockings, the scuffs on my Mary Jane shoes. Casualties from racing out of Baylor Medical and tripping in the parking lot.

Placing strong hands over mine, Nick loosens my grip on the candy bowl, my fingers aching from holding on so tightly, and sets it on the ground by my feet. "Got any new food jokes?" He hesitates, pain etched in his features. "The last one you told me was about a tomato turning red because it saw the salad dressing."

"No, Nick," I say after awhile. "Not today." My voice sounds fractured, like I'm coming unhinged.

He brushes his thumbs under my eyes, collecting the tears as if to save me from drowning in them. "I brought you something." Digging in his back pocket, he produces a bag of candy corn and offers it to me. "Are they still your favorite?" he asks with a small, rueful smile.

"Yes," I say, then pop a few pieces into my mouth. For a moment the sweetness makes me feel like I'm full of something again.

"Can I sit?"

I nod, moving over on the step to make room for him. He lowers himself beside me, his jean-clad leg grazing against mine.

Nick rakes a hand through his hair, still wild as ever despite years of attempting to tame it into something manageable. I hope he never succeeds. His hair deserves to be this way. No amount of control can set straight what's meant to be crooked.

When he catches me watching him, he stops and sighs, focusing his gaze on the mansion he used to call home. There's a sad expression on his face, and I wonder if he's thinking about his childhood. If he's remembering a pigtailed little girl and a gap-toothed boy smitten with each other.

Hugging my knees, I look away from him, my eyes fixed on my father's covered front porch. Cauldrons, spiderwebs, and cardboard tombstones clutter the nooks and crannies. Bats made from socks dangle from hooks. A straw-stuffed scarecrow, wearing an old pair of Levi's jeans and a flannel shirt, slumps in a rocking chair next to the door. I squeeze my eyes shut, memorizing the scene, picturing my father setting it all up this morning before—

I shake the thought away.

"Talk to me, Lillie," Nick says, his tone earnest as he wraps an arm around me.

I lean into him, tucking my head into the crook of his neck. His skin smells like soap and spice and safety. Like comfort. "My dad eats water chestnuts as a midnight snack."

There's a long pause, and I wonder if I've spoken too softly, but then Nick says, "Jack taught me how to play the guitar and how to parallel park."

"He makes a wicked chili dog."

"His laugh is infectious."

"He chats to the food while he's cooking it," I say, fresh tears carving tracks down my cheeks, soaking into Nick's shirt. "He's particularly fond of hash browns."

Tangling his fingers into my hair, Nick rests his chin on top of my head. "You're his entire world, Lillie."

"I know," I cry. An image of my father lying in the hospital bed flashes through my mind. A strangled sound works its way out of my mouth. My hands clench as the fissures inside me finally break. Heaving sobs wrack my body, the harsh movements vibrating deep in my bones. Why didn't I fight harder to stay with him this morning? Why did I let his stubbornness dictate my actions? What if I never got to say good-bye? Nick anchors me against his chest, tracing circles over my back, as fear and grief swallow me whole. I cry for what feels like hours until finally I'm able to calm myself down.

"What if he doesn't recover from this?" I ask, hiccupping through the tears, my hair sticking to the side of my face.

"Jack's strong."

I swipe at my nose and pull away from him. My eyes burn and my throat feels raw. "I've been so selfish," I say, bowing my head. "So, so selfish." This whole time, I've been blaming everyone else—Wes, Annabelle, Sullivan Grace, Nick, even my father—but the person I should have been pointing at is me. "I didn't even tell him I love him before I left this morning. Why didn't I tell him?"

"Jack knows how you feel about him, Lillie. He raised you to let you go." Placing a finger underneath my chin, Nick tilts up my face. His expression is concerned, but also determined. "He's only ever wanted you to be happy."

I shake my head. "Look at me now. I'm still being selfish, making this all about me, when it should be about my father. I guess . . ." I draw in a shaky breath and start over. "I guess what everyone says about me is true."

"What is?"

"That I'm my mother's daughter," I say, picking at a weed growing along the steps. "I even look like her."

"Lillie . . ." Nick reaches out to touch me.

I dodge him, scooting away. "I'm all my father has, and

I abandoned him, just like she did. Now he's sick, and I can't get that time back."

"Don't do this to yourself."

"He *needed* me, Nick, and I wasn't there." I clear my throat. "I haven't been there for a long time."

"You're here now."

"Because he tricked me. He knew I'd never come back to Dallas on my own, and he had too much pride to tell me he was hurting, that he's *been* hurting," I say. "I hate that the biggest thing I have in common with my mother is also the worst thing . . . and that those I love have suffered because of it."

I swore up and down I would *never* be like her. The kind of person who could desert her husband and three-year-old daughter without a word of good-bye or forwarding address. The kind of person who could find a replacement family effortlessly and without regret. Only no matter how far I try to distance myself from her, I seem to end up right back where I started.

"Lillie, if Elizabeth were still here, I think you'd discover that many of the wonderful things people love about you come from her. Or at least that's where the building blocks originated from."

His words, so simple, so sincere, hit me straight in the heart. I lock my gaze with his and look, really look, into his eyes. Gone is the naive boy from my childhood and the bitter, angry man he put in his place. Now all I see is a stripped soul, laid open and bare. Yet behind each blue fleck are glimpses of the Nick I never left behind.

How could I? The wind won't let me forget him, even if I wanted to. It follows me around, whispering his name like a secret. Like at this year's Chicago Pitchfork Musical Festival—something Nick and I promised to attend together someday. Only our someday never came. Instead,

Drew surprised me with tickets. For hours we lost ourselves in the music of indie-rock bands, swaying to the rhythm. The stage lights flashed against the stainless steel ribbons that framed the Jay Pritzker Pavilion, reflecting vibrant colors into the night sky. When the music began to fade away and the crowd with it, Drew dropped to one knee, ring in hand, and asked me to make him the happiest man in the world. It was in that moment, right as I said yes, that a breeze tickled my ear and I heard it. So faint I nearly missed it. *Nick.*

"I ran out on a lot of things, didn't I?" I say, thinking about how Nick may have left me first, but I still left.

For a moment Nick only stares at me, his mouth turned downward. "Only because I pushed you."

"You can't push what goes willingly."

"No, Lillie." He shakes his head. I open my mouth to protest but he holds up a hand. "Let me say this while I can. Please." He takes a deep breath. "I'm sorry. I'm sorry for all of it—for blaming you, for the cruel things I said, for pushing you away. You meant *everything* to me, and I let you become a stranger."

"We both did."

"I never believed I could hurt you, *us,* the way I did," he says, his shoulders sagging. "I was so angry all the time. Angry at my parents because nothing I did ever met their expectations. Angry at myself for feeling like a failure every time I looked in the mirror. Angry at you for not understanding how hard I was trying to . . . keep it all together."

I bite my lip. "It wasn't just you, Nick. I didn't know how to be there for you . . . to be what you needed. So instead of fighting harder, I did nothing at all," I say, overcome with shame. "I was supposed to be your biggest supporter, and I turned my back on you . . . and on myself. I'm so sorry for that."

"I forgave you a long time ago, Lillie."

"I'm sorry it took me a little longer to do the same."

Silence stretches between us.

When Nick finally speaks, his voice is unsteady, hoarse. "That day on the Junior League porch you said you weren't enough. That was never the case. *Never.* I wasn't in a place to show you any different," he says, shifting his body toward mine. He grabs my hand, callused and capable holding soft and small. "I hate myself for not listening to you that night, for every horrible thing I said. You needed me to be there, to talk about your mother, and I dismissed you like you were nothing. I'll never forgive myself for that."

My stomach twists, remembering the harsh, dismissive way Nick spoke to me, how my heart shattered into fragments, the desperate feeling swirling inside me, pushing me to *go.*

Nick clears his throat and continues. "It took me a long time to realize that you needed to leave—had to leave. It was like you received this gift, like you'd been released from the hell we were living in. I only wish it didn't mean losing you for me to finally get my shit together. Because I always wanted to keep you, Lillie. *Always.*"

I suck in a breath, his words jolting through me, rattling something loose. Our conversation in Montgomery Park comes into sharp focus. *Maybe this is exactly how it's supposed to be.* I understand now what he was trying to tell me that morning after our run: that me leaving allowed us to be here now, at a place of forgiveness.

My eyes roam over his face, taking in his strong jawline, high cheekbones, the tiny wrinkle between his brows. I can see his pulse beating in his neck.

His name falls from my lips. A murmur so quiet I'm sure the sound didn't travel far enough to reach him, but then Nick narrows his eyes, and I know he heard me. My skin tingles, buzzing with overwhelming urgency. A feeling that life is fragile, something to be savored, and if I don't act with intention, it could all slip away from me again.

I *can't* let it slip away again. I have to grab it and never let go.

I have to—

I rise up on my knees.

Fist my fingers into Nick's hair.

And crash my mouth against his.

22

THE KISS IS DEVASTATING AND *OH, SO INCREDIBLE.* IT TASTES of regret, longing, and a soul-deep realization that it has never been—and will never be—better than with him. From somewhere far off I recall that my father is lying in a hospital bed, but my mind is in a haze.

All of a sudden strong hands push me away. I sit back on my heels, my chest heaving. "What . . . ?"

Nick combs his fingers through his hair and exhales a ragged breath. "This isn't right."

Isn't right? Crushing humiliation washes over me. Will I *ever* be enough? After everything we talked about, I thought maybe, but no. I'm still not worth the sacrifice. Tears prick my eyes as I stand on wobbly legs.

He reaches for me. "Lillie, wait. I need to tell you—"

I lurch for the door. I stumble into my father's darkened house, *my* house. When I get to the kitchen, I bend over the table and rest my forehead on the cool surface, trying to breathe, to rid myself of this feeling that I got punched in the gut.

"Lillie."

I whirl around. Nick blocks my escape route. He studies me, his nostrils flaring. There's something dangerous in his gaze, as though I'm the deer and he's the hunter.

"I came after you," he says, low, hoarse.

I shake my head. "Margaret's the only person you should be going after."

He lets out a frustrated growl. "There is no me and Margaret. Not anymore."

I look at him, confused.

"I ended things last night, Lillie, though I should have done it after our kiss," he continues, taking a step forward, his body illuminated in moonlight. "You said that desperation is a powerful motivator. So is loneliness." Another step. "I never should have started a relationship with Margaret for that reason, but after everything she did for me, I thought I owed her my loyalty." Another step. "But she deserves more than just that, which is something I can't give."

My heart hammers in my chest, his confession a tether connecting us. We stand there for a second, staring at each other, as if we're playing a game of chicken daring the other person to move. Then Nick crosses the kitchen. Or maybe my feet propel me forward. Doesn't matter. We slam together; our mouths collide in a frenzied kiss. When his tongue grazes against mine, everything inside me ignites, awakened by his taste, his touch, his smell. Brilliant white stars burst behind my eyelids. I tremble, wanting his fingers, his mouth, his body everywhere, all over me.

His hand cradles the back of my head, tangling in my hair, while the other presses into my hipbone. I curl my fingers into his shirtfront, drawing him closer so that the solid planes of his chest align with the soft curves of my own. It's as though our bodies never forgot each other.

We stumble backward without breaking the kiss. I hit a solid edge. A beat later my legs are off the ground, locked around his waist. When he places me on the counter and I feel his weight against me, my mind goes blank, all thoughts spiraling away except for Nick and how fundamentally right this is. I've only ever belonged to him.

"Oh, God," I gasp, my heels digging into the back of his thighs. My urgent, greedy fingers dip under his T-shirt and glide across his smooth back, his chest, his shoulders. They weave in his hair, pull at the roots. Nick lets out a deep, sexy grunt that coils around me like the red stripe of a candy cane.

"Lillie," he pleads. His mouth grazes the sensitive spot behind my ear, runs across my cheek, and down my neck. The stubble on his jaw whispers promises against my skin. Everywhere he touches leaves a trail of fire. I don't even care about the ridiculous, desperate sounds I'm making.

His tongue darts out, skimming the hollow of my throat. His impatient hands tug at my costume, dance up and down my thighs, tease purple lace, then rip it away. I gasp. My stomach tightens, warmth pooling there, as Nick brushes his thumbs over my nipples through the fabric of my dress. His teeth nip at my collarbone. And oh, the pressure is delicious, causing me to ache in all the right places.

"Don't stop," I beg, as a current of energy thrums through me.

Nick captures my mouth again, hungry and desperate. I whimper, drowning in kiss after kiss. He breaks away, eyes hooded and dark. His stomach muscles contract in rhythm with his short breaths. I yank the shirt over his head and discard it on the floor, then work on unbuttoning his jeans. I pull down his boxer briefs just enough to free him, gripping and stroking his hard length the way that used to drive him insane. Based on the curses and guttural noises echoing around the kitchen, and the way he pushes and pulses against my hand, it still does.

"Fuck, Lillie." His voice is rough in my ear and *so completely* destructive. "*Fuck.*"

Lust and yearning and control jolt through me because I brought him to that.

Nick picks me up and braces me against the wall, cupping my bare skin, my dress gathered around my waist. His gaze burns with intensity, watching my expression as he lifts me slightly and slides my body down onto his. We both groan, and Nick mutters phrases that resemble *gorgeous* and *so good* and *perfect* against my collarbone.

The world dissolves. Nothing exists but the two of us, moving together. Touching, kissing, making up for so much lost time. The only sounds between us are grunts and moans and quiet urging. I grip Nick's shoulders as his thrusts grow harder, faster, more jagged, his hips hitting my thighs.

My eyelids flutter shut and my head drops back against the wall. Heat builds inside me, spreading between my legs, a tingling sensation that causes my toes to curl. Then I'm unraveling, clutching him as I cry out. Moments later, Nick comes undone, his back muscles flexed and slick with sweat. For a second, everything is quiet. Our bodies stay entwined, chests heaving, hearts pounding.

Matching the banging on the front door.

"Fuck," Nick says, his face buried in my neck, breath hot on my skin. He disentangles. Cool air rushes between us. My body hums with the memory of his touch.

There's more knocking.

"Who the hell is that?" he says, throwing on his shirt, then zipping and buttoning his jeans.

"I don't know. Probably a drunk trick-or-treater." With shaking arms, I straighten my own clothes and smooth down my hair, attempting to regain my composure. My underwear is in scraps on the floor. My lips are swollen and tender, and my legs feel as if they may give out at any moment.

"Lillie?" a voice calls out.

Sobering dread floods through me. *Shit.* It's Drew. *Shit, shit, shit.*

What happened to him giving me space, us taking a break?

"Whoever is out there obviously wants to see you," Nick says, though the coldness in his voice indicates he already has a good idea of who it is. "Maybe you should answer it." He cuts his gaze away, his features concealed in shadow.

I open my mouth to respond when more pounding and yelling interrupt me.

Shaking my head, I shout, "Coming," as I race to the door and fling it open.

"Thank God," Drew says, almost breathless. He stands on the porch crowned in moonlight, wearing a navy suit and red tie. A brown leather bag rests against his leg. "Your phone's been off all day. I was just about to leave and try the diner next."

My engagement ring is in my dress pocket rather than on my finger, my costume is a rumpled mess, and I'm sure my expression shows everything that transpired between Nick and me. Only Drew doesn't seem to notice anything is off. *How can he not notice?* Instead he wraps me in a hug and presses his lips to my forehead.

Wiggling out of his embrace, I blurt, "What are you doing here?"

Drew furrows his brow and says, calm and steady as always, "Baylor Medical Hospital called the apartment this morning. The person I spoke with wouldn't tell me much, only that you're listed as your father's emergency contact. I tried your cell, and when I couldn't get ahold of you, I took a flight here. I'm not sure what's going on, but it sounded serious. I thought you would want the support."

My heart clenches. I did want the support, just not from him.

"Is your father okay?" Drew asks. "Is it his knee?"

"No, it's not his knee. He collapsed from a heart attack and underwent bypass surgery. He's recovering now," I say, lacking the energy to elaborate further.

"I'm sorry to hear that."

Drew starts to loop an arm around my waist when the porch light flips on. I jump a little, nearly stumbling on a cardboard tombstone. Sucking in a breath, I peer over my shoulder. Nick leans against the doorframe, arms crossed, jaw set, eyes piercing in a way that twists my stomach into knots.

Drew glances between us. I can only imagine the questions running through his mind. *Who is this guy? What's he doing at my father's house with all the lights off? Why is his shirt on inside out?*

Wait. Nick's shirt is on inside out.

He put his shirt back on inside out?

This whole situation is a disaster. I squeeze my eyes shut, hoping to become invisible. These two men were never supposed to meet. Yet here they are, my past and my present.

Drew continues to glance between Nick and me. For a moment I think he's connected the dots, that he read the flashing sign above my head proclaiming my feelings for Nick and is finally about to get upset. Then Drew steps forward, his face composed, and extends a hand, as if he honestly expects Nick to take it. "Hi. Drew Harrington. Lillie's fiancé."

Nick remains motionless. Several seconds pass before he turns to me and says, "Doesn't it get exhausting?"

"What?" I ask, forcing myself to speak, to maintain eye contact.

"Pretending to be someone you're not." I feel the sharpness in his voice like a harsh, biting wind.

Before I can respond, Nick stalks off the porch, hops into his Mercedes, and drives away.

Drew looks at me, his forehead crinkling. "What was that about?"

"That was Nick . . . The ex I told you about . . ."

Sinking down onto the top step, I press my palms into my eyes, breathing hard through my nose. Drew takes a seat beside me and rests a hand on my knee. I place mine on top of his. Simple, easy.

Suddenly it's all so clear. What I've known in my soul but only now am willing to fully admit. For the past two years I have allowed myself to exist in this safe little bubble with Drew where there's no real intensity or challenges, an anesthetized version of what life *should* be about. That's no way for either of us to live.

Our first date flashes through my mind. I remember how we met in front of Wrigley Field, where Drew purchased a pair of nosebleed tickets from a scalper and escorted me through the main entrance gates into the park. We made our way to the highest spot in the stadium, laughing as we stumbled to our seats, arms filled to the brim with hot dogs and baseball cap sundaes dripping hot fudge down the sides.

While we watched players move around the field like ants attacking a picnic basket, we devoured our ballpark fare and joked about needing gloves to catch all the fly balls whizzing around and made bets about each at bat. Sometime in the ninth inning, amid a group of drunken fans celebrating a Cubs home run, Drew cupped my face in his hands and leaned in so close I could see the smattering of freckles across his nose and the gold flecks in his amber eyes, and kissed me, sweet and soft and sure.

I remember thinking at that baseball game I had found someone who could offer me stability, comfort, happiness —things I lost with Nick but so desperately craved. Things I still crave but now realize aren't enough to sustain a relationship in the long term. Where is the passion, the messiness, the euphoria of taking chances? The tingling sensation that separates loving someone from being *in love* with someone? The emotions I feel with Nick?

I take a deep breath and exhale as though I'm blowing out a hundred birthday candles. "Drew, we need to talk."

For a moment, he stares at the straw-stuffed scarecrow in the rocking chair, his leg bouncing. Then he sighs and says, "Yeah, I suppose we do."

I know I need to be the one to begin the conversation, but how do I break a heart that has no business being broken?

"I'm not going back to Chicago with you," I say finally.

He nods, as though anticipating this response. "I called the management company from the airport. They've agreed to let us out of our lease early. I can be down here permanently in a month."

"No. I mean, I can't marry you, Drew," I whisper. "I'm sorry. So, *so* sorry. But I can't."

My vision blurs as tears sting my eyes. A few tumble down my cheeks. I wipe them away. My face feels hot and blotchy, and there's an ache throbbing inside me that touches me at the core. Even though I know this is right— letting Drew go so he can be with someone worthy of his love, someone who can bear witness to his life and give him everything I can't—it's also one of the hardest things

I've ever done. Harder than leaving Dallas, scared and alone. Maybe even harder than discovering the truth about my mother and abandoning my dreams of someday running the diner. This time the decision is coming from an honest, pure place, not one fueled by desperation or anger.

For the first time I see a crack in Drew's usually relaxed, easygoing facade, his gaze shining with worry, his mouth pulled down into a frown.

"I don't understand," he says. "We're well suited. We have a content life. We love each other."

I gulp down a breath, trying to get myself together. "I do love you, but not in the way that's enough. Not in the way that's fair to either of us."

Drew shakes his head, as though he refuses to believe it. "I think you're just confused, Lillie. With everything that's been happening with your father, it makes sense. We don't have to get married this February. We can take the break you said you needed and reevaluate later. Whatever it is, we'll figure it out together. I don't want to lose you. Not like this."

For a second I feel my resolve crumbling. I picture the two of us fifteen years down the road, holding hands as we stroll along Michigan Avenue, people watching and window-shopping. Or the two of us lounging around in flannel pajamas and slippers on a Sunday morning, sipping coffee and reading the newspaper. I could live that life, maybe even learn to find happiness in it, but then I hear Nick's taunting voice in my ear. *Keep pretending to be someone you're not.* I know I have to remain strong, see this through to the end.

I shift on the step to look directly into his eyes. "I'm not confused." My voice is gentle yet firm. "You shouldn't want to marry someone who isn't passionately in love with you because that's what you deserve and what I can't give you," I say, echoing Nick's words from earlier.

Drew studies my face. He must notice something in my expression that tells him everything he needs to know because he asks, "Is this about him? . . . Nick?"

A fist squeezes around my heart. Maybe I should deny it, spare Drew more pain, but I can't lie to him. Not in addition to everything else. I've had enough of the secrets and the lies, because, truth be told, the only difference between a secret and a lie is that a secret is a lie not spoken aloud.

I swallow. "Yes, but this is more about *me*," I say as the tears continue to flow. And I mean it. This *is* about me. I want something real and messy and complicated, no matter what happens between Nick and me in the future. "I'm so, *so* sorry, Drew. I never meant to hurt you." Removing my engagement ring from my pocket, I set it in his open palm and close his fingers around it.

Drew's eyes stay glued to his clenched hand. He's quiet for a long time. When he meets my gaze, his lashes are wet, but there's acceptance on his face. He kisses my forehead and whispers good-bye. The finality of his words feels like jumping into a cavern, endless, yet somehow freeing. Drew stands, and I watch him move farther and farther away from me until he vanishes under a blanket of darkness.

Out into a world where I can't follow.

23

WHEN I ARRIVE AT THE DINER THE NEXT MORNING WELL before dawn, it's dark and empty. Peaceful. It seems to be sleeping, its windows half lidded, waiting for its caffeine injection of clanging dishes, happy chatter, and jukebox songs.

I flip on the light in the back room and look around. The last time I stood in this exact spot, clutching my mother's apron, I felt overcome with dread. This time, when I tie my father's dancing clams apron around my waist, the soft, faded fabric roots me here.

I step around the bags of flour stacked on the floor beside the industrial mixer. The schedule posted on the corkboard nailed to the tile wall indicates today's breakfast Blue Plate Special is pancetta and pear waffles with cinnamon honey syrup.

Grabbing the boom box off the shelf above the prep counter, I pop in the copy of *Resolution* Nick gave me and let the band's music keep me company while I gather the ingredients from the walk-in pantry and refrigerator.

I rummage around in a drawer for the paring knife

with the duct-taped wooden handle and take a pear from a wicker basket. Pressing the blade into the fat end, I turn the pear around and around, the skin falling onto the prep counter in one long curl. I repeat the process with another, then another. With each pear I peel, images of my father in the ICU, what happened with Nick the night before, fade away. For the first time in years I allow myself to just be. Before long all the pears are peeled, halved, cored, and arranged cut-side-up in baking dishes for roasting.

I pull the plug on the power cord as I hear the lock turn on the side door. A beat later, Ernie strolls into the back room, yawning. He stops when he sees me and whistles.

"You've been busy," he says, hanging his jacket on a hook before putting on an apron. "I didn't expect to find you here. I thought you'd be at the hospital."

"Visiting hours haven't started yet," I say as I wipe down the prep counter. "Plus, I figured you may need some help." In truth, I don't know *why* I'm in the diner's kitchen, only that when I woke up this morning, something primal and deep was pulling me to it. The desire was so strong I don't know how I survived the last five years without it. Or why I ever allowed it to die in the first place.

Ernie rests a hand on my shoulder. "How are you holding together, Lillie?"

"Oh, you know. Fine." My voice cracks. Tears fill my eyes. I blink them away. I'm so sick of crying. "I've been better," I say, then fill Ernie in on everything Dr. Preston told me.

"Despite all that, I'm sure Jack will be in good spirits when you see him later," he says.

"Yeah, probably too good," I say with a laugh, though there are more holes in it than Swiss cheese. "I hope he takes his condition seriously."

"Jack knows what's at risk," Ernie says. "Why else do you think he asked you to come back here? He needs you to force him to see sense when he's too stubborn to see it for himself."

I smile, surprised at how genuine it feels. Ernie's always had this special way about him. How he can cut straight to the heart of the matter, remind you of exactly what's important. I remember his first shift at the diner, nearly twenty years ago and without a lick of cooking experience. He jumped right in anyway. Before that, he repaired engines at a local body shop, and at night, played in an amateur baseball league with my father. Somehow my father suckered him into a career change. I'm glad he did.

Ernie squeezes my shoulder, then heads off to the kitchen. I finish the pears, drizzling lemon juice evenly over each half, dotting them with butter, and sprinkling the whole thing with vanilla bean–infused sugar. When I enter the kitchen, baking dishes in hand, Ernie has fired up the flat-top grill and preheated the oven for me. While the pears roast, I render some pancetta until crispy, combine cinnamon and honey in a large saucepan for the syrup, and prepare the waffle batter, which includes beating egg whites into soft peaks to add air into the mixture. Down the line, Ernie preps the ingredients for the usual breakfast staples: biscuits and red-eye gravy, overstuffed omelets with all the fixings, fried chicken and waffles, corned beef hash. My mouth waters over the different scents floating around me, familiar and welcoming.

With a pastry brush, I grease the waffle iron with vegetable oil, then pour batter into the center and scatter the pancetta bits on the top. Three minutes later, I pluck the fluffy waffle out of the iron and taste it immediately, burning my tongue and the roof of my mouth in the process. Still, the flavor is heavenly—slightly sweet with subtle savory notes. The perfect complement to the tender, grainy pears and warmed spiced syrup. Though the waffle texture isn't quite right. I retrieve the wooden box containing my mother's recipes from the office safe and flip through it.

"Searching for something?" Ernie asks, coming to stand beside me.

"There's an ingredient missing in the batter, but for the life of me, I can't remember what it is." I bite my lip. "Where's the card for this recipe?"

"Not in there."

I meet his gaze. "Why not?" My father guards the contents of this box like an oyster guards its pearl. He notices when the cards get out of order, let alone if one disappears altogether.

"Because it's not your mother's recipe."

"Then whose is it?"

Lines appear around Ernie's eyes, extending down to his mouth in a frown. "It's yours, Lillie."

What is he talking about? Sure, a few Blue Plate Specials are inspired by my high school newspaper columns, but all the regular menu items trace back to my mother.

"What do you mean?"

"The original recipe used your mother's classic Belgian waffle batter, but sometime during your middle school years, you revamped it, added your own touches like the pears and pancetta and syrup. We've been serving your version ever since. So if you want to know what ingredient is missing, you're going to have to rack that pretty little brain of yours."

Ernie stares at me the same way Sullivan Grace did that morning in my father's kitchen. Like there's something I'm supposed to understand but haven't figured out yet.

It feels as if I'm running out of chances.

———

By the time I climb behind the wheel of my truck, my body feels as though it could snap apart. I forgot how much filling orders, rushing about the kitchen, and pushing food down the line wreaks havoc on my muscles and joints.

I grab my cell phone out of the glove box and power it on. The icon for my voicemail inbox pops up. I cringe as I listen to the messages.

"Lillie, Thomas Brandon here. Kingsbury Enterprises wants to move up the product launch by a month. We need you on the next flight to Chi—" Delete. *"It has been two hours since my last voice-mail. I thought we already discussed your dedication to this project. If —"* Delete. *"It appears your phone has been turned off. White, Ogden, and Morris provides all employees with company cell phones with the expectation that—"* Delete.

I toss the phone onto the seat beside me and merge into traffic, driving in silence to Baylor Medical. As I'm parking in the visitor lot, my cell vibrates. Thomas Brandon. That man is more aggressive than a pit bull attacking a pork chop.

"Hello," I say, entering the hospital through the sliding glass doors.

"Why haven't I been able to reach you?" he barks.

I start to respond, but he cuts me off, spewing a tirade about my lack of commitment, my failure to complete tasks, my poor work ethic. I block him out as I walk down a hallway that reeks of antiseptic to the elevators. As I step into the ICU waiting area, Thomas Brandon transitions to ranting about my inability to function as a team leader, how brownnosing Ben is better suited to handle the responsibility. I can hear him breathing hard into the phone.

Finally he clears his throat and says, "You're off the project, Lillie. I suggest you start looking for another place of employment."

I stare at the screen as a laugh bubbles up. This is all so ridiculous. My father has a potentially fatal heart condition and everything with Nick is a mess and my friends have been lying to me for months and Thomas Brandon thinks I care about this job or a stupid promotion?

Just like with Drew, I know Annabelle's right. If this career path were truly my passion, where I'm meant to be, I would've better managed my work obligations from Dallas. I would've prioritized my life in Chicago rather than sinking so easily back into my old life here.

"You have impeccable timing, Mr. Brandon."

He grunts. "Why is that?"

"Because I quit."

————

My father is awake and causing trouble as usual when I arrive at his room. Apparently not even a heart attack can slow him down.

"Baby girl, explain to Nancy here that I'm as ready as a Cornish game hen on plucking day," he says as soon as he sees me come in. His skin still appears sallow, eyes sunken. The bruises marring his arms somehow seem even darker in the daylight. There's a lipstick mark on his cheek that matches Sullivan Grace's signature color.

I look at the nurse, Nancy, I guess, who is replacing an empty IV bag with a new one.

"Jackson is attempting to charm the hospital staff into discharging him early," she says. "Which will only occur if the doctor grants the order. Until then, he's staying in this bed."

My father exhales a long breath, his cheeks puffing out. "What if I offered you free peach cobbler at the diner for a year? That's a darn good deal if I do say so myself."

"I don't think that bribery is your lucky golden ticket to freedom," I say, pulling up a chair beside his bed and settling into it. "Try amping up the flirting instead."

The nurse laughs and excuses herself with the promise to return in an hour. My father mutters under his breath and glares at the muted television mounted on the wall.

I tuck the blanket tighter around him, then grab his hand. "How are you feeling?"

He says nothing. The room fills with the noise of medical equipment beeping, whirring, humming. When my father does respond, the words fly from his lips. "Baby girl, you need to get Ernie on the phone and confirm the Spoons hasn't collapsed."

"I was already there this——"

"Remind him that all floats are half price until closing."

"Dad."

"Tell Ernie he needs to get the pumpkin mac and cheese in the oven by three o'clock or else it won't be ready in time for the dinner rush."

I lean forward and say his name again, firmer this time.

"Then you need to help him prepare the——"

"Dad!" I shout, then soften my voice. "You could have died."

He blinks, momentarily stunned. "Nonsense," he says, recovering quickly and patting my hand as though placating a child. "I'm not going anywhere."

I shake my head. My father has always been too stubborn, too prideful, to the point that it's a detriment. Standing, I pace in front of the windows and peer out at the world below. In the reflection of the glass, I can see my father watching me, a wrinkle between his brows.

A knock on the door makes my heart jump like water droplets in hot grease. Dr. Preston strolls in. "How is my happiest patient today?" he says, a stethoscope around his neck. He nods and smiles when he sees me, one side of his mouth lifting higher than the other just like his son. An orderly trails after him, carrying a tray.

"Never better, Doc. Never better," my father says, wincing as he struggles to sit up.

"Easy," I say, propping the pillows behind him.

The orderly sets the tray on the bedside table and removes the plastic cover before exiting. My father sniffs at the bowl of chicken broth and pokes at the blob of green Jell-O. "Doc, I ain't touching no food that resembles sea foam salad and probably tastes just as questionable."

"Then it appears that starving yourself is the only other viable option because from now on your middle name is Nutritious," Dr. Preston says. He performs a physical examination, listening to my father's chest, inspecting his incisions, checking his tubes and vital signs.

My father grumbles something about convincing the nurse with the pretty green eyes to sneak him pancakes later.

Dr. Preston scribbles notes on a chart, then spends the next ten minutes explaining to my father the severity of his prognosis and his updated treatment plan. I write down Dr. Preston's instructions word for word, even though he already outlined all of this to me yesterday.

"Do either of you have any questions or need me to go over anything again?" Dr. Preston asks.

I tell him no, while my father continues grumbling. A voice crackles over the PA system, requesting Dr. Preston's presence in the OR immediately. "My apologies. If you'll excuse me," he says, then dashes out of the room.

"We have quite the journey ahead of us to make you healthy again, Dad," I say after the door clicks shut.

"I don't know why everyone's got to be such dream crushers. Even Nick's sayin' I've got to lay off the mashed taters."

"Nick was here?" I ask, surprised, but then, of course, Nick would visit my father. No matter what Nick's feelings are toward me, my father is still hugely important to him.

"Sure did. Stopped by earlier," my father says. "He seemed more exhausted than a coffeepot after the morning rush hour. If you ask me, that boy's been working too hard —" A violent coughing fit racks his body, the sound echoing off the floor and walls.

I reach out to rub my father's back, but he waves me away. "I'm fine," he says once the coughing subsides. He draws in a ragged breath. "No need to baby me."

I clench my jaw, my hands curling into fists. Doesn't my father understand that if he doesn't regard his condition with the severity it deserves he may never witness my wedding day or cradle a grandchild in his arms? Doesn't he know that his death would destroy me?

"I won't survive it if I lose you," I say. "Do you realize that?"

"Don't be so dramatic, baby girl," he says, back to poking at the wiggling Jell-O. "I ain't going anywhere."

"No, Dad. This is serious," I say as heat floods my cheeks and tears sting my eyes again. "You're sick. Pretending otherwise is selfish and careless. Mom already left. Please don't leave me, too."

My father frowns. Deep lines are carved in his forehead. He opens his mouth, but no words come out.

His silence speaks for both of us.

———

My father falls asleep a short time later, and I sneak quietly out of the room. As I turn to grab a chair in the waiting area, I spot Annabelle at the far end of the corridor, a fruit bouquet and a bundle of balloons in hand. With everything that's happened, it's hard to believe it's only been a day since I last saw her. When Annabelle notices me, she hesitates for a second before continuing her path down the hallway.

"Shouldn't you be at the Ritz Carlton for the Upper Crust run-through?" I say, which is also where I'm supposed to be.

"Sullivan Grace and Paulette Bunny are handling it." Annabelle shifts the fruit bouquet in her arms, causing the purse on her shoulder to slide to her elbow. After a beat she says, "We promised each other no more secrets and I broke that. I'm sorry, Lil." The apology catches me off guard. Coming from her, those words are as sacred as an heirloom bridal gown.

I pull her into a hug. "Me, too. I'm glad you're here," I say, squeezing her shoulders as I lean back to look at her. "My father's sleeping right now. You hungry?"

Annabelle wrinkles her nose. "For hospital food?"

"Coffee?"

She nods. I wait while she slips into my father's room and drops off the goodies inside the door.

We make our way to the café in silence. After ordering our drinks, we sit at an open table near the atrium market, beside a nurse slurping soup from a thermos. The air smells faintly of stale cookies.

"I need to know why, Annabelle."

She rips open a packet of artificial sweetener and pours

it into her large Americano, avoiding my gaze. "Because Old Man Jack asked us not to."

I furrow my brow. "And you listened to him?"

"He's your *father*, Lillie. Of course we listened to him. He said he'd tell you in his own time, on his own terms. We had no choice but to respect that, and don't lie and act like you wouldn't be angry hearing about his situation from anyone other than him."

Annabelle's right. My father owed me that. If only he wasn't such a professional at being evasive or wearing his pride and stubbornness like one of his beloved plaid shirts.

"I see you've been spending time at the diner." She jerks her chin at the bits of waffle batter on my shirtsleeve. "I'm glad."

Biting my lip, I say, "I couldn't leave Ernie to fend for himself. Some of the regulars are worse than rabid foxes."

Annabelle smiles, eyes bright, and I wonder if she can sense there's more I'm not saying—that the desire is still there, simmering under the surface, threatening to spill out.

I wrap my hands around the paper cup to warm my fingers. "So you and Wes," I say. "What's happening there?"

Sighing, she takes a sip of her coffee and says, "I don't know . . . We're talking, I guess. He says he's not sure if he can ever trust me again, which I know is justified. At the same time, how can I trust that he'll change? What if we somehow find a way to put my infidelity behind us and he still doesn't believe in marriage? What then?"

"Annabelle, no," I say, shaking my head. "Don't let a defeatist attitude like that infect the progress you've made with Wes. You're the one who told me not to play the victim or give up."

She stirs more sweetener into her coffee. "Sometimes it's easier to dish out the advice than accept it."

We're quiet a moment. Then with her usual abruptness, Annabelle changes topics. "The album release party at the House of Blues is in a couple of days. You'll be there, right?"

"I don't think that's a good idea . . ."

Arching an eyebrow, she asks, "Why is that?"

Inhaling a deep breath, I launch into the events of the past twenty-four hours. I tell her about what happened between Nick and me in my father's kitchen, about his confession regarding Margaret. I tell her about Drew showing up unexpectedly and Nick storming off, about me permanently ending things with Drew and me quitting my job in Chicago.

Annabelle's mouth drops open. I can see her processing my words. Finally, she slaps the table so loud people turn to glare at us. "Shut up, you little hussy! Are you still on birth control?"

"Annabelle!" I hiss, glancing around, a fake smile glued to my face. "Yes. Now shhh!"

She snickers to herself. "Damn. Is it wrong that I'm proud of you? Well, not because you screwed over Drew."

I cringe and take a sip of my vanilla chai latte. The liquid burns my throat.

"But because it's been years since you've acted so bold," she continues. "Do you regret it?"

"Which part?"

"Any of it."

"Hurting Drew, yes. The rest . . ." I shrug.

Annabelle hits the table again. "I knew it." Her expression grows serious. "Lillie, you need to come to the album launch party."

I want to protest, but the imploring look in her eyes and the edge in her tone force the words back.

Besides, what more do I have to lose?

24

THE HOUSE OF BLUES IS LIKE A SKILLET OF JAMBALAYA with its rustic, southern vibe and juke-joint charm. There's flavor in every aspect, from the crazy-quilt curtains framing the stage, to the custom-painted murals and funky patterns covering the walls and ceiling, to the folk art and exotic furnishings adorning the music hall. The mass of fans, radio personalities, music reporters, and photographers crammed into the space add extra spice.

A bartender hands me a pint of Shiner Ruby Redbird, garnished with a lemon wedge. I squeeze the juice into the glass and take a long pull. The sharp kick of ginger and tangy grapefruit hits the back of my throat and fills my whole mouth. The Randy Hollis Band must have pulled some major strings to get this particular beer on tap for their album launch party. It's typically a seasonal selection available only in the summer months.

Rising on tiptoes, I peer above the crowd. I lost track of Annabelle an hour ago. Since I got here, she's been rushing around like a crazy person, coordinating vendors, answering questions, fixing last-minute catering problems.

Near the entrance, I spot Margaret chatting with some suits. I wonder if they're from the band's management company. In front of them, the guys sit at a table, autographing copies of *Resolution* and snapping photos with adoring fans.

"Need a boost, shorty?"

I turn. Wes stands off to my side, hands stuffed into his pockets.

"No. But I could use some company," I say with a smile, hooking my ankle around a bar stool leg and sitting down. "Care to join me?"

"You drive a hard bargain, Jelly Bean," Wes says. After he orders a Ruby Redbird for himself, he sinks onto the open stool beside me and we lapse into silence, allowing the buzz around us to do the talking.

"I visited Old Man Jack this morning," Wes says after our beers are half gone.

"He told me."

"So he gets released tomorrow?"

I nod. "Yeah. Heaven help us."

"Listen, Jelly Bean. I'm sorry I didn't say anything about Jack. I thought for sure he'd told you about his condition and that's why you came back. Then when he started in on you managing the diner, it became clear you still didn't know. He said he'd tell you in his own time, and when he didn't, I guess I sort of felt like you deserved more than hearing about his condition from anyone other than him—"

"Wes." I set a firm hand on his arm. "It's okay. Really. I understand why you didn't say anything. It wasn't your place."

His shoulders relax. "What do you say we go park ourselves on one of those couches along the wall? I think the show's about to begin."

"I get the cushion near the armrest," I say, nudging his side.

"Not on your life," he says with a wink.

We weave through the swarm of bodies. As I move around a server balancing trays of empanadas and mini pulled pork sandwiches, Nick steps squarely into my path. From the startled expression on his face, I gather he didn't expect to run into me at the House of Blues, even though he knows I was invited. Maybe he didn't think I'd actually attend. For a second we stand there, a silent impasse. My chest tightens.

"Hi," I say when it's clear he's not going to. My voice sounds strange, not like my own.

"Hello, Lillie," he says finally.

The way Nick looks at me makes me feel stripped bare like an exposed nerve. I'm tingling all over. My mind floods with white-hot images of him bracing me against the wall, thrusting inside me, watching as I come undone around him, when there was nothing but skin between us. Then I remember his harsh words after Drew surprised me, and the tiny firecrackers exploding inside me fizzle out.

"What's up?" Wes says. "The big night's here, huh?"

"Yeah," Nick says. He backs up a pace, raking his fingers through his hair that is in desperate need of a cut. It's even wilder than usual, as though he stuck a fork into an electrical outlet, which he dared me to do when I was twelve. His eyes dart around, and I wonder if he's searching for Drew, or maybe he's simply planning his escape route.

"Listen, man, we were about to snatch some ass real estate over there, if you're game," Wes says, gesturing to the couches along the wall.

I glance at Wes. Does he know what happened between Nick and me? A lump forms in my throat.

"Thanks, but I need to deal with some things," Nick says. "I'll see you guys later. Enjoy yourselves tonight."

I want to ask him to stay. There's so much that demands to be said, but before I can get the words out, Nick disappears into the sea of people as abruptly as he appeared. The squeezing pressure in my chest amplifies.

Wes turns and stares at me, a question in his eyes. I shake my head. This isn't the time to explain.

The overhead lights flicker and dim. Cheers erupt around us. I look at the stage to see the Randy Hollis Band taking their places behind well-loved instruments. Karl throws several guitar picks into the audience as Jason twirls his drumsticks and Tim's bass riffs reverberate throughout the room. Gripping the neck of a Gibson Les Paul electric guitar, Matt saunters up to the microphone, a grin illuminating his whole face.

"How you feeling, Dallas?" he says as the opening guitar-driven strains of "Shadows and Dust"—the first track off *Resolution*—fill the House of Blues. He's answered by a chorus of whistles and hollering.

By the time Wes and I fight our way through the crowd, the couches are all occupied and it's standing room only. We find a spot near the side of the stage and join in with the other fans singing along to the lyrics. Purple, yellow, and blue stage lights pulse as bodies sway and dance to the beat of the music. Arms wave in the air. The band rolls right through the set with "Autumn Green," a hard-rocking country track that highlights the raw, earnest emotion in Matt's lead vocals, and then straight into "Concrete Rodeo."

"We want to thank y'all for coming out tonight," Karl says when the song comes to a close. "Years ago we were four guys tinkering around in a college apartment. We used to play in bars around town and give away our independent records for free with dreams of someday selling out stadium shows. Now we're actually making money off those records and that pipe dream is becoming a reality. We're no longer a bunch of fairy-tale chasers. We've captured ours, thanks to y'all's support."

Shrills from the audience grow even louder. Camera flashes bounce around in the darkness.

"We've spent the majority of our careers lugging gear to club after club, holding down multiple jobs to make ends meet, tearing relationships apart with our hectic sched-ules," Matt cuts in, swapping out his electric guitar for an acoustic one. "The past few years have been a whirlwind for us. We've achieved some big milestones—landing a major record deal, hearing our music on the radio for the first time, debuting on the *Billboard* country charts with our single 'August.' We've also experienced personal heartbreak —death, cheating, divorce, drugs. All this terrible life shit that no one prepares you for."

A couple of guys wearing T-shirts with staff written across the chest bring out stools, guitar stands, bongos, and shakers.

"When we went into the studio to record *Resolution,* we knew we wanted to reflect all that, to reach deep inside and explore all those warring emotions," Matt continues. "So, naturally, we had to work with the best in the business. Lucky for us, one of our closest friends, who was going through some of the same crap as we were at the time, happens to be one helluva songwriter. And, lucky for y'all, he's here tonight and has agreed to play a set with us."

Wes elbows me and shouts in my ear, "You ready for this, Jelly Bean?"

Squinting at him, I yell back, "Ready for what?"

Wes grins and jerks his chin toward the stage.

I follow his gaze to see who everyone is going crazy for.

I try to process it, but I can't. My brain has vacated my body. It's like converting recipe measurements doped up on cough medicine, it's that impossible. There's no way Nick is walking across the stage carrying my father's old Taylor acoustic guitar, no way Nick is claiming the empty stool between Matt and Karl and adjusting the microphone, no way Nick is throwing the worn leather strap over his head and tuning the pegs.

Only it is him, seeming completely in his element, right there on that stage.

"Let me introduce you to our buddy Nick Preston, one of the best damn songwriters in country music," Matt says, slapping Nick on the back. "Please give him a warm, Randy Hollis–style welcome."

The crowd breaks into catcalls and thunderous applause. Nick waves, then rubs his hands up and down his thighs. His eyes are like flames, so bright they could light me on fire.

"We're going to slow things down a bit and play a song for you off the new record called 'Unwinding.' It's about a guy and a girl who have severed the thread that once tied them together and are now trying desperately to pedal backward and reconnect it," Karl says as he strums the guitar. "Hope y'all enjoy it."

A hush settles over the room as the progression of guitar chords and bongos create a sad, beautiful melody. Matt begins to sing, Karl and Nick adding the harmony, though it's only Nick's smooth tenor I hear. An arrow to my heart. It breaks through the shock and the awe.

I blink several times, but Nick is still onstage singing and strumming my father's old guitar like he never stopped. Like the ugly chapters in our past are a bad dream.

Wes places a hand on my shoulder, concern etched on his face. "You okay?"

I shake my head, unable to speak.

Understanding dawns. "Shit. I'm sorry, Jelly Bean. I thought Nick explained everything that night at Otto's Corner."

Is that why Nick gave me the advanced copy of *Resolution*? Was that his way of telling me about . . . whatever *this* is?

I choke out something about needing to clear my head. Wes calls my name and reaches for me, but I turn and push through the crowd, hoping the bodies bumping into me will knock me out of this twisted reality I seem to be caught in. Only no matter how fast or far away I move from the stage, Nick's voice follows me.

I'm almost to the entrance when manicured fingers close around my wrist, pull me up against a wall. Margaret stares at me with a fierce glint in her gray eyes.

She crosses her arms and says, "Nick has me to thank, you know."

"For what?" My throat feels dry.

She points at the stage. "For him holding that guitar. For him falling in love with music again. When everyone else deserted him, it was *me* who stayed, who encouraged him to quit medicine to pursue songwriting. *Me.* Not you. Yet it still wasn't enough." Her face shifts as she spits out the last part, the hard exterior slipping before it's put back in place.

It takes several seconds for her words to register; my mind is clouded, trapped in a dense fog. "What do you mean Nick quit medicine?" I ask, certain she must be lying.

My gaze flicks toward the stage. From my vantage point, Nick is hidden behind the mass of people, but I can still hear his voice, smooth and deep and, *God*, so sexy it steals my breath. I picture him with his head bent down, pouring raw emotion into every chord, every lyric. And I know with bone-deep surety that Margaret is telling the truth. When Nick said he abandoned his surgical residency, I thought he meant he switched to another area within medicine, not that he gave it up entirely.

All this time, I've been gripping tightly to this expectation of who Nick has become, but I've been so very, very wrong.

I don't know who Nick is anymore.

Margaret laughs a small, resentful laugh. "Of course you have no idea about that. You have no idea about anything."

Guilt and frustration rise in me as I am once again reminded of all the things I've missed these past five years, all the history I need to learn. It's all too much. Pushing off the wall, I head for the door, desperate for air.

"You have no idea what it's like competing with a ghost." Margaret's tone is acidic.

I stop and face her.

"Even after Nick went up there, he still wouldn't let go."

My brow furrows. *When he went up where?*

"To Chicago," she says, as if reading my thoughts.

Everything freezes, then the crowd and the music thaw back to life. All I can concentrate on is sucking air into my lungs. Nick came to Chicago? When? Why didn't he tell me?

I remember what Nick said in my father's kitchen. *I came after you.* At the time, I thought he was referring to right then. Now I realize he did tell me, but why didn't he *find* me?

I look at the stage as the opening chords of "A Tragic

Trajectory"—the final track off *Resolution*—surround me. The sea of people have parted a bit so I can see the top of Nick's head, bent down, as I suspected. It hits me that while I may not know everything about him anymore, I still know him. He's lived inside me since our world was one block wide and I thought clouds were meringue cookies floating in the sky. Our roots are so entwined they can't be separated.

"Eventually Nick did let go and move on. With *me*," Margaret says, recapturing my attention. Her eyes are alight with anger and hurt and sadness, emotions I recognize all too well—I've seen them in my own eyes enough times. "You just couldn't stand to see that happen, could you? You had to sweep back in here and destroy everything I've rightfully earned."

The bitterness in her voice settles like a brick in my stomach as I recall Nick confessing that he shouldn't have entered a relationship with Margaret out of a sense of loyalty. I can't blame her for her anger, and while not intentional, maybe I am a reason for her pain. I feel as if I owe Margaret an apology, but more than that, my gratitude. For her honesty, for being Nick's anchor when I wasn't strong enough, for helping him get here, to this point.

"I'm sorry," I say, hoping she senses that it comes from a sincere, real place.

She shakes her head, as though rejecting it, and says, "You'll run away again—it's all you're capable of. Except this time I won't be there to pick up the pieces." Shouldering past me, Margaret storms away.

Her words are aimed to strike at my heart, her fury about the situation acting as fuel, but I refuse to grant them that kind of power because she's wrong. I'm not running anymore.

The music fades out, and Jason speaks into the microphone. "We're going to play one more song in this acoustic set, then get back to what y'all came here for." He taps a short beat on the bongos.

"You won't find this track on *Resolution* because it's not our story," Tim adds, his fingers poised over the frets of the bass guitar. "That doesn't mean it shouldn't be told. So we're going to hand this one off to our boy Nick to lead."

Nick glances at Tim, an unspoken conversation passing between them, then rakes a hand through his hair and exhales a deep breath. "This song is called 'Ripped Stitches.' It was written during a particularly dark period in my life . . ." Nick clears his throat, his gaze scanning the audience. My skin prickles, and I swear he's searching for me. "It's about leaving people behind who don't want to be left . . ."

Closing his eyes, Nick counts down from three and begins to play. The band joins in. A slow, somber melody reverberates around the House of Blues. Nick sings with such rawness and intensity I feel his voice running through every inch of my body.

I can't do anything but stand there, listening as the lyrics, so full of sadness and betrayal, chain me to their honesty. The way they talk about abandoning the people we love the most. How every choice has a cost, and no matter how high the stakes, the consequences are great just the same.

A fist squeezes my chest as I remember clutching a suitcase and whispering good-bye to Nick while he slept, the moment before our paths moved in opposite directions.

The moment before I left him behind.

I fold the memory inside of me, tuck it away. Maybe someday it won't hurt so much to remember. Maybe someday time won't carry so much weight.

I understand finally what Margaret meant when she talked about competing with ghosts. Just as Nick's ghost has haunted me these past five years, perhaps mine has lingered with him as well. Perhaps that's the true motivation behind why Nick ended things with Margaret—we're both still clinging to each other. At least I want that to be the case. I know now that running isn't the same as moving on or letting go, and I have to believe that Nick hasn't done the same either. Otherwise, where does that leave me?

I move back toward the stage and work my way to the front as the song ends. The crowd roars with cheers and applause. Nick gives a slight bow, then lifts the strap over his head and rests my father's old guitar in the stand beside his stool. He exits off the stage, and I intercept him when he steps into the crowd. His face is composed, unreadable as a label-less can.

"Why didn't you tell me you gave it all up?" I ask. "Why the half-truths?"

Nick remains silent, his deep blue eyes studying mine, his mouth a thin line. "Would it have mattered?"

I consider his question. It occurs to me that until recently I wasn't in a place to hear him, even if he had told me. "No, and it still doesn't because that's not what this is about."

A muscle twitches in his jaw. "Oh? What *is* it about, Lillie? I don't even think you know."

My throat constricts, but I press on. "It's about how it always comes back to you and me . . . how we never really left each other behind."

Shaking his head, Nick turns and walks to a pair of double doors at the side of the stage.

The hope starts to drain out of me.

Hope is dangerous that way. Once it sparks, it grabs hold and devours everything it touches until it's the only thing keeping you breathing. To put it out would mean death, swift and absolute, but without it what's the point of living at all?

I cling to the small sliver of hope still flickering within me and follow Nick into a corridor lined with framed concert posters. "Now who's running away?"

Nick stops in front of the bathrooms and faces me. "What do you want, Lillie?"

"Why didn't you find me?"

"What?"

"In Chicago," I say.

"Because I went there expecting the girl I remembered. Who I discovered was someone else." He glances at my bare left ring finger. "It's been so easy for you—new job, new *life*." His voice is controlled, but I hear traces of something I can't pinpoint simmering underneath.

"You think it was easy? It took everything I had to piece myself back together. There was no one there to catch me if I fell. I was alone, left to figure out how to navigate a whole new world of firsts on my own," I say, remembering when I moved into my tiny apartment with only my name on the contract, scoured job sites for positions I was in no way qualified for, ventured out into a city that was now my home but in no way felt like it.

He stares at me, his gaze impenetrable. "Yet you were able to move on so quickly."

I shake my head. "Drew and I . . . We're no longer engaged . . . because the thing is . . ." I take a deep breath. The truth is messy and scary and sometimes it hurts, but I must tell it, trust that the risk is worth it. "I love you, Nick."

There it is: the bravest thing I've ever said.

His eyes, his expression, it all hardens. "You don't even know who you are. How could you know what you feel?"

"You're wrong. I may still be figuring myself out, but

not this," I say. "Loving you is the biggest, most honest thing I know. It's consumed my whole life."

Nick's quiet a moment. When he finally speaks, his voice is a cold nothingness. "Listen, Lillie, if I've learned anything in the last five years it's that I have to be in charge of my own happiness. I have to make choices that are good for me. I know exactly who I am now, unlike you, and I won't fall back into old habits. I won't repeat my same mistakes."

At his words, my stomach drops, but then I realize it's actually my heart, which is so much heavier and more fragile. I watch as it shatters at my feet, strewn across the floor. Everything inside me is anguish.

Nick turns and stalks back down the hallway toward the main room, without hesitating, without glancing over his shoulder.

As if I mean nothing to him—as if I've *never* meant anything to him.

25

There's a spot in my father's backyard near the fence line, where if I lie on my back, feet facing the house, it's as though the trees touch the sky. They stretch and stretch and stretch like taffy until it's impossible to decipher where the branches end and the clouds begin. There, I can knock on the floor of heaven. There, time stands still.

Sometimes, back in Chicago, when it was late at night and I couldn't sleep, I would squeeze my eyes shut and imagine I was in that spot again, floating toward the sky, the leaves haloed in light. Curling my fingers into the sheets, I'd pretend the soft cotton was damp grass and the noisy traffic passing on the street outside our apartment was the next-door neighbor boy with the blue eyes and crooked grin strumming a Taylor acoustic guitar in his own backyard. I'd breathe in deep and convince my senses that the lingering greasy odor of Thai delivery was the scent of my father's famous chicken and dumplings drifting out the kitchen window.

Because if I returned to that place in my head, then nothing had changed.

I visit that spot now, minutes after driving my father home from the hospital. Kicking off my ballet flats, I lie down, wiggling my toes in the sun-bleached grass, and stare up at the sky, waiting for that floating feeling to overtake me, for time to pause. My body feels heavy, my limbs filled with crushing disappointment. Everything is different, lost. The trees have been trimmed, no longer climbing high, some of the branches stripped bare and reduced to stubs. I can see the side of Nick's old house through the gaps in the leaves and hear the impostors that are the Rosenbloom family discussing their choices for the upcoming Oscar nominations on the covered veranda.

That's the bitter thing about loss; there's no going back to what once was, and nothing stays the same after.

All I can do is move forward, but how am I supposed to do that when everything inside me wishes it could rewind, erase my mistakes, forge a new path where I never left and my father is healthy and Nick is still mine?

I close my eyes. The events of last night dance across my eyelids in a constant loop. *I won't repeat my same mistakes.* Nick may have forgiven me, but he won't forget. Only now do I fully comprehend the meaning behind the lyrics of "Ripped Stitches," when he sang about choices and consequences. Me leaving, our history, all the pain, it will forever stand between us. How could I have been so foolish to assume otherwise?

I wonder how many songs Nick has written with the blood of our failure; if the process has healed him. I wonder if channeling all his hurt and anger and betrayal into every verse and bridge and chorus, purging our history, allowed him to let go of us as thoroughly as he did. If only I could do the same.

If only I wanted to.

LATER IN THE DAY, I rummage under the bed for my old memento box, dust motes flying in the air. I can't seem to find it anywhere. Did my father toss it into the garbage? Panic wells inside me, but then I spot it shoved in a corner by the headboard, the word "Life" written in cursive on the side. Grabbing the scissors off the desk, I slice through the duct tape, fold back the flaps, and turn the box over, scattering the contents across the floor.

It's funny, most people would consider this stuff sentimental junk, but these items were my most prized possessions, and in a way, they still are. Each one carries a mark —the splotches on a stack of photographs from being displayed directly in the sun's path; the frayed edges of my newspaper columns because I was too lazy to cut them out properly; the chips in the guitar picks from an overzealous musician; the curled corners and creases in the cover of a small spiral notebook from years of shoving it into apron pockets, the pages filled with recipes, some unfinished.

With my back resting against the foot of the bed, I sift through it all, remembering. At some point, I hear the floorboards creak. My father stands in the doorway, his salt-and-pepper hair sticking up in weird directions. He's wearing his usual uniform. The sleeves are rolled up on his ratty plaid shirt. His skin still has a sallow quality but the dark bruises have yellowed a bit.

"Dad, you should be in bed sleeping. Dr. Preston's orders."

"Nonsense. Doc ain't nothing but a dream crusher," he says, stepping into the room. "I'm healthier than asparagus. Besides, it's my ticker that's messed up, not my legs."

I sigh. My father's been home from the hospital less than four hours and already he's up to his old tricks. I even caught him sneaking a bowl of peanut brittle ice cream for lunch, claiming it was included in the list of soft foods he's approved to eat. At least he tried to appear sheepish while I searched the house, ridding it of all junk food and hidden stashes. *Perhaps some things do stay the same,* I think as my father settles beside me on the floor.

"That's an oldie," he says, tapping the photograph in my hand.

I nod, smiling at the skinny, knobby-kneed versions of Nick and myself sitting on a mound of haystacks, my lips pressed against his cheek. A sign reading 14TH ANNUAL OAK HILL CORN MAZE hung from a gnarly tree in the background. Even with the hollowed-out pumpkin perched upon his head, Nick's hair ran wild beneath the makeshift hat. Our shoulders glowed golden in the afternoon sun.

"You were so in love with that boy, even back then."

I swipe my thumb across Nick's grinning face. "Yeah, I was." I am. I think we both know I never stopped. Even when I tried to push those feelings away, they always came back, more consuming than before. I hoped Nick hadn't stopped loving me either, that he could see past the worst parts of me, but just as I was wrong about so many other things, I was wrong about that, too. Now I have no choice but to accept it as punishment for my actions, for running away.

"I'm glad you stayed close with him," I say, but more than that I'm glad Nick was there for my father when I wasn't.

"It wasn't always like that. For a long time after you left, the boy wouldn't show his face anywhere, but then he did some growing on his own. Now I can't seem to get rid of him."

His words make my heart feel as though it's been ripped open. While I was out there trying to discover the real me, Nick was actually doing it. Now it's too late for us. As much as I want Nick to belong to me, people aren't items on a grocery shelf—they can't be owned.

My father must be able to tell I don't know how to respond because he says, "If my brain's working right, I think you threw a terror of a tantrum after I snapped this picture."

"That's because you wouldn't let me do the barrel ride when you gave Nick and Wes permission."

"Baby girl, all the barrels were occupied at the time. I told you to wait in line for the next available one, but you weren't hearing any of it."

"I was seven. What did you expect?"

My father laughs, his eyes crinkling in the corners. "You've always been too stubborn for your own good."

I nudge his side. "Who do you think I inherited that trait from?"

"Don't be pointing fingers at me. I'm the very definition of open-minded."

"Whatever you say, Dad." I rest my head against his shoulder.

My father picks up the spiral notebook and flips through it, his fingers dancing over the pages. "I remember this. You carried it around everywhere, always scribbling little notes or some such in it. Do you ever plan on finishing some of these?" He's paused on a French onion soup recipe that's only half complete. I got frustrated figuring out the correct sherry-to-cognac ratio to balance out the broth and gave up on it.

"I don't know. Maybe."

He smiles, wistful but also sad. "You're so much like her—your mother. When inspiration struck, there was no standing in her way. She'd jot down recipes on napkins, cracker boxes, old egg cartons, anything she could get her hands on."

I tense. "Dad, I don't want to talk about her."

"Even when you run your mouth off. She used to do that when she got flustered or annoyed at something. And the way you blush when you're embarrassed . . ."

My stomach twists. "I think we should get you back in bed." Straightening up, I reach for his arm, but he waves me off.

"Now, listen close, baby girl. You listening?" My father brushes the hair off my forehead. "You've got the best parts of your mother inside you, but you've also got some of me in there, too. It's what separates you from her. Don't ever forget that. Promise me you won't forget."

"I promise," I say, automatic, as I'm reminded of the day I discovered my mother's peach cobbler recipe, when I vowed something similar.

A vow I broke.

I wonder if I'll break this one, too.

For several moments, we're silent, lost in thought. I hear the rooster clock crowing downstairs, familiar, comforting. Until now I never realized how much I missed that annoying sound.

"I'm sorry I abandoned you," I say after a while, my eyes welling with tears.

"Don't go apologizing for that. You needed to get out there, do some searching on your own for a bit," my father says, setting the notebook aside. "Besides, you dropped a trail of crumbs when you left. I always knew you'd follow them home someday, even if it did take a little prodding from me to get you moving."

"I didn't. Still, I wish you would've told me the truth when you suffered the first episode. You shouldn't have kept something like that from me."

"I thought I could handle it on my own, and I didn't want to worry you."

I shake my head. "And your scheduled bypass operation and cough? Why were you so evasive about all that?"

My father sighs and says, "Parents make mistakes, baby girl. I've been thinking about what you said the other morning in the hospital, and I promise I'm going to try harder, do better. That situation with the ice cream was a minor slipup."

"Sure it was," I say, concealing the break in my voice with an attempt at a laugh.

"Hey, now." He cups my face, wiping away the wetness with his thumb. "Someone's got to keep you on your toes. Otherwise, you'll get rusty as an old tuna fish can."

This time I do laugh, and it fills me with a weightless sensation.

My father chuckles softly to himself like he does when he's musing. "It seems like yesterday you were no taller than the counter. I remember how you used to dress up as the Chef Boyardee man, but my old white coat was too big on you and the chef's hat didn't fit your head, so it was always dropping into your eyes."

I smile, remembering how I would stand on a step stool gesturing with a wooden spoon as though I was the conductor of our kitchen, bossing my father around and dictating recipe instructions to him.

"Now look at you," he says. "All grown up with a master's degree and a career of your own. You're strong and beautiful and independent. You don't need me protecting you anymore, but sometimes it's easy for me to forget that. You'll have to forgive your old man for his stupidity."

"I'll always need you, Dad," I say, squeezing his knee. "Always."

He covers my hand. The calluses on his palm scratch against my knuckles. "I know that, but I also know you've got a life to return to. It was unfair of me to pull the rug out from under you like that. If Chicago is where you want to be, then I'll get Ernie to run things until I arrange for something more permanent. Just promise to visit every now and again. But don't even think about bailing on the Upper Crust. Sullivan Grace will have my hide if you do."

"I'm not going anywhere, and I'm not bailing. The only place I want to be is right here with you." *Which is where I should have been all along.*

My father frowns, the lines around his mouth and eyes deepening. "What about that boyfriend of yours and the big promotion?"

I bite my lip. "I sort of quit my job and broke up with Drew . . ." Now I don't know what I'm going to do. All I know is the life I had planned in Chicago isn't what I want.

My father is quiet a second. Then pats my leg and says, "You know sometimes you have to lose who you are before you can find who you are. Even if that means starting from scratch, making a whole new life for yourself here in Dallas —with or without the diner—I know you'll figure out how to get yourself found again."

I gulp in some air, fighting back a sob. Somehow my father always knows the exact words I need to hear. I don't know what my future looks like, but that's okay. *I'm* okay. "I love you, Dad. So much."

"Love you, too, baby girl." My father wraps an arm around me and kisses the top of my head. I hug him as if I'm five again, so tight he may burst. The soft fabric of his shirt smells like hash browns, even though it's been washed since he wore it last.

"Easy there," he says, loosening my hold. "I ain't no Tonka truck anymore. Now get going. You need to practice for the Upper Crust. Second place isn't in this family's vocabulary."

I smile as a tear slips down my cheek. Right then, I've never been more thankful for my father's antics and stubborn ways, for bringing me back here. Despite how jumbled everything is in my mind, I'm also overcome with certainty that I'm finally on the right path.

————

WHEN ALL ELSE FAILS, cook. That's the motto I followed anytime life turned upside down. *None of this making lemonade outta lemons nonsense. The acid will rot your teeth,* as my father likes to say.

Yet I turned my back on all that, fought against it, and I don't even know why anymore. Right now there's nowhere else I'd rather be than here in my father's outdated kitchen with only my thoughts and the promise of fresh ravioli on the horizon. Maybe that's what happens when you run so far from the place you belong you end up lost. Maybe that's what happens when you lose everything, period. I thought I had it all decided—my relationship with Drew, my career, my life in Chicago—but that's all disappeared. My father's right. Maybe I had to lose who I am before I can find who I am. Now it's up to me to do that.

I measure a trio of paprikas—hot, smoked, and sweet —into my palm and dump it onto the ground pork and other spices. As I combine the ingredients, an image of Nick playing with the Randy Hollis Band, my father's old acoustic guitar under his arm, crystallizes in my mind again. How when he sang, his voice sounded almost haunting, unguarded. The image fades, replaced with another, the day Nick received his acceptance letter to medical school. I remember how after he shared the news, he looked me in the eye and said that dreams died every day, especially silly, childish ones like writing songs for a living. That was part of growing up—accepting the future for what it was and not what you wanted it to be. Besides, becoming a surgeon was what he'd been working toward since he was a kid.

Except sometimes a dream rises like a phoenix from the ashes and rebirths itself as reality, changing course and altering a person's history forever. A sense of pride rushes through me for all Nick has accomplished. I only wish he would have achieved those dreams *with* me, not *because* of me, because I was a coward.

I set aside the homemade chorizo to allow the flavors to meld. I wash the gunk from under my fingernails and watch as birds sweep between the trees in the front yard, their wings rustling the leaves. The sky is a vivid reddish pink. Across the street, a little girl in a baggy swimsuit plays in an inflatable pool, while an elderly couple supervises from Adirondack chairs.

There's something special about seeing the world from inside this kitchen. How it seems to make things move slower, make worries lighter. Even when I tried to pretend otherwise, I still gravitated toward its familiarity. I think back to the morning with the cinnamon griddle cakes and the knowing look on Annabelle's face. I wonder if she suspected it was only a matter of time before I was back here permanently.

The floorboards creak above my head. Who knows what kind of trouble my father is causing now. He refuses to stay in bed like Dr. Preston instructed. He claims remaining sedentary forces him to twitch. I think I should order that therapeutic massager chair as soon as possible. Maybe it'll help him relax and adjust to his new normal.

I wipe down my work area and gather the ingredients for the pasta dough. After forming the flour into a mound, I create a large well in the center, then crack some eggs into the hole and add olive oil, salt, and water, beating it all together with a fork. It takes several minutes to incorporate the egg mixture into the flour, but the result is a tacky dough the color of clarified butter.

My shoulders throb as I knead. It's a good ache, one I haven't felt in years, but somehow it's like my body remembers. I thought slipping into my old routine would feel strange, but the burning in my muscles and the delicious smells invading the kitchen fill me from my toes to the tips of my ears.

It's more than that, too.

The raw physicality of rolling out paper-thin sheets of dough, the cadence of dropping small dollops of the chorizo filling along each, the precision of sealing and cutting out the ravioli, anchors me here.

I plate up a steaming portion and top it with a corn and basil sauce thickening on the stove. When I take a bite of ravioli, the sweet kernels burst on my tongue, melding with the spiciness of the meat and the rich egg pasta, cooked perfectly al dente. I take another bite and close my eyes because *darn it's delicious,* sighing as my body collapses against the counter. It's warm and creamy and tastes just like home. Like where I'm supposed to be.

It's all so ridiculously obvious I laugh. I understand now what Nick meant about pretending and what my father said about finding myself. This is what I want. This is all I've ever wanted—to discover and create and experiment, with new recipes and new ingredients. How did I ever think I could fight against something that's as unconscious to me as breathing?

A single, sharpening thought rises within me: *I want to win.*

I'm a bit rusty at the whole baking thing, but the process of crafting something from the palms of my own hands is second nature. The deconstructed strudel may have started out as a way to spite my father, but that doesn't change that it's a champion recipe. That it's *my* recipe.

The thought flashes again: *I want to win.*

No, I *will* win the Upper Crust.

My way and on my own terms.

26

THE RITZ CARLTON BALLROOM IS A CIRCUS.

I've participated in various amateur culinary competitions over the years, but none have compared to this. The Upper Crust committee has spared no expense for the event. Individual kitchens have been set up along the perimeter, each stocked with a freestanding gas range and convection oven, minirefrigerator, and ingredient storage bins. Wooden tables, configured in a U shape, act as prep and work areas for each kitchen. In the center of the room, the judges' table is perched on a raised platform. Seven chairs line one side, a cast-bronze nameplate in front of each. Floral arrangements are scattered throughout the ballroom, and there's even a news crew staked outside the entrance, interviewing people as they pass through the doors.

"How's Old Man Jack handling being cooped up at home all day?" Annabelle asks me as she leans against one of the prep tables and pops a peach slice into her mouth. She's eaten almost a whole peach already. If she keeps it up, there won't be enough for the deconstructed strudel.

"He's going stir-crazy. Laziness isn't in his DNA, or so he likes to remind me every chance he gets. Dr. Preston has him on house arrest for another week," I say, measuring the ingredients for the phyllo dough into a glass bowl. "Will you preheat the oven to three fifty for me?"

She nods, setting the temperature as instructed. "Think he'll break out anyway to come to the awards ceremony?"

"That's a given."

Annabelle snickers.

"What are you laughing about?"

"Nothing," she says. "I'm picturing Old Man Jack sneaking out of his bedroom window like we used to do."

"Yeah, except with my luck, he'd take a tumble off the roof and shatter every bone in his body. Then I'd have to deal with that, too."

"At least he'd be bedridden and wouldn't be able to slip off somewhere," she says, then switches gears with her usual abruptness. "When are you adopting a cat?"

"Excuse me?" I say as I incorporate the ingredients together until the dough is soft and sticky.

"You know. Because of 'the unmentionable.'" Annabelle's been referring to Nick dismissing me at the House of Blues as "the unmentionable." "How long until you become one of those bitter old ladies with twenty cats instead of children?"

"Hey," I say, flinging cider vinegar at her nose. "There's still hope for me, and I like cats."

"Not with the way you've been moping around."

"I haven't been moping."

"Liar. Though you could have saved yourself the grief if you would've read the liner notes or listened to me all those times I tried to tell you."

"I know, I know," I say. "He really quit medicine? Just like that?"

Annabelle nods. "After the incident at the football tournament, Nick went to his parents' house and told them he was done with all of it. That same day, Nick picked up his guitar and started writing songs again. I think he used it as a form of therapy, but mostly I think it made him feel closer to you."

"I sincerely doubt that," I say, remembering the way Nick referred to us, what we shared, as a mistake.

Annabelle shrugs. "Believe what you want."

A Junior League volunteer races over and whispers something in her ear. Annabelle sighs and looks at me. "One of the other competitors told Paulette Bunny that whipped cream reduces wrinkles. Apparently she got some up her nose and is now experiencing shortness of breath." She rolls her eyes. "I need to handle this. I'll check in on you later."

"Have fun—" She's gone before I can finish. I dump the mixing bowl over on the floured prep table and form the phyllo dough into a mound.

There are forty of us participating in this year's Upper Crust competition, each working furiously. Well, everyone except for the guy in the kitchen beside me. He's wearing an actual chef's jacket with his name embroidered above the breast pocket. Steve Ayers, it reads in blue thread. He's garnered the attention of half of the Junior League volunteers, including Bernice Rimes, who is carrying on like a girl with a playground crush, batting her eyelashes and rambling on with those goldfish lips of hers. The guy, Steve, is offering the ladies bites of chocolate and regaling them with stories of his culinary successes. He's acting as though he's a celebrity chef rather than a competitor. Maybe he should be more concerned with baking his chocolate stout cake than with entertaining if he intends on finishing in the allotted time.

Bernice must catch me staring at her because she barrels over to me, a pinched expression on her face. Her overly processed yellow hair doesn't budge with the movements. Even the curls, which should sway, stay put. It reminds me of the two-dollar cranberry sauce that plops out of the can still shaped like the can, with the ridges and everything.

"I heard Nick rejected you," she says, her southern accent dragging out the words. "You know, *everyone's* talking about it."

"Is that so?" I say, kneading the dough.

"Sure is," she says. Bernice is waiting to get a rise out of me. "Is it true you burst into tears?"

"That's the rumor going around?" I say as I lift the dough and dust more flour underneath.

"Oh no. The rumor is *much* worse. I was being polite."

Of course she was. "I've been too busy worrying about my sick father to cry over something like that." Truth be told, I did cry to Wes and Annabelle about what happened with Nick, but I'm not about to admit that to Bernice or give her the satisfaction. "Now can you go back to your pathetic attempts at flirting with Steve over there so I can do something productive?"

She gapes at me. I fight the urge to squeeze her cheeks together to make her goldfish lips pucker even more. With a scowl, Bernice turns on her heel and stalks away. Finally, some peace and quiet.

My back aches as I continue to knead the phyllo dough. I sprinkle more flour on the prep table, then press the dough with the heel of my hand, fold it over, and rotate it twenty-five degrees. Ordinarily I'd let the hook attachment on the stand mixer knead the dough for me to save time, but the competition guidelines state that all items in the recipe must be made on site and without the aid of special cooking equipment unless otherwise authorized. Since I'm supposed to be creating my mother's summer peach cobbler, which only requires a rubber spatula and two large bowls, I couldn't exactly ask Sullivan Grace for permission to bring in a stand mixer without drawing attention to myself.

After another few minutes of kneading, I shape the dough into a ball, brush it with vegetable oil, wrap it in plastic wrap, and leave it on the table to rest. While the phyllo dough proofs, I prepare the sweet cheese and peach mixture, adding in pomegranate seeds at the last minute.

"Your entry is looking divine, sugar. Like something you might find at one of those discount grocery stores," says the older woman in the station next to me. Her tone is sweet and warm, but her upturned nose and disapproving features betray her.

She's been cutting butter into flour with a fork for the past ten minutes, throwing away at least as many batches. Good thing she brought plenty of extra ingredients. I want to tell her that the butter isn't cold enough because she left it on the table instead of in the minirefrigerator, and the mixture should resemble split peas not cheese puffs, but I don't think my father would approve of me fraternizing with the enemy.

I arrange my face into a smile, and channeling Sullivan Grace, say in a phony voice, "Well, bless your heart, aren't you so nice? I wouldn't want you to feel intimidated, so here's a helpful hint. Maybe consider cheating next time. Bad pies in a box are just as effective and significantly less effort than you're exerting. That's a little tidbit for you to noodle on."

The woman mutters something under her breath and returns to destroying her piecrust. She should've taken my advice.

I unwrap the dough and separate it into chunks. It should rest more, but rolling out the dough into layers is going to consume a large portion of my time and patience. I grab a French rolling pin and get moving, flattening and stretching until the sheets are the thickness of card stock. Before long, all the dough is used up. Several of the sheets have rips in them, but those can be hidden. I only need one perfect layer for the top. I start assembling, placing the sweet cheese and peach mixture on the bottom of a baking dish and then topping with the phyllo dough, generously buttering between each sheet.

As I'm coating the final layer with butter, Annabelle rushes up to me. "Better get that in the oven pronto. Sullivan Grace is on her way over. One peek at that," she says, waving at my deconstructed strudel, "and she'll feed you to the Dumpster rats out back."

"I'm hurrying. I'm hurrying," I say, picking up the dish and sliding it onto the middle rack. I kick the oven door shut behind me, but I lose my balance in the process and collide with the prep table. Flour billows in my face. I sneeze.

"Lillie, dear, why are you wiggling your nose like that?" Sullivan Grace taps one of her low-heeled shoes on the carpet.

I brush off my apron. "Why, is that considered unattractive?"

"Yes. Very," she says, smoothing her already smooth navy couture dress. The rose-gold bangles adorning her forearm wink under the ballroom lights. "Now, what is the status of the cobbler?"

"Everything's in order," I say with a thumbs-up, because I know it will irritate her, even if she doesn't show it. Sullivan Grace's always so composed, but it's like my father said, someone has to keep her on her toes.

Annabelle snorts.

"Good, good," Sullivan Grace says. Then she stands there, staring at me expectantly. I stare dumbly back. Finally with a flick of her wrist, she says, "Well, stop dilly-dallying, dear. You don't have all day."

"I'm not," I say, but then I remember she thinks I'm submitting my mother's peach cobbler for judging, which takes significantly less time to prep and bake than the strudel. I wouldn't need to start making it until an hour before the competition ends. So I have no real choice but to play along. "I was about to—"

"Uh, Lillie?" Annabelle interrupts.

I look at her. There's a crease between her brows. "Yeah?"

"The oven is smoking."

27

Ribbons of smoke are curling out around the oven door.

Please don't be ruined, I pray, then run over and turn on the oven light. I peer through the window. Flames are licking up from the bottom and around the sides of the strudel. *Crap.* This has never—and I mean *never*—happened to me before. Did I preheat too early? Set the temperature too high?

Panic pulses through me. I turn off the oven, allow the fire to die out, and slowly open the door. A blast of smoke shoots out. Coughing, my eyes burning and watery, I try to wave it away but the oven keeps exhaling plumes of smoke. I shove on some mitts, stick my hands into the inferno, praying my dress doesn't catch a lingering spark, and yank out the dish, hurling it onto the stovetop. The deconstructed strudel is burned but recognizable. Maybe Sullivan Grace won't notice it's not my mother's peach cobbler.

No such luck.

"I'm disappointed in you, dear," she says as wisps of

smoke continue to rise. Shaking her head, she walks away, tugging the pearls around her neck.

An audience has gathered around me now, comprised of a handful of other challengers and several judges, who have been wandering around the ballroom and observing since the competition started.

One of the judges, an instructor at Le Cordon Bleu— at least according to his chef's jacket—inspects inside the oven. He removes a palmful of ashes and a small scrap of paper with burned edges. I recognize the handwriting on it as mine. Somehow my recipe notes went into the oven with the strudel and caught fire. Frustration sweeps through me. How could I sabotage myself like that? Why wasn't I more careful? I was in such a hurry to get the strudel into the oven I didn't bother to check that there wasn't anything stuck to the baking dish.

"Well, this is unfortunate," the judge says, wiping his hands together over the trash. "I hope you have a backup plan."

A fellow competitor, a woman about my age with sucked-in cheeks and glasses that are probably supposed to be fashionable but instead distort her eyes, pokes at the blackened phyllo dough. "Perhaps she just can't cook and should give up now," the woman says, wrinkling her nose.

"Or maybe the oven had heartburn and thought burping flames would solve the problem," I deadpan, pulling off the mitts and tucking them into my apron pockets.

Some people laugh, while others have blank stares on their faces. The bug-eyed competitor glares at me. Wannabe celebrity chef Steve Ayers is still too busy stroking his ego to notice the commotion happening around him, but the woman in the station on the other side of me has a smile plastered on her face. I suppose I deserve that.

Another judge rests a hand on my shoulder. I recognize her as the food critic from *The Dallas Morning News*. "Per Upper Crust guidelines, you won't be granted extended time or provided additional ingredients. You'll need to make do with what you have, which includes using the oven designated for you specifically."

I nod, contemplating my options, which at this point are limited.

"All right, people. Show's over," Annabelle says with a clap of her hands. "Quit gawking."

The crowd disperses, Annabelle trailing behind like a shepherd herding a flock of baffled sheep. I chuck the strudel, dish and everything, in the trash, wondering how I'm going to fix this. The whole thing would be hilarious if I wasn't so screwed. I spread my hands flat on the prep table and press my fingers into the top, forcing all the frustration out of my body and into the wood.

Think, think, think.

Resigned, I sift through the minifridge and storage bins, removing the ingredients for my mother's peach cobbler. There isn't enough time to make another batch of phyllo dough, and my pride will never recover if I don't submit *something* to the judges for consideration. Not to mention my father will murder me.

I spot my mother's handwritten recipe card wedged between the baking powder and cornstarch. It's not like I need it for reference; the five steps have been branded on my brain like a kitschy commercial jingle since I found the card in my father's kitchen all those years ago. Still, I read them anyway. A lump forms in my throat.

As I scan the ingredient list and instructions, I notice

the recipe calls for yellow peaches instead of white and a batter topping rather than a drop-biscuit. I frown.

It's as if my head has been clogged all this time and it's finally cleared. I understand what everyone's been trying to tell me.

None of this has been about my mother.

It's been about *me*.

The peach cobbler may have started out as my mother's recipe, but somewhere along the way, it became *my* recipe, made special with my own personal touches like so many other recipes that make up the diner's menu and daily Blue Plate Specials. With each recipe, I removed a little something here or added a little something there, tweaking the original until I created a dish uniquely *mine*.

My father's right. My mother lives in me, but she's only a small part of who I am, not all that I am. Her actions don't define me, they never have. It's not her blood that flows through the Spoons. It's mine and my father's and every other person who crosses its threshold, keeping it breathing and thriving. My mother has no presence there anymore.

Something unlocks inside me, a truth I've denied for far too long. My heart seems to know my decision before it crystallizes in my head.

I'm taking over the diner. It's a strong thought, beating in rhythm with my heart. "I'm taking over the diner," I say aloud. There's an edge of urgency in my voice. I've never been so sure about anything in my life.

A microphone squeals, startling me. Sullivan Grace's voice comes through the speakers set up around the ballroom. "Challengers, you have one hour remaining until entries are due to the judges. Good luck."

All at once, the desire to win surges up again. I spring into action, slicing the remaining thawed, flash-frozen white peaches, and combining them with sugar, cornstarch, and cinnamon in a glass bowl. While the peaches release their juices to form a syrup, I whip together the biscuit dough and melt butter in a large cast-iron skillet I smuggled from the diner, tossing in the peach mixture and letting it cook for a bit. *I'm taking over the diner,* I think again, even stronger than before. It's a chant, spurring me on as I dollop spoonfuls of biscuit dough over the fruit so it resembles a "cobbled" effect. I put it in the oven, crossing my fingers that there isn't another episode that necessitates calling the fire department.

Normally I have the self-control of an obsessive health nut, but right now I feel like a fad dieter faced with a room overflowing with cheeseburgers, because I can't help cracking open the oven door and peeking at the cobbler while it bakes. If my father were here, he'd scold me.

I switch to cleaning my station. As I'm organizing the dry ingredients in the storage bins, I catch a glimpse of Margaret entering the ballroom, gold envelopes and stacks of papers in hand. She's been avoiding me since I arrived this morning, not that I blame her. Our eyes meet. There's none of the usual hardness in them, nor is there any smugness on her face. Or maybe I'm seeing Margaret differently now, as she really is: someone of worth. Someone important to Nick. Someone he maybe even loved.

I nod at her, but she cuts her eyes away. Margaret walks over to the judges' table, placing an envelope and a stack of what I assume are the ballot cards at each spot. Challengers can submit an entry in one of six categories—cookies, cakes and cupcakes, brownies and bars, chocolate, fruit desserts, and pies. The winner of each category will be eligible for best in show.

"Eight minutes," Annabelle's voice rings out as the judges settle in their seats. A flurry of activity erupts around them as competitors scramble to put the final touches on their dishes. Lucky for me, part of the charm of cobbler is the rustic way it's displayed—straight from the oven in a cast-iron skillet—so all I can do is wait for the timer to ding. Some people may finish with a scoop of vanilla-bean ice cream or a drizzle of heavy cream at the end, but in my universe serving cobbler with anything other than a fork and a bib is a sacrilege.

I notice the woman next to me has abandoned the pie idea and is instead frosting a single-layer Hummingbird Cake. To my surprise, it actually smells edible, bordering on tasty. I wonder if the woman will be deemed ineligible for changing her entry or if Sullivan Grace's been lying to me this whole time.

Somehow Steve Ayers has managed to complete the chocolate stout cake. Now he's pouring Double Brown Stout from Dallas's own Deep Ellum Brewing Company into pint glasses—one for each judge, it seems—and adding a scoop of ice cream for a grown-up float. As much as I hate to admit it, the whole presentation looks so professional it could grace the glossy pages of a food magazine. Maybe he really is some kind of celebrity chef.

For a moment, my confidence wavers. I underestimated my fellow competitors' skill level and the seriousness in which they'd approach the Upper Crust.

The timer dings. I pull on some mitts and take the cobbler out of the oven. The peach juices, thick and bubbling, threaten to escape the skillet, and the drop biscuits are golden brown. Perfection. The smell alone is enough to declare me the winner. The worry squeezing my chest relaxes. I grate some nutmeg over the top as a horn sounds.

"Time's up, time's up. Utensils down, everybody. Utensils down!" I guess it's Bernice's turn at the microphone.

Around the ballroom, people step away from their dishes with their hands raised, though one guy continues working. Sullivan Grace strides over to him, still a picture of poise. The guy is so focused on cutting a pan of Hello Dolly bars into squares he doesn't see her standing there. Sullivan Grace marks something on a piece of paper and sets it on the prep table in front of him. He glances at it, then finally at Sullivan Grace. With pleading eyes, he says something to Sullivan Grace, but she shakes her head in that admonishing way of hers. I bet he's been disqualified, which is unfortunate for him because those Hello Dolly bars look divine. As if in confirmation, the guy unties his apron and throws it in Sullivan Grace's face, then storms out of the ballroom. The news crew captures the whole thing on camera. I've never seen Sullivan Grace appear so shocked.

Bernice rattles instructions into the microphone. Challengers are to deposit their dishes in Dessert Heaven, a small room off the ballroom lined with tables designated for each category. The fruit desserts will be judged first. Thank goodness. While cobbler is delicious at room temperature, it's best enjoyed warm.

As I enter Dessert Heaven, I notice each table has roughly an equal number of dishes. Placing the skillet on a hot pad, I scope out the competition. There's traditional apple pie, mint brownies, chocolate turtle cheesecake, violet macarons, key lime pie, cherry turnovers, and even snickerdoodles. Still, none compare to my peach cobbler. Best in show is mine to win.

Junior League volunteers sweep into the room, each grabbing a fruit dessert. I follow behind the girl carrying my skillet. The scent of cinnamon and ripe peaches floats past my nose. My stomach gurgles. The volunteers deliver the entries—a loganberry tart, a banana trifle, pear clafouti, a plum crumble, mini citrus pavlovas, a triple-berry crisp, and my peach cobbler—to the judges and divvy out small, individual portions of each. Without hesitating, the judges pick up a fork in one hand and a pen in the other. My eyes are glued on them as they take their first bites and scribble something on the ballot cards. Their expressions betray nothing. The atmosphere in the ballroom feels tense.

The judges continue to bite, taste, scribble. Bite, taste, scribble. All with poker faces.

Doubt creeps in again, pricking up and down my spine.

When the Junior League volunteers bring out the pies, I return to my station, unable to watch any longer. My father is there, chatting with Annabelle.

"Baby girl, what's this I hear about you almost burning down the hotel?" he says with a frown. "You know we ain't got the insurance to cover that." A part of his bandage peeks out from under his shirt collar, hiding the scar that runs down the middle of his chest. I wonder if I'll ever not blame myself for not being here when my father needed me. Maybe someday when the scar fades my guilt will fade, too.

"There was only a little smoke," I say, leaning against a prep table.

Annabelle snorts. I peg her with my oven mitts. She nudges my side and winks.

"Dr. Preston is going to chain you to the bed if he finds out you snuck out of the house," I say.

"Don't be dramatic, baby girl." My father scratches the scruff on his jaw. "Besides, Wes drove me, so it's his fault."

"What'd I do now?" Wes says, joining us. He's eating a white chocolate chunk macadamia nut cookie.

"Kidnap me," my father says at the same time Annabelle says, "Where'd you get that?"

"From that room over there," Wes says, pointing to Dessert Heaven.

With his attention diverted, I steal a bite of cookie. *Darn, it's good*—soft and chewy with the right amount of sweetness. The macadamia nuts are so buttery they melt on my tongue.

"Wesley, those aren't for public consumption," Annabelle says, hitting his shoulder.

"Well, then maybe there should be a sign indicating that." He breaks off a piece of cookie, launches it in the air, and catches it in his mouth.

Annabelle mutters something about how Wes better have left enough for the judges and beelines over to the room.

"Why's she so upset?" Wes says, polishing off the cookie. When he finishes chewing, he adds, "You'd think she'd be thanking me for wiping out some of the competition for you, Jelly Bean."

"Turners don't win by cheating," my father pipes up. "We've got too much talent for that. Or we did before baby girl nearly burned the place down."

I shake my head. Will he ever listen to me?

"How much longer until the winners are announced?" Wes says.

I shrug. "No idea, though I'd guess not too long. The judges have already moved on to the brownies and bars category."

"I'm gonna check it out. Stay out of trouble, you two." My father cracks his knuckles, then wanders off in the direction of Sullivan Grace.

Wes looks at me. "Shouldn't we be the ones telling him that?"

I laugh. "You read my mind."

While we wait for the judging to finish, we chat about

SMU's upcoming football game against its biggest rival, Texas Christian University. Wes explains how he has the linebackers running stairs in full gear and dragging tractor tires up and down the field in preparation.

"I promised the boys some stick-to-your-ribs home cookin' when it's all over," Wes says, patting his stomach. "Maybe after I get back from my trip, you can whip us up some brisket and coleslaw?"

My brow furrows. "Where are you going?"

Wes's face turns serious. "Tennessee."

My eyes widen. It takes a moment for his words to sink in. Tired of the passive-aggressive comments and constant pulling, Wes distanced himself from both his parents until they stopped putting him in the middle. It took some time, but eventually he and his mother mended their relationship, but as far as I know, Wes hasn't visited his father since the summer after his college graduation.

"Why now?" I say, though he doesn't seem to hear me. His focus has shifted to Annabelle emerging from Dessert Heaven. I tap his leg with my shoe, snapping him out of his daze.

Wes picks my oven mitts off the floor and tosses them into one of the ingredient bins. "Pops called yesterday. He's getting married again, Jelly Bean. This Sunday. Her name's Wendy, a secretary in his office. She's got three kids, all grown."

"Yeah?"

Wes nods. "He asked if I'd consider attending the ceremony."

"What'd you tell him?"

"No, at first." He hesitates. "After thinking about it some more, I changed my mind. I leave after the game on Saturday."

I study his face. "Wes, that's . . . I don't even . . ." I trail off, overcome with rightness. "Is Annabelle going with you?"

He shakes his head. "No, we're not at that point yet. This is something I need to handle on my own, you know?"

I squeeze his arm, understanding all too well. Wes conjures a weak smile. "I'm getting there, Jelly Bean."

"I also have news," I say.

Wes raises his eyebrows. "What's that?"

"I'm taking over the Spoons. Officially," I say, happy to finally tell someone.

"That isn't exactly news, Jelly Bean," Wes says, bumping my shoulder. "We all knew you'd come around eventually. You don't fit anywhere else but here."

I grin because he's right, feeling grounded for the first time in years.

"Challengers, the judges have finished tallying the scores." Sullivan Grace's voice fills the ballroom. "Please make your way to the stage for the awards ceremony."

"Here goes nothing," I say, removing my apron and smoothing the fabric of my dress.

Wes tugs on my ear. "Knock 'em dead, Jelly Bean."

I swat his hand away, then head over to the stage at the far end of the room. Apart from the Cordon Bleu instructor standing behind a lectern, the rest of the judging panel has assembled off to the side with the Junior League volunteers and Upper Crust committee members. I notice Margaret is absent. Several news crews and photographers line the walls surrounding the stage. In the area in front, competitors have formed into groups, one for each category. I join the others in the fruit desserts section.

Paulette Bunny, who seems to have recovered from the whipped cream incident, walks onto the stage and hands a stack of envelopes to the Cordon Bleu instructor. I wonder

if he's been designated the head judge. She whispers something in his ear. He steps back from the lectern and
gestures for her to take his place. Paulette adjusts the
microphone, then clears her throat, gathering everyone's
attention.

"Challengers, on behalf of the Junior League of Dallas
Park Cities, we would like to offer our sincerest gratitude
for your fundraising efforts and participation in this year's
Upper Crust competition." Paulette leans away from the
microphone and claps. The crowd echoes with their
applause. When the sound dies down, she continues.
"Additional thanks to the Upper Crust planning committee, the panel of judges, the various corporate sponsors,
each individual contributor, and the League volunteers
who devoted their time and energy to make Junior
League's biggest event another rousing success." More
applause erupts. "All funds raised will be donated to the
Dallas Food Bank and will provide assistance to families in
our community. Once again, thank you. Now on to the
awards ceremony."

The instructor from Le Cordon Bleu resumes his
stance behind the microphone. "Each category will be
announced in the reverse order of judging," he says,
straight to business. "I ask all winners to please remain on
stage for best in show. Let's begin."

A hush falls over the ballroom. My heart hammers.
The anticipation makes me feel as though I'm a warrior
battling in Bocuse d'Or—the world's most prestigious culinary contest—rather than a participant in an amateur
baking competition for charity.

One by one, the judge reads off the first-place winners
in each category—a hazelnut and fig linzer cookie, a
funfetti blondie, a classic strawberry cake. The woman with
the modelesque cheeks and bug-eye glasses nails it with her

toffee crunch butterscotch pie, while Steve Ayers dominates the chocolate category with his chocolate stout cake and grown-up float. No shocker there.

"It's time for the final category, the fruit desserts." As the instructor from Le Cordon Bleu says this, all doubt flies from my mind. A calmness settles over me. "In first place, with her skillet peach cobbler, Lillie Claire Turner."

Even though I was expecting my name to be called, my heart jumps in my chest. A grin spreads across my face. People slap my back and offer congratulations. From somewhere behind me, I hear Wes whooping. I meet the other first-place winners on stage. A camera flashes in my eyes. I can't stop smiling.

"Well done," the judge says, peering at each of us. "Now the moment everyone's been waiting for. The grand prize recipe, deemed best in show, will be showcased in the Junior League of Dallas Park Cities cookbook. The winner will have a feature in *D Magazine* and earn bragging rights for a year."

Hollering and whistling sounds from the audience.

"And this year's Upper Crust champion is . . ." The Cordon Bleu instructor opens a gold envelope and pulls out a card.

Here it comes. I can see my name forming on his lips.

I step forward, away from the other category winners, ready to claim my title.

"Courtney Higgins, with her hazelnut and fig linzer cookie!"

28

I LOST TO A LINZER COOKIE?

Cheers and applause sweep through the ballroom. A surprised-looking Courtney Higgins steps around me and crosses the stage to accept her prize. Bernice hands her a trophy, then Courtney ducks her head so the *Dallas Morning News* food critic can drape a medal around her neck. The gold medallion dangling from the striped ribbon twinkles under the chandelier lights.

Shaking my head, I hop off the stage and into a sea of fellow competitors and people with photo ID press badges clipped to their clothes. My father is waiting on the periphery of the crowd, arms folded across his chest. I expect disappointment to be etched on his features, a frown weighing down his mustache. Runner-up isn't in our family's vocabulary, after all, but his eyes are bright and shining, brimming with pride. I smile, pride blossoming in me as well. My father squeezes me tight against him, the fabric of his plaid shirt soft against my cheek.

"Them judges must have wonky taste buds, is all," he

says, ruffling my hair. "There's always next year. You've got plenty of time to create a game plan. If you want."

"Well . . ." I look up at him as a grin spreads across my face. "My schedule's going to be pretty packed with running the Spoons full-time, but I suppose I can figure out something."

My father opens his mouth to speak but no words come out. Finally he kisses the top of my head and says, "That's real good, baby girl. Real good."

"Lillie."

I jump, my breath catching in my throat at the sound of Nick's voice behind me.

I spin around to face him, but I should have gathered my bearings first, prepared myself more. Nick stands in front of me in a crisp charcoal-gray suit that conforms to his broad shoulders and muscular arms before tapering to his trim waist. Paired with a checked shirt and tie . . . God, he looks incredible. Before, I would've assumed he'd been at a Baylor Medical event, but now I wonder if he came from a meeting with another musician about a potential project.

"About time you showed up, son," my father interjects, giving Nick a hefty pat on the shoulder. "Now if you'll both excuse me, I'm gonna ask that pretty lady over there if she wants to grab a fruit smoothie with me since I'm the poster child for health these days." My father strolls toward the stage, where Sullivan Grace is presenting a five-figure check to a representative from the Dallas Food Bank. More cameras flash.

"I thought you were adamant about not taking over the diner," Nick says.

"I guess I changed my mind . . ." I bite my lip. "The Spoons is in my blood, kind of like you and songwriting."

He steps toward me. "I knew you'd figure it out."

His eyes are an intense, startling blue, and as I gaze at him, I feel myself falling—as I always do—under his pull, a slow, golden warmth that spreads through me. I notice he attempted to style his hair, and my fingers twitch to comb through the silky strands to bring back the unruliness.

"What do you want, Nick?" I ask, keeping my tone neutral even as my stomach clenches and unclenches.

He pins me with a steady stare, and my pulse quickens. "There were snowflakes on your eyelashes," he says. "When I saw you walking down Michigan Avenue. You were bundled in a million layers and had on this knit cap with a crochet flower on one side, and there were snowflakes on your eyelashes. You looked *so fucking beautiful.* Like Christmas morning, like the soul of every song I've ever written."

The ballroom noises, the conversations floating around me, the overhead music—it all goes quiet. All this time I swore my mind was playing tricks on me when I saw him standing outside Crate & Barrel that winter afternoon, but as it turns out he really was there.

"I was honest when I said you were different from the woman who left me behind. You were *smiling,* Lillie, happy and unburdened and living life," he continues, taking another step forward. "It took seeing you like that for me to understand that loving you meant leaving you alone. And I do love you. I've *always* loved you. You're the bedrock of everything that matters in my life."

My heart pounds against my chest, echoing in my ears. I'm struck dumb by his confession. Any second now I'll wake up and this will all have been a dream.

I shake my head, still not believing it. "But . . . you called us a . . . *mistake,*" I choke out. My voice isn't working properly, and my body is aching from the effort of holding myself together.

"Trying to move past you—*us*—has been fucking impossible for me, while it seemed so effortless for you. I meant what I said. I can't repeat my same mistakes, not anymore." Nick inhales a deep breath, as if bracing himself. "My biggest mistake was losing you, Lillie, and I refuse to lose you again. I want all of you, forever."

Goose bumps break out over my skin, energy thrumming through me. I've been waiting years to hear him say those words, and now that he has it feels too good to be true.

"So much has happened between us," I say.

He nods.

"It won't be the same as it once was."

"No, it won't." Nick steps even closer, close enough for me to reach out and touch him, to smell his familiar, natural scent of spice and citrus. "It'll be better, because *we're* better. I promise you that, and together we'll prove that promise to each other every day."

"It's not going to be easy," I say, feeling dizzy with the nearness of him.

"When have you ever backed down from a challenge?" Nick wraps an arm around my waist, and the electric current inside me surges to a million volts. My breath hitches, and a slow smile stretches across his face. "Though I think we both know you're going to let me win this round."

I start to reply, but Nick shuts me up with a kiss, and I know with certainty that this is good and true. Here is my passion and my comfort. Here is my heart and my desire. Here is my past and my future.

Someone whistles, and we jerk apart. Blood creeps into my face as I look at the crowd gathered around us.

"It's about freaking time," Wes hollers, pumping a fist in the air, his dimples on full display.

"No kidding," Annabelle adds.

"Really, dear, where are your manners?" Sullivan Grace says, twisting her pearl necklace, though I notice she seems to be fighting a smile.

My father only nods at us, pride still beaming in his eyes.

Nick stares at me, a cocky, crooked grin on his face. "So how about you let me try some of this second-place peach cobbler?"

"Hey! I dominated my category." I pinch his side. "And besides, I'm rusty."

"Good thing you have a lifetime to practice then," he says, his words a hope and a promise.

EPILOGUE

It's the night before my father officially starts his retirement and the Spoons is packed with regulars, young and old, who have come to celebrate the end of an era. Bundles of balloons are tied to chairs, and a banner shouting HOORAY FOR OLD MAN JACK! LONG LIVE THE LEGEND! is draped across the ceiling.

I'm in the kitchen with Ernie, filling orders. I drop some battered okra into the fryer, toss a skillet of onions and bell peppers softening on the stove, and serve up a hearty portion of smothered pork chops over rice with a side of green beans. Placing the steaming plate in the window, I ring the delivery bell and wipe my hands on my apron. The fabric is splattered with grease and covered in food stains, and my back and feet ache from working eight hours without a break, but the familiar pulse and smells of the diner act like fuel to keep me energized.

Today's menu is dedicated solely to my father's favorite dishes—southern classics like chicken-fried steak with mashed potatoes and peppered cream gravy, barbecue spare ribs with collard greens and corn bread, and shrimp and grits. For dessert my father insisted on banana pudding, pecan pie, and, of course, peach cobbler. Items that are off-limits to him, but since it's a special occasion, I agreed to allow him a small helping of meat loaf and macaroni and cheese as long as he first ate his weight in heart-healthy produce to balance everything out.

Right now my father is slumped on a stool at the counter, wearing a party hat and a frown, pushing steamed broccoli and asparagus around with a fork. I thought he would've consumed the vegetables quickly so he could move onto the good stuff, but perhaps parting with the diner, something that's defined his existence for the past twenty-five years, has robbed him of his appetite. Even as patrons offer him their thanks and congratulations, my father only grunts and nods. Not that I blame him—I understand how difficult it is to let go. While I know he's thrilled I'm back home running things, carrying on our family's namesake, it's going to take time before he fully adjusts to all the drastic changes in his life.

Above the din and cheerful chatter, I hear the slow opening chords of James Taylor's "Something in the Way She Moves." I glance over to where Nick is strumming a guitar on the small stage set up in front of the wall cluttered with rusted signs and my framed newspaper columns. As part of the evening's festivities, Nick's been shuffling through the list of my father's favorite songs, though I know he chose this one specifically for me—it's what he played the first time he claimed me as his, two teenagers tangled together in the bed of my truck surrounded by a canopy of oak trees.

Nick meets my gaze from across the room, his lips curling up into a mischievous grin, as he continues to pluck the guitar strings. Under the fluorescent lights, his eyes appear electric, a blue so vivid I could drown in it. My heartbeat speeds up in anticipation of later when I can be alone with him in the dark, those eyes and mouth and nimble fingers all over me. My expression must betray my thoughts, because Nick winks at me before he refocuses his attention on the music and starts singing.

While I was gawking at Nick, five new orders came in. I sprinkle an herb-spice rub liberally on both sides of some Texas catfish filets and combine melted butter, lemon juice, and garlic powder in a bowl to drizzle over the top. I'm popping the sheet tray with the fish into the oven when Wes pokes his head in through the kitchen window.

"Yo, Jelly Bean, I'm gonna need more of that pimento cheese."

"Already?" I ask as I switch to whisking a beurre blanc sauce to keep it from separating.

He peers at the various pots and pans simmering away, a look of childlike glee on his face. "Blame Annabelle. She's the one hoarding it."

Wes returned from his father's wedding emotionally exhausted but also hopeful. While I prepared the brisket and coleslaw I promised to make for the football team, Wes told me about his trip, how he and his father finally got their issues out in the open, how he's not sure if they can ever fully repair the rift between them but that he's willing to try. As for the status of his relationship with Annabelle, they arrived at the diner tonight hand-in-hand.

"I'm slammed right now, so you'll need to get it yourself," I say. "I made extra and put it in the walk-in fridge."

"I'm on it," Wes says, retreating to the back room. I check on the short ribs braising on the stove, tweaking the seasonings and adding more red wine.

The oven timer dings. Removing the fish, I spoon a generous amount of beurre blanc on the bottom of three plates, divide a medley of roasted vegetables equally among them, and place a catfish filet on top of each serving.

From my vantage point in the kitchen, I see Sullivan Grace wedge her way through the crowd, weaving around tables to the stainless steel counter. She reaches my father as Nick begins playing an acoustic version of Peter Gabriel's "In Your Eyes."

"Jackson, enough of the sulking," I hear her tell him. "Now be a proper gentleman and ask me to dance."

My father mumbles something about being born with two left feet. For all his charm and wit, he really is the most unskilled dancer. My father often says bacon is like duct tape—it can cure almost anything. If only he could use it to cure this particular endearing flaw.

"Jackson." Sullivan Grace puts her hands on her hips. "I'm shriveling into an old woman waiting for you."

I hide a smile, watching in amusement as my father leads her to the makeshift dance floor and wraps his arms around her waist, swaying side to side like he's in middle school. Sullivan Grace doesn't seem to mind; she rests her head against his shoulder and closes her eyes.

I glance away, leaving them to their private moment, and get back to work.

Later, after the rush has died down and my father has gone home, Nick sneaks into the kitchen and comes over to where I'm cleaning the flat-top grill.

"Want some help?" he asks.

"I'm just about done," I say, pushing the scraper along the griddle, removing the last bits of food stuck to the surface.

He moves to stand behind me, his hands resting on my hips. "In that case," he says, his mouth brushing the shell of my ear, "I need to show you something in the stockroom." Warmth spreads like hot caramel through every inch of my body at the sudden roughness in his voice.

"We can't. Ernie's still here," I say, though the words sound unconvincing even to my ears.

Placing kisses against my neck, Nick pulls on the strings of my apron and slides a hand under my shirt, his palm splayed flat against my stomach. My muscles tighten beneath his touch. He turns me around, a lopsided grin stretching across his face as he tries to look innocent but fails miserably. "I swear my intentions are honorable."

I laugh as Nick walks backward toward the stockroom, tugging me along with him. Here we are, at the start of a new journey together. There isn't a recipe to guide us, and I don't know what the future holds, but that's the thrill of it. Life isn't about perfect pielike pieces, with everything symmetrical, rigid, planned. We've experienced enough of that already. We're some of the lucky ones who get a second chance.

I know it won't always be easy. There'll be times when he grips tighter than I do. Other times, it'll be me carrying him through. None of that is important. All that matters is that we're holding on.

Then again, isn't that the whole point? To protect the good and fight together through the bad? To laugh and learn and refuse to surrender? To cherish the big and savor the small? Because even when life veers off course there's a silver lining.

We can always build from scratch.

THANK YOU

THANK YOU for reading FROM SCRATCH! I hope you loved Lillie and Nick's story as much as I loved writing it.

If you enjoyed this book, please consider leaving an honest REVIEW at the outlet of your choice. Reviews are wonderfully helpful to every author, big or small, and are both welcome and appreciated.

For the latest NEWS, SALES, and SPECIAL OFFERS for all of my current and upcoming novels, friend me on my Facebook Author Profile, like my Facebook Page, and follow me on Twitter and Instagram. For more information on all of my bookish happenings, head to my website: www.rachelgoodmanbooks.com

Keep reading for a sneak peek of SOUR GRAPES, book 2 in the Blue Plate Series, a Southern romance set in Texas Hill Country. On sale now!

SOUR GRAPES SNEAK PEEK

BLUE PLATE SERIES BOOK 2

Chapter 1

Bitterness is as classic as Chanel.

Tonight I'm wearing it as armor under my black flowing silk chiffon gown. At any moment guests will start arriving for Baylor Medical's annual gala—the hospital's biggest fundraiser and the most ambitious PR/event planning project I've ever tackled. After ten months of intense preparation, I'm ready.

Nick should be celebrating the success of the evening with me, but I'm here alone after he tossed me aside for his first love like last year's Christmas present. Tonight is my chance to prove to everyone that a failed relationship won't keep me down.

It's be hurt or be hardened, and I pick the latter.

I adjust my headset and glance around. The modern concrete building of the Dallas Museum of Art is bathed in jewel tones, complemented by the mosaic wall opposite the entrance. The Moroccan music playing in the sculpture garden drifts on the wind, carrying the scent of incense and fruit from the hookah lounge. Photographers flank the red carpet leading into the main atrium, and valets surround the rectangular drive in preparation.

As if on cue, a train of limos and luxury vehicles pulls up. A fluttering sensation ignites in my stomach. Gathering my bearings, I inhale a deep breath and say, "All right, everyone. Look sharp."

I polish off a glass of Dom Pérignon, the taste light and crisp with a dry finish. Life should never be wasted on unremarkable champagne. Hiding the flute in a manicured bush, I click on the headset and ask my assistant, "Is everything finalized for the live auction and dinner?"

"Yes, Captain," she says, as though we're some ridiculous crew at sea. "Can I take a breather now? My feet are *killing* me." She's a psychology major straight out of college with no experience or work ethic—she's chronically late, frequently leaves early, and spends most of the day fighting with the coffee machine. Last week she barged into my office complaining about the workload and begging for an assistant, not even comprehending that she *is* the assistant. I only hired her because our mothers are tennis partners at the club and my mother demanded I do her a favor. Never again.

Only if you'd rather be unemployed, I think as a valet opens the first car door. To my shock, Dr. Greg Preston, Nick's father, steps out.

I knew Dr. Preston would make an appearance this evening—he's the head of cardiology at Baylor Medical—but I thought I could avoid him in the throng of the three hundred people attending the gala. Panic builds in my chest, my heart thumping an erratic rhythm. Cameras flash as he walks the red carpet, talking and shaking hands with the other benefit goers all dressed in their finest formal attire. His resemblance to Nick makes my stomach tighten—the tousled hair, the eyes so blue I could dive into them, the movie-star features.

Nick was supposed to be mine, I think, as resentment latches on to me, strengthening my suit of armor. When everyone else abandoned him—his family, his friends, his *fiancée*—during the darkest point in his life, it was *me* who picked him up off the floor and helped him rediscover his passion for songwriting. *I* saved him. *I'm* the one who deserved his trust, loyalty, devotion. Yet Nick chose Lillie, the girl who destroyed him when she ran off, only to return five years later to steal the man I had rightfully earned.

Dr. Preston turns in my direction, but I duck out of sight before he can see me. I sneak behind the receiving line of belly dancers greeting guests to the festivities and move past the check-in area overflowing with the event programs and promotional materials I'd spent months creating.

The atmosphere in the main atrium feels as warm and exotic as the spices in Marrakech. Luxurious silk fabrics in vivid shades of teal and purple are draped across the ceiling, the walls lit up to match. A Moorish tile pattern is projected onto the floor, while pierced iron lanterns adorn tallboy tables covered in linens the colors of precious gemstones. Servers in traditional dress, from fez-capped heads to feet in heelless leather slippers, offer mint tea mojitos and caramel-fig martinis to attendees when they enter the cocktail reception. Several people gasp as they scan the room, and I hear a woman comment that it feels as though she's been whisked away on a flying carpet.

I spot my parents near the stage set up in front of the windows framed by beautiful Chihuly glass. My father looks regal in a tuxedo and my mother sparkles in a beaded couture gown, exuding confidence and feminine sophistication with impeccable posture. Her red hair, identical in color to mine, is styled in an elegant French twist, and diamonds are dripping off her neck.

When my mother notices me, her megawatt smile disappears into a thin line and her eyes narrow, displeasure evident in her features. It's an expression I'm all too familiar with given that I'm always on the receiving end of it, though she's typically more conscientious than to show it in public for fear someone may see past her perfectly constructed persona. Knowing it'll only make her more upset if I delay, I pull my shoulders back and go greet them. My mother embraces me in a hug, her nails digging into my shoulders.

"Margaret, sweetheart, you decided on a black dress. How lovely," she says. To a bystander, her tone sounds smooth and inflectionless, as though she's doling out a compliment rather than thinly veiled criticism.

My mother thinks black is too harsh for redheads and our fair skin. She prefers midnight blue or emerald green. *To accent the gray in your eyes*, she reminds me often. But tonight? Tonight is *my* time to shine, so I'll wear whatever I want, even if I'll be admonished for it later when we're behind closed doors.

"Thank you," I say with a grin so believable it could pass as an authentic Birkin handbag in Chinatown.

She tucks a loose strand of hair into my updo. "That's better. I wouldn't want you mistaken for a slob." She raises an eyebrow, daring me to respond. When I don't, she laughs, but there's an edge to it. "Your father and I were just talking with the Westways. You remember their daughter Harper? I think she was three years behind you in school. She got engaged last night. Yale educated, investment banker, comes from a long line of politicians. The wedding will be next summer at his family's estate in East Hampton."

It's her subtle way of reminding me that I've embarrassed her, marred her pristine reputation, for wasting years of my life on an inappropriate man who, despite his sterling upbringing and pedigree, abandoned his family legacy of medicine to pursue such a tasteless ambition as songwriting. No amount of success—monetary, awards, or otherwise—could change my mother's impression of Nick. To her, he'd always be an indiscretion. That he then chose a *waitress* over me, thus subjecting our family to a fresh round of gossip and scrutiny, has only fueled her anger.

If only my mother could understand that I never expected Nick to be a lesson I had to learn, or that I would be the one left standing on the sidelines.

"Do let me know if they need an event coordinator," I say, refusing to let her elicit a reaction from me, then turn toward my father and peck him on the cheek, careful not to leave a lipstick mark. "Daddy."

"Hello, honey." He brushes a kiss against my forehead in return. "The food so far has been delightful. Particularly these tasty little things," he says, snatching a bacon-wrapped date off a passing tray.

"Don't be ridiculous, Roger," my mother chides.

He pops the date into his mouth, blithely ignoring her —something he excels at. There's a reason he's one of the best family law and divorce attorneys in Dallas—he spends the majority of his time at the office and away from home in order to avoid my mother. I've often wondered why they're still married, or how they ever got engaged in the first place. If their current relationship is any indication, I imagine the whole thing was more of a business transaction my mother probably suggested—"It's the next logical step in our courting," she'd have said— than an over-the-top romantic gesture. Perhaps the reason my father stays with her is because he's witnessed firsthand how vindictive and cruel people can be when it comes to dividing assets.

"I'll have a box of dates delivered to your office," I whisper to him with a conspiratorial wink. "I'll even include some fig and pear pastilla for dessert." He smiles and pats my shoulder.

"Margaret, your father and I were discussing tonight's theme—Arabian Nights. Interesting choice," my mother says. Her voice is breezy, but the underlying reprimand is obvious.

"Moroccan," I correct.

"What's that, sweetheart?"

"The theme is centered around Morocco," I say, the fragrant aroma of turmeric and cinnamon heavy in the air.

My mother waves me off, the diamond tennis bracelet on her wrist glinting in the light. "Same thing."

"Arabia is in the Middle East. Morocco is in Africa. Different continents," I say.

"Either way, we wondered if you'd considered its appropriateness for a hospital gala. Isn't that right, Roger?" she says to my father. He's staring at a group of people admiring their newly applied henna tattoos, not even pretending to listen.

I don't bother to tell my mother that I selected the theme to separate the benefit from every other bland black-tie fundraising event so I could give people a night they'd remember. Once she's cast judgment, any attempt at explaining is as futile as waiting for a Louis Vuitton sale.

"Roger," my mother says again, touching his arm. "Explain to your daughter the importance of fulfilling client expectations."

My father glances at her, then over at me, and shrugs. "In my experience, it is important to consider all sides of an issue before moving forward," he says noncommittally, finishing off his scotch. After a lifetime of conversations with my mother, he's built an entire arsenal of platitudes. It's unfair how he gets stuck in the middle of us, how he often has to act as Switzerland in the battle between my mother and me. "When is dinner served? The small bites are great, but not nearly enough to hold me over."

"Soon," I say. "I hope you're ready for an authentic feast."

My mother opens her mouth with no doubt another jab, but I cut her off. "Speaking of which, I should go check on the meal. Please excuse me," I say, striding away at a speed just shy of fleeing. *Where did I put that flute of champagne?* A server balancing a tray of mint tea mojitos brushes past me. I swipe a glass and take a few sips. The alcohol burns my throat, the hint of lime tart on my tongue.

While attendees mingle and nibble on lamb skewers and beef phyllo cigars, I ensure everything is still on schedule and running smoothly. So far no issues, apart from my mother's condescending voice echoing in my head. The invite list is completely crossed off. It's go time.

Not surprisingly, my assistant has vanished. I try reaching her through the headset, but all I get is silence. I find her in the sculpture garden smoking a hookah with a group of her friends from the country club whose parents paid for their tickets.

My expression must reflect my annoyance, because when she sees me, she stands so fast her knees bump the center table, nearly causing the hookah pipe to topple over.

"The last guests have arrived," I say, sharp enough to bite.

She mumbles a *sorry* and quickly shoves her heels back on.

"I don't want your apology. Just do your job. I need you with catering to make sure the food service is expedited properly. Can you please handle that?"

"Yes . . . I mean, no, I mean—I'll take care of it."

"Good." As I turn away, I hear her mutter what sounds like *bitch* and *slave driver*. The rest of the group snickers. *Tomorrow you can fire her.*

I paste a smile on my face before returning to the atrium and motion the mistress of ceremonies, the Medical Center Foundation director, to start. She nods, adjusts the microphone on the podium, and calls for attention.

"Ladies and gentlemen, it is with great pleasure that I welcome you to 'A Faraway Land,' Baylor Medical's annual gala, benefiting programs and services for the hospital. I'd like to express my sincere appreciation for your support and generosity, which help ensure our patients and their families have access to outstanding care and facilities. Thank you for being a part of this special event. Please enjoy your evening of enchantment."

The audience applauds as cameras flash. The woman from Christie's leading the live auction steps behind the podium and begins introducing the first item. People sink into plush velvet banquettes, cocktails in their diamond-adorned hands, ready to bid. As the prizes—the VIP luxury suite season tickets for the Dallas Cowboys; a long weekend of golf at the exclusive Shadow Creek in Las Vegas; a ten-day yacht cruise in the Caribbean—go quickly and expensively, I breathe easier. The paddle-lifting concludes as the final item, a magical three-week getaway to Morocco, sells for the price of a Lamborghini. My heart swells with pride. Between the auction and the donations, the gala raised more than two million dollars—nearly double last year's amount.

Staffers escort the guests to the Chilton Galleries for an

authentic Moroccan feast served family style, save for dining on the floor and eating with their hands. Little bowls of olives, hummus, smoked eggplant, and harissa are scattered around the table to accompany flatbread. Red wine is poured into colorful tumblers, while platters arranged with roasted vegetables in flavorful marinades are passed around. I watch as faces transform with delight at the first bite of carrot and chickpea salad, and grin. Keeping the menu consistent with the theme was a risk, but it seems to have paid off. Soon the museum is filled with sounds of people sharing good food and conversation.

As the second course is served, a waiter taps my shoulder. "Excuse me, miss," he says, shifting on his feet. "There's a problem at table fifteen."

Great.

I follow him into an adjacent gallery, where Mr. Dugan —Dallas's most successful car dealership owner—has wedged himself between two women, one on the verge of throwing a clay pot of basmati rice, the other gripping a fork, armed for combat. My earlier excitement fizzles. *Shit.* How did I put his wife of thirty years in the same vicinity as his thirty-year-old mistress? The tension in the room is thick, everyone transfixed by the scene.

"Let's move this outside," I say, approaching with caution. The women don't hear me, each focused solely on the other.

"He bid on the trip for me, you saggy old hag. Do you really think he'd spend ten days in the Caribbean staring at *you* in a bikini?" the mistress hisses at Mrs. Dugan, slashing the fork in the air. Mr. Dugan grabs her wrists and pins them against him.

Mrs. Dugan's mouth opens and closes like a fish, but no words come out. She looks at her husband, but he won't meet her gaze.

"Ladies, please. This is neither the time nor the place." I keep my voice calm but don't dare intervene for fear of getting stabbed.

The mistress flings out a graphic comment about her favorite sexual position with Mr. Dugan, and the cord snaps. Mrs. Dugan hurls the clay pot at the mistress's chest, nearly knocking her off her feet. The pot crashes to the ground and shatters. Basmati rice flies everywhere. Then, as if she were doing nothing more than brushing away a speck of lint, Mrs. Dugan adjusts the shawl on her shoulders and strolls away.

The air feels thin in the sudden silence. The mistress clutches her chest, rage burning hot in her eyes. Mr. Dugan stands frozen like an ice sculpture. A staffer rushes around me to wipe up the mess. Someone giggles and hiccups, and the fog around Mr. Dugan evaporates. He glares at me with a coldness that causes a prickle to run down my spine, then whispers to his mistress and guides her to the exit with his back straight and head held high, as if determined to ignore the awkward hush around him and the people gawking.

I don't manage to be so collected—my heart is lodged in my throat and my stomach is tangled into knots—especially under the weight of my mother's deprecating stare. I know she'll say this entire scene is my fault, that I'm in charge so it's my responsibility to have my finger on the pulse of our social circle's ever-evolving spats.

Desperate to get the evening back on track, I instruct the waiters to immediately start serving the main course. Still, even as the guests enjoy steaming tagines of lamb chops with pomegranate molasses, roasted chicken with preserved lemons and olives, and couscous with raisins, almonds, and saffron, they continue to discuss and dissect what transpired.

No doubt it'll make the rounds in the next few days, ensuring this event will be the talk of the town, though not in the way I'd hoped. Still, if this is the worst thing to happen tonight, I'll consider it a success. After all, when money, alcohol, and society mix, something is bound to go wrong. And the only thing worse than a scandalous event is one no one talks about.

The lights dim and the music rises, signaling it's time for the real party to begin. After the last person leaves the galleries in search of the hookah tents and dance floor and I'm alone with only the servers and cleaning crew, my heart returns to my chest and the knots in my stomach loosen. The hard part is over. I survived.

I allow myself one more moment of solitude before I rejoin the guests back in the main atrium. My mother intercepts me as I enter, pulling me off to the side by the fleshy part of my arm. Pain shoots into my fingers and tears sting my eyes. I remember during my sixth-grade cotillion dance when I removed my white gloves because my hands broke out in a rash, my mother dragged me out of the ballroom away from the other attendees, squeezing the skin so hard the bruise took weeks to fade, and scolded me until my eyes were bloodshot and snot ran down my nose. Since then I've learned it's better to swallow the pain and the scolding.

"You sat Mrs. Dugan at the same table as her husband's mistress?" she hisses. "How could you be so incompetent? These are our family's friends and your father's colleagues!"

I don't respond. Answering will only prolong the torture.

A belly dancer takes position in the center of the floor, and a hush falls over the room. The music changes, and the dancer's hips begin to sway. My mother *tsk*s in disapproval even as guests create a large circle around her, clapping in rhythm with her movements.

"The whole gala has been a disaster. First the theme. Then your inability to handle something as *basic* as a seating chart. Now this?" she continues, gesturing to the performance. "And the menu! Did you even consider people's food sensitivities? The foundation committee trusted you to plan an elegant affair, but all you've managed to do is embarrass yourself and this family." She glances over her shoulder, scanning for nosy eavesdroppers. "You've been slow to understand this, so let me spell it out for you, Margaret. You're only as meaningful and valuable as others perceive you to be. And tonight no one envies me my daughter. An experience I expect not to repeat in the future—" She breaks off, ordering me through clenched teeth to smile as the newly appointed Junior League president approaches us. I rub the tender spot on my arm where I know a bruise is already blossoming.

The League president greets my mother and faces me, kissing my cheeks. The scent of caramel-fig martinis is heavy on her breath. "Margaret, you outdid yourself! What a memorable event. Truly spectacular."

"Thank you," I say.

"Nancy, you and Roger must be so proud," she says to my mother. "This night is going to be all anyone talks about."

My mother loops an arm around mine, the megawatt smile ever present, and pinches the soft skin above my elbow. I bite my tongue to prevent myself from wincing. "Of course. We're proud of everything Margaret does."

A coldness rushes through me, as if I've been doused with ice water. At thirty-two and a professional businesswoman, I shouldn't feel such crushing disappointment at her words. After all, my mother hasn't been proud of me since I was a little girl, before I could form my own opinions and dreams. Still, I'd hoped this time would be different, that she would recognize how important this night is to me, how hard I've worked even if it isn't the event she would've planned. How idealistic and foolish of me to assume I could ever be good enough.

The League president starts to speak as my earpiece crackles. "Margaret, we've got a man out here trying to reach one of the guests inside. He's insisting on entering the gala, but he's not on the list. Can you come talk to him?"

I sigh. It never ends. Why security can't turn away some party crasher is beyond me. I click on the mouthpiece. "I'll be right there." Wiggling out of my mother's grip, I walk away without a good-bye or second glance. Later she'll reprimand me for my rude behavior, but I don't care. Not tonight, anyway.

Weaving through the crowd, I step outside and come face-to-face with Nick.

OTHER BOOKS BY RACHEL GOODMAN

Blue Plate Series
SOUR GRAPES

Margaret Stokes is bitter. And not in the robust fine wine or tangy dark chocolate kind of way. She just got dumped, is fed up with her job as a glorified party-planner for the rich, and can't possibly listen to one more veiled insult from her impossible-to-please mother. So she retreats to the comfort of her grandmother's ramshackle bed and breakfast in Texas wine country, where the wide open vineyards are filled with surprises, from the shockingly delicious Tempranillo to the aggravating yet oh-so-tempting man who makes it.

Ryan Camden's easy approach to life encourages Margaret to loosen up and have a little fun, despite her better judgment. She resists the urge to micromanage every detail, embracing the welcome distractions of her surroundings and letting their relationship unfold at a natural rhythm. But when a health scare forces Grammy J to give up the B&B, Margaret begins to wonder if Ryan really is the man he promises—and whether the problems she tried so hard to escape ever really went away.

ABOUT THE AUTHOR

RACHEL GOODMAN is the critically acclaimed author of the Blue Plate Series (light women's fiction/contemporary romance/chick-lit). She was raised in Colorado on Roald Dahl books and her mother's award-worthy cooking. Now an engineering professor at her alma mater, Southern Methodist University in Dallas, Texas, she has not lost her passion for culinary discovery or a well-told story. A member of RWA, she continues to hone her craft through the Writer's Path at SMU while seeking to create the perfect macaroni and cheese recipe.

Follow Rachel
www.rachelgoodmanbooks.com

 facebook.com/RachelGoodmanBooks

 twitter.com/mojitomaven

 instagram.com/mojitomaven

Made in the USA
Columbia, SC
22 April 2020